Unwelcome Mail

by

Kayla Danoli

Copyright

First published in 2020
Copyright © Kayla Danoli 2020

Cataloguing-in-publication data
Creator: Danoli, Kayla, author

Cataloguing-in-Publication details are available from the National Library of Australia www.trove.nla.gov.au

ISBN: 978-0-6483950-7-2 (paperback)
ISBN: 978-0-6483950-8-9 (digital)

Cover by T A Marshall, Mackay, QLD Australia

Contents

Also by the Author

Revenge is not Enough
Harbour Plaza: built on dreams
On the Way to Istanbul
An Unsuitable House
A Land Too Far
Paradise Interrupted

Chapter 1

"No. No, not again; not another one please," I whispered as a large white envelope slid through the letter slot and fluttered down to the carpet. Why don't I just ignore it; throw it away? I don't have to look at it to know it will be like the others: no stamp, no postmark, no return address… In fact, the only thing written on the envelope will be the address of this house, '10 Minstrel Court'. Hand delivered again of course. What have I done to deserve this? Who is sending them … and, perhaps another question is: who delivers them?

Halfway down the stairs on my way to the kitchen when the envelope made its appearance, I froze on the spot. After a few heartbeats, I tiptoed cautiously down a couple more steps. Maybe whoever shoved it through the slot is lurking about outside waiting for me to come to the door to collect it. So… What if they are? What can they do? The door is locked. I suppose they could push something else through the slot … something worse.

Get a grip, I told myself. Go and retrieve the envelope. I took a deep breath, and started down the stairs again

"What are you doing?" Jo's voice so close behind me in the otherwise silent house made me jump. "Mel, what's going on? Why are you sneaking down your own stairs? You look like a teenage girl trying not to wake her parents as she sneaks out to a midnight assignation?"

Nothing I could say would sound even vaguely intelligent. So, I settled for just a shrug. If I tried telling her what's been happening, she would think I'd been at the cooking sherry. The response I offered didn't help. "It's not midnight. It's morning and it's breakfast time. And that's why I was heading to the kitchen – to prepare breakfast."

"Oh look; you've got mail. Bit early for the today's first post isn't it? I don't remember seeing the envelope there last night, so I suppose it arrived in the early morning delivery. Anyway, whenever it arrived, I'm sure it won't contain a bomb, or anthrax, or anything else equally deadly. So why are you sneaking up on it?"

"I wasn't 'sneaking up on it' as you put it. All I was doing was tiptoeing around so as not to wake you." I knew Jo wasn't likely to swallow that explanation. It didn't sound credible even to me.

"Well, I'm awake now, and I'm here at the bottom of the stairs with you. So, let's continue to the kitchen to make breakfast, and collect the envelope on our way past"

Her slow and deliberate reply left me in no doubt she didn't buy my explanation. I know more questions will be forthcoming, questions she won't let me avoid answering. It makes sense to answer them before they are asked. I realise that, but what is there to tell her? I don't know anything. The sum total of it all can be summed up in a few words: unpleasant hand-delivered notes arrive periodically, and on significant dates.

When we reached the front door, Jo was a step or two ahead of me. Without breaking stride, she swooped down, picked up the envelope on her way past, and continued to the kitchen. Over that short distance, I watched Jo examine every part of the envelope before throwing it onto the kitchen table. In a bid to delay, if not avoid, what I knew was coming, I went straight to the kettle. It only took a few moments to fill it and set it to do its thing. Then, I had run out of diversions.

The time had come to face Jo. She sat unmoving at the table, her eyes never leaving me. With the envelope remaining where she tossed it, she paid it no heed, not even glancing in its direction. Jo's face showed no emotion. It gave no clue as to what was in store for me, but her eyes told another story. Hard and analysing, they were latched onto me with an intensity that made me squirm. Unsure what to do I hesitated by the stove. Then all was lost. Jo took command and the cross-examination began.

"So, Mel, what is this all about?" Without taking her eyes off me as she spoke, Jo gestured towards the envelope still lying at the end of the table. "Come on, talk to me about it. It's obvious the envelope's arrival unnerved you. Why?"

"I don't know why they are happening… and that's the truth. So, there isn't anything I can tell you about it."

"This isn't the first time it has happened?" I shook my head. "So, unmarked, unstamped, hand-delivered envelopes arrive and you do nothing about them? Were the others you received the same?" This time I managed a shrug and a half-hearted nod.

We sat in silence for what seemed like a long time but probably was no more than a minute. I found myself wishing she would get on with the questioning; go into full-on inquisition mode. It would be easier to endure than this stony silence. Almost on cue, my wish was granted.

"You don't appear to be in a hurry to open it, so I'm assuming you know what it says. Have they all said the same thing? And, when I say 'all', how many have there been?"

"There have been three I know of so far. No, they don't all say the same thing, but their wording amounts to the same message."

"As it is obvious they upset you, what have you done about them?" I hesitated, not for any reason other than to find the right words for a succinct – albeit brief – explanation. "You have done something…? I hope you're not going to tell me you chose to ignore them."

"Of course not; I talked to the police about them. And no, they didn't appear too interested. They claimed the letters were harmless enough, and didn't constitute sufficient threat, or provide enough information for them to initiate an investigation."

"Am I correct in assuming the letters are a recent innovation? I mean, did they only start arriving after James' death?"

"They only started arriving after I bought this place. Now, there's a thought. Does buying this place have something to do with it?"

"While I don't want to make you revisit what must've been a horrible time for you, it would help if I knew what happened. I have to admit to not knowing much about it at all. I was overseas when I received word from someone in the office here. All they told me and, therefore, all I knew was your husband had died. I still don't know the details. Nevertheless, I can understand if you don't feel inclined to discuss such a terrible time."

"Maybe examining everything to do with what happened could be a good thing for me as well as for you. The kettle is boiled. Why don't I tell you over breakfast?"

Chapter 2

Faffing about making breakfast and settling ourselves at the table allowed me time to arrange my thoughts in some logical order. Stirring my coffee and buttering my toast provided a further brief procrastination. But, Jo's hard look from across the table told me she was running out of patience. After a sip of coffee and a deep breath, I began my painful story.

"I'm not being evasive, not really. My problem is working out where to begin. If truth be told, I don't when this situation began or what triggered it."

"You said you received three letters. Suppose you start by telling me about when the first one arrived. It's probably as good a place as any to begin."

"As I said, nothing happened – nothing I'm aware of any-way – until I bought this place. While it was exactly what I was looking for, you know how it is, there's always a bit you want done to it before you move in. This place was no different. It took me a while to work out what I wanted. There were the usual delays involved in having the building assessed and drawings for the new work produced. After details were finalised, there were further delays in selecting, engaging and informing the contractor who would do the work.

Once they made a start, I kept out of the workmen's way for much of the time, only coming to the house every couple of days or when they needed me to check on something. I was impatient to move in, and frustrated when it seemed to take longer than I imagined. But, like all good things, the work finally ended, and I was cleaning up and settling in. While in the process of moving in, I came across an unopened envelope with this address hand-written on its front; just the address and nothing else."

"You say you found it. You weren't here when it arrived?"

"No, and I didn't want to open it. I guessed it arrived during the renovations, and was intended for the contractor. When I called him about it, he claimed no knowledge of it, but would ask his workers if any of them remembered its arriving."

"When he didn't know anything about it, did you open it?"

"No-o, not right away. I didn't touch it again until after the contractor called me back a couple of days later. It seems his apprentice remembered it. He wasn't sure whether it was the first or second day they worked on the house, but probably the first day. The apprentice arrived before the others to open up and set up ready for the day's work. On the day in question, the letter was on the floor when he walked in. To prevent the others tramping over it when they arrived, he picked it up and put it 'somewhere safe' – and then promptly forgot about it."

"Okay. So, the envelope was here for a while before you found it, and then for a bit longer after that before you opened it. What was in the envelope?"

"There was just a folded single sheet of paper containing the words *he's waiting for you*. The envelope was the same as this. I have no doubt, today's will contain only a single sheet of paper too. It's why I'm not in a hurry to open it. I know it sounds hard to believe, but that first note really unnerved me."

"While I understand how you found it disturbing, what was the most upsetting thing about it?"

"That's a good question. Everything about it bothered me. I suppose, it was its short message. It seemed a direct threat. But, as well as the message, there was something else unnerving about its arrival. While I still don't know when it was delivered, if the apprentice's memory serves him right, it arrived on the date of James' birthday, or perhaps the day after."

"Yes, that would upset you, but I don't think you can rule out the possibility of coincidence. How many people knew James' birth date? I didn't – and still don't – although I've known you both for years. I spent a lot of time with the pair of you, including celebrating a lot of other people's birthdays with you."

"I know. After I found the envelope, I reminded myself few people would know it was James' birthday. I almost managed to convince myself it wasn't meant for me. My mind kept suggesting it was intended for the contractor working on the place, or maybe one of his workers. To me, that made more sense than someone sending me such a cryptic message. After all, not many people knew I bought the place. And, who could possibly be waiting for me?"

Jo giggled … and then spent some time apologising. "I'm sorry. I know it's not funny, and I understand how upsetting it is, but a rogue thought tickled my sense of humour. For a moment, the thought of someone sending you a message to intercede on behalf of some shy would-be-lover was hilarious."

"Shy would-be-lover…! What are you on about? I live an almost cloistered existence. My life doesn't allow me time even to read a book, let alone be out there attracting potential male suitors. And, if I had spare time, I would find plenty of things to do with it other than that."

"Keep your petticoat on straight. I didn't mean anything by it. Anyway, one day you might be so inclined. Have you ever considered the possibility you might remarry?"

"No-o, not really. I think mine is a classic situation: been there, done that, have the scars to prove it. Lesson learned. None of us knows what the future holds. Maybe one day I will feel differently but, at the moment, I doubt it."

"It was just a passing thought. Let's move on. What about the second envelope you received, when did that arrive?"

"I think it was about three months later. Yes, it was ... and I think it goes some way to eliminating any suggestion of coincidence. It arrived on the anniversary of the day James disappeared. I know information about his disappearance exists in the public domain, but I can't imagine why it would be of interest to any-one after all this time."

"Maybe any interest they had goes back to the time when it happened; perhaps even earlier. I don't know what happened to James. If you remember, I had been based overseas for a while by then. My only knowledge of it came after the event, when a work colleague mentioned it in an email. I appreciate it remains difficult for you to talk about it, but it might help if you tell me what happened. You mentioned he disappeared… It's the first time I've heard that."

"Well, it was almost two years ago now. Time has taken some of the sting out of the memory, and allowed me to realise life goes on in spite of the loss. The word *coincidence* again comes to mind."

"How so…? What has coincidence to do with the second letter? No, don't answer that yet. First, tell me about James' disappearance. Is 'disappear' a euphemism for something else? Was there more to the story, or did he just 'disappear'?"

Yes, he just disappeared. The short version of the event is he was lost overboard. For all intents and purposes, the mystery ended when the coroner's inquest found James was presumed dead after being lost at sea. It happened after the big annual sailing race around Rock Island."

"I don't know much about it, but I remember the race was a big event around here … and I remember it being James' favourite race. I also remember you weren't overly fussed about sailing."

"True; and I haven't sailed since. Weekends on the boat were fine, but I wasn't into racing. I liked to pick the conditions under which I went sailing. If it looked like blowing a gale and raining or drizzling the whole time, I wasn't going. The Rock Island race that year was different for us. James had been in bed for about ten days with the flu, and wasn't out of bed for more than a few minutes at a time until the day before the race. He was as weak as I'd ever seen him. I tried telling him he wasn't up to a long, hard day's racing, but he insisted on competing."

"There would be others on board too, wouldn't there? Surely he could take it easy; stay in command, but let someone else do the heavy work."

"He always raced with only one crew member. The one guy who sailed with him for years moved away a few months before. James took on another young bloke, but they only sailed a couple of races together before the Rock Island one. With my concerns about James' health and the new crew member's experience, it seemed I should go too. As luck would have it, the day turned filthy the moment we hoisted the sails, and became progressively worse. A squall came up … The waves were huge … Everything and everywhere was wet … It was cold … and we were so busy with the sails the whole way, there wasn't time or opportunity to eat during the race."

"You picked a good time to go sailing. Sounds like conditions were ideal for a disaster to occur. When did the tragedy happen? Was it during the race?"

"No. Wet through, freezing, battered and bruised, we managed to finish the race. I have to take my hat off to Damien, the young crewman. James shouldn't have raced. He wasn't fit to be there, and he didn't take into account the new crewman's not knowing how he liked things done. Nevertheless, while Damien put up with James' yelling at him and did a brilliant job, we wouldn't have managed even to finish the race if I hadn't been there. James couldn't accept how tough things were as a result of the weather and his poor health. He was disappointed we only came second.

Until then, he had won the race a few years in succession. By the time we crossed the finish line, I was exhausted. I think Damien was too. James wasn't too bad, probably because we took as much load off him as we could during the race. Anyway, after the race, there always is a party. The organisers put on food and drink, the trophies are presented, and then dancing and entertainment goes on into the night. I wasn't up to partying, and James didn't appear keen to participate either. Maybe it had something to do with receiving only the second-place trophy."

"It fits with what I remember of James. Second-best was never good enough for him, particularly when it came to sailing. Okay, so all three of you survived the race, and nobody was keen on partying. Then what happened?"

"That's not quite true. Damien was as exhausted as the pair of us but, being young and fit, was all set to party on into the night. Our plans were to spend the night at the marina and sail home the following morning. Then, as Damien was about to go ashore for the night, James announced we would head home instead of overnighting at the marina."

"If Damien was all set to party, James' change of plans wouldn't go down well."

"I expected Damien to be disappointed. I prepared to argue for us to stay the night. An early night on board appealed, and Damien was looking forward to partying all night. In the end, there was no argument. The change of plans didn't worry Damien. He said he would get a lift home tomorrow with a mate crewing on one of the other boats. His mate also was spending the night ashore."

"While I hope you'll tell me you had more sense than to leave straight away, that wasn't the case, was it?"

"Oh, I kicked up a fuss about it. I had endured more than enough sailing for one day, but I didn't have much of an argument. By then, sailing conditions were perfect; flat sea, light breeze… We could be tied up at home within a couple of hours and spending the night in our comfortable bed. After a light meal on board, we set sail for home. I stayed topside for a while keeping James company. Sailing was pleasant, but I still had to clean up after dinner. I left James at the helm and went down to the galley.

By the time I cleaned up, packed up the few things we would be taking off with us, and freshened up, a bit of time had elapsed. As I was about to go topside again, I sensed things were not right. I don't know whether I heard something, or what it was. I raced up on deck. White water was boiling all around us. We were close into shore – too close in – and almost on a rocky outcrop."

"Christ! What did you do? Did you end up on the rocks?"

"I yelled to James to warn him about the rocks and that we were almost being on them. At the time, it struck me as odd he wasn't aware of what was happening. It wasn't yet dark; twilight at best. The rocks were obvious, as was our situation. I kept yelling at James until I realised he didn't correct our course. We were heading closer to the rocks. That's when I discovered nobody was at the wheel."

"Nobody was steering the boat and you were about to flounder on rocks…? Was the boat badly damaged?"

"No, we didn't flounder. I raced back, grabbed the wheel, and somehow managed to keep us off the rocks. The whole thing left me a bit weak-kneed, and not thinking too clearly. As soon as things were under control again, and I was functioning normally once more, I looked for James. I'd kept calling him after I first noticed he wasn't at the helm, but there was no answer. With the boat luffed up, I searched everywhere on board. There was no sign of him. He was gone ... just disappeared. I set course for home."

"You didn't find any sign of anything untoward happening; no evidence to suggest James went overboard?"

"There was nothing out of the ordinary at all. It took me a while to accept the situation but, by then, I was entering our home marina. As soon as I was on the mooring, I raced to the coastguard building to tell them James was missing and what I thought had happened. They went out straight away to search the area where James most likely went overboard. There was no trace of him that evening, or over the next few days after they extended the search to the wider area. They expended a lot of energy mapping currents and tides to predict where James' body might turn up. It never did."

"Why did you continue on to the marina before alerting anyone? I don't think I would be capable of going anywhere if I were in your position. My most likely approach would be to chuck the anchor over and sit there bellowing over the radio until someone came to see what all the fuss was about."

"Yes, that was my first thought too, but circumstances conspired against me. I don't really understand the radio and don't know how to operate it properly. Apart from that, it wasn't working anyway. There's always a bit of banter during a race between James and one of the other skippers. When we were more than halfway around the course, and James hadn't heard anything from the other bloke, he decided to stir things up. That's when we discovered the radio wasn't working. So, I had no option other than to carry on to the marina to raise the alarm. It was lucky I was close to the marina when it happened. I only had to sail for about another ten minutes before dropping the sails and motoring to our mooring."

"I imagine his disappearing in such a way raised a few questions, particularly when his body never was found. It must have been a rugged time for you having to live with not knowing – not having closure – to compound your loss."

"I don't remember much about the days immediately after the event. Everything around me was a blur. I spent the whole time in a zombie-like state. While the search was called off after several days, issues associated with his disappearance lingered for weeks."

"His disappearance would have captured everyone's attention; police, media, social gatherings, pub patrons… And, everyone would have an opinion."

"It was rough going for quite a while. Some of the police made no secret of the fact they believed I had done away with him. Those months before the coroner pronounced James presumed dead impacted on every aspect of my life. Even bank accounts were frozen. It was fortunate I could still operate one of my personal accounts."

"Something just occurred to me. You and James did not share the same surname. If I remember correctly, McCarthy was your maiden name. You never took James' name when you married. Why was that?"

"I'm not sure. My solicitor asked the same question when we were preparing for the coronial inquest. I didn't have an answer then, but the question nagged me afterwards. Perhaps subconsciously I was making amends to my father. He became so protective of me when mum died while I was in my early teens, it led to friction between us as I grew older. There are times when I wish he was still around so I can thank him for all he did for me, and tell him how I now understand some of the stuff I railed against back then."

"Perhaps the most amazing story lies in how you managed to resurrect your life and move on after losing James."

"Let's make a fresh pot of coffee before we examine that time of my life."

Chapter 3

"So, how did you cope in the aftermath of James' disappearance? I imagine the temptation was to curl up and hide inside the beautiful home you lived at the time."

"Well, it was hard to move on. But, with responsibilities demanding my attention, I didn't have a lot of options other than to get on with it. Of course, the company was a major part of the motivation. Legally, it was my company after I inherited it from my father. About a year after we married, I appointed James managing director. The appointment solved a couple of domestic issues. It meant he ran the company, and I only attended management meetings when necessary."

"How did the arrangement work out? It was brave of you to hand over the reins when you had run the company for so long. You proved you were capable when you took over after your father became ill, and continued running it after his death."

"Yeah, but my owning and running such a large company was difficult for James. At the time, he was unemployed and had no real prospects other than to become a kept man. Neither of us was happy with that prospect. It affected our marriage. I had to do something and, as it turned out, he made a reasonable job of running the company."

"Your father must have turned in his grave when you appointed James. As I recall, he wasn't particularly happy when things looked like becoming serious between you and James. After James' death, how did the staff react to your taking up the reins again?"

I squirmed as I searched for an appropriate response. Jo noticed, and continued before I could answer. "Only an honest answer, or none at all will do, thank you."

"If I must be honest…"

"You must ... or don't answer and I will draw my own conclusions. While I applaud your diplomacy – or perhaps it's out of loyalty – this is not the time for it, and not with me."

"Truth is, I don't think James was well liked by managerial staff or employees. I know he made mistakes. We all do. It's only human. But I think it went deeper than that. Nevertheless, it was difficult for everyone for some time after I took over again."

"How so...? Weren't they pleased to have you back?"

"I think most were relieved, as opposed to happy, but I hadn't been involved in day-to-day operations for quite a while. Over the first few months, I almost drove senior staff mad with my question as I tried to come up to speed with everything. And, there was the small matter of accounts being frozen. We had a battle to have the court recognise me as the legal owner of the business, and grant a permit for the company to continue operations until the matter of James' death was settled. We had to prove James had no legal claim to the company.

While it was embarrassing and difficult for me, it also was difficult for the company. Money was tight. We had to downsize operations. Somehow, we managed to avoid having to lay off staff or employees. Regardless, yes, those eight months prior to the coroner's verdict were tough for all concerned. Most coroner's inquests don't happen until at least twelve months after the event. We were lucky to have James' scheduled after only eight months, and to come away with a verdict at the end of it. It allowed not only me, but also the company, to regain some degree of normality."

"What have you done since then? Since I lobbed on your doorstep, you haven't appeared to be working full-time. I hope you're not taking time off to entertain and keep me company."

"No, it's nothing like that. I made a few changes at the company. One of the long-time senior staff is now the production manager. He looks after day to day stuff. Until the place settled down under the new arrangement, I went in to the office for at least a few hours every day. Now, I only go in two or three times a week, and spend just enough time there to deal with whatever I must do. I've developed other interests to keep me as busy as I want to be."

"So, how do you see the future? Is this how and where you think you'll spend the rest of your life, with only being involved with the company part-time?"

"…Not sure I've looked too far ahead yet. Some days it feels like I lost James ages ago. Other days, it seems like only yesterday. One day I will have to take a long, hard look at my future, but not yet. Anyway, that's enough about me. What about you? What are your plans for the future? Whatever they are, you know you are more than welcome to stay here with me for a long as you like. I'm enjoying the company … but don't take any obligation to stay here from that comment."

"At the moment, I'm indulging in long overdue holidays. I know people think being a forensic accountant is a cushy number. It's not like that at all; not from my experience any-way. I confess to being happy to be home again after four years. When the firm sent me overseas to work on a couple of major investigations they were involved with, it was supposed to be for about twelve months. Then, when they were contracted to undertake other jobs over there, they already had me in place to oversee the work, and had me stay on."

"You said you had about three months' leave due. Will they send you back overseas when you return to work?"

"I'm not sure I'm going back to work. I mean, I'm not sure I will return to work for the same firm. After doing the same thing for so many years, both here and overseas, maybe a change would be nice. Who knows? By the time my leave finishes, I might feel differently. In the meantime, if you can put up with me, I'd love to accept your offer and base myself here at number 10 Minstrel Court … and have the tenant continue leasing my unit."

"Having you here this last couple of weeks has been wonderful. We get on well together, but we still do as we want as individuals without feeling constrained by the other's presence.

I'm enjoying the company, and the fact that we share an interest in many of the same things makes it even better."

"Good; now that's settled, perhaps we can return to thinking about these anonymous letters you've received … and what we are going to do about preventing more of them arriving."

Today could turn into heavy going. When Jo gets an idea, she is difficult to dissuade. I put the kettle on again – for a pot of tea this time. I have a feeling we might need sustenance as well to help cope with this morning's agenda.

Jo said she needed a notebook in which to scribble pertinent points and ideas we discussed as we again reviewed the period from shortly before the commencement of the fateful Rock Island race. As it was the first glorious day in more than a week, we agreed to adjourn to the garden. While Jo galloped upstairs for her notebook, I collected my 'clippings folder' from the office. The file contained not just clippings, but anything and everything I collected to do with James' disappearance.

As soon as we settled in the garden, Jo resumed her interrogation. "Some time earlier this morning, you commented the second letter put paid to any suggestion of coincidence. What makes you think so?"

"The second letter arrived on the anniversary of the day James disappeared overboard. The media was full of it at the time, and for some time afterwards. Anyone interested in what happened would have no difficulty researching it. As with the first letter, the second letter suggested someone – the sender presumably – knew all the details."

"As a third letter has now arrived, I think the first thing we should do is go back to the police. We now can show a continued campaign being waged against you."

"No, I think it would be pointless. The police are so busy, and probably short-staffed, they don't bother even investigating domestic break-and-enters anymore. A woman from one of the groups I belong to had her house broken into on three occasions over the last two years. Items were stolen, damage was done, and the whole place generally turned upside down. On each occasion, she reported it to the police. The police came, interviewed her, took photos and were sympathetic. The bottom line on each occasion was they wouldn't be pursuing the matter. It was not police policy to tie up resources investigating domestic break-ins. When she took them to task about it, the police suggested the break-ins probably occurred because she, the householder, hadn't kept the place secure. So, no, I won't be going back to the police."

"While I too sympathise with your friend, I can't help wonder if the police's inspection of the property after the break-in found some degree of casual approach to protecting the property. You know the sort of thing I mean: a door left unlocked for a teenager to return late; the placed left unlocked for just a few minutes during a quick trip to the corner shop; a window left partially open on a hot summer night. Sometimes it's the things we've done for years without serious consequence that suddenly turn against us."

"I hear what you are saying, but my answer remains unchanged. I would need something more concrete – more solid evidence – to take to the police before I talk to them again. When I spoke to them previously, they treated me like some Nervous Nelly who should go home and take another Valium."

"Right, more evidence is needed. So, how do you plan to find that, Sherlock?"

"Elementary, my dear Watson; by investigating the matter of course … just don't ask me how."

"Maybe a couple of thoughts I had might help make a start. I think I'd like to create a timeline of the various events. I know everything's recorded indelibly in your mind, but a visual reference would help me understand it quicker."

"Okay, where do you want to start?"

"The usual response would be *at the beginning* but, that's not where I want to start. I'd rather talk about this place and how and when you bought it. Was it purchased soon after James' disappearance?"

"No, it was some time later. A lot of things happened before

I thought about selling up and moving. Remember, I wasn't in a position to buy anything straight after James disappeared. All of the company's trading accounts were frozen pending the outcome of a coronial enquiry and probate being granted. I was using my private money to keep both the company and myself afloat until the company's accounts were released. Money was tight. I didn't have spare cash to buy a packet of crisps, because I didn't know how long the situation would last."

"You said the inquest and verdict happened sooner than expected."

"It still had to go to court to have the accounts released. There wasn't a problem with that so much. It was the delay in getting it into court which made my life difficult. The problem was that mine was a civil case and, every time a criminal case was to come before the court, civil cases were bumped to the bottom of the list. So, thanks to the system, there was a considerable delay."

"Yes, that's the usual complaint you hear in relation to civil cases being heard. How long did it take?"

"We finally had our day in court not long… Uhmm … I thought these details were chiselled into my mind forever, but already they aren't quite so clear. Our case was heard not long before the Coroner's Court hearing. I think it was about six and a half months … Yeah, about six and a half months after James disappeared before we went to court to establish James had no legal ownership of the company. He only held the salaried staff position of managing director, and was a signatory on the company's trading accounts. The hearing lasted one day before we were back in court a couple of weeks later to hear the judge's verdict. Whatever the process was, it then took quite a while before I could operate on the accounts again. While I waited, we still had the coronial enquiry to look forward to."

"You said you had to downsize operations but didn't lose any staff that period. It seems a remarkable feat."

"Full marks to staff and employees; without their cooperation, we faced a different outcome. Everyone with annual leave or long service leave due, stepped up and volunteered to take their leave during that difficult period. By doing so, they reduced the number of staff operating at any time. With leave being paid out of the accumulated leave holdings, the amount of wages and salaries being paid out was reduced. While our production was reduced, we were fortunate sales remained strong. Looking back on it now, it seems like nothing short of a miracle we managed to survive."

Jo finished scribbling in her notebook before asking her next question. "So, the first milestone after James' disappearance was accessing the company's trading accounts, and that was about six and a half months later. It sounds like the next milestone on my timeline is the coroner's hearing. You said that was not long afterwards…?"

"It was almost eight months to the day after he fell overboard, and we were lucky to have it scheduled so soon. My legal team told me the court had set aside two weeks for the hearing. I couldn't understand what could take two weeks. But, then it began, and it felt as though anyone who even heard of James was called to give evidence: me, Damien, the Maritime authority who did all the calculations of tide and current, just about everyone involved in the search, even the former crewman. I don't know why they called Damien to the stand. He wasn't on the boat when it happened.

I think every police officer and forensic person who went over the boat in search of evidence was called to the stand. The forensic mob fingerprinted just about every inch of the boat's surface and every piece of equipment on it. Of course they found a host of fingerprints: James', mine, Damien's, the former crewman's, and some of the rescue people who came on board as soon as I was back in the marina. Even the skipper of the other boat, with whom James usually had a running banter during a race, was called to testify. He told how he tried to call James a few times during the race but our radio wasn't responding. At least that backed up some part of my statement."

"Did the hearing last the two weeks?"

"No, thank God. It lasted four days and the early part of the fifth day. My legal team expected the coroner to delay his verdict until the following week, but he didn't. After the last of the hearings in the morning, the coroner adjourned the court until three o'clock that afternoon. When we came back in, after a long summation of the evidence he received, the coroner handed down his verdict. So, it was all over in five days."

"It must have been a relief when it was all over, and so quickly must have felt like a bonus."

"You would think so wouldn't you? I expected to feel relieved, as though the load was lifted from me, but it wasn't like that. It's hard to explain how I felt. I was numb and felt as though I was floating in limbo. It was all over. I should have been rejoicing. Instead, I was an emotional wreck; couldn't even think straight."

"Right, I've added the coroner's hearing to my timeline at the eight months mark. So, by then, you had full control of the company again. The matter of James' disappearance was settled and the legal team could apply for probate on James' estate. How did it go with probate; any surprises?"

"No … well, yes, I suppose there was. James didn't own much: wardrobe of expensive clothes. Expensive camera, few pieces of jewellery – most of which I gave him over the years, but that was about it."

"What about cash?"

"That was surprising. In spite of his handsome managing director's salary over so many years, there wasn't much cash in any of his accounts. Once funeral expenses came out of it, only a few thousand was left."

"You didn't mention the house or the boat – or his vehicle."

"I owned the house and all the contents, and both our vehicles. I bought the boat, but it was in both names. It didn't really matter who owned what. Everything came to me anyway. His estate was so straightforward, the probate process was smooth and quick."

"Did you decide to sell your beautiful big house straight after completion of all the legal matters?"

"No, I think I was still a bit shell-shocked by everything. Thinking back on it, I suspect the idea of selling and moving to a smaller place was somewhere in the back of my mind, but I never thought on it until several months later. I wanted everything to settle and return to normal before I thought about the future or making any changes."

"But you did sell the big house and move into 10 Minstrel Court – which I love, by the way. How did it happen? Was it just some happy, serendipitous accident?

I felt a wry smile slide across my face as I thought back on it. "Serendipitous…? I suppose it was in the end. It took me a few months to realise I couldn't settle in the old house; didn't want to be there. Then there was the long process of deciding what sort of place I did want to live in. That took at least another couple of months. In the end, I decided I wanted a smallish cottage with not too much yard to look after, somewhere quiet, and close enough for the daily commute to work not to become unbearable. An advertisement caught my eye. I set out to look at the place before arranging an inspection … and became lost.

Having driven past the turnoff I wanted, it was almost impossible to make a U-turn on the highway. So, I continued to the next side street … and found myself in Minstrel Court. Intending to turn around on the quiet street before re-entering the highway, I drove to the turning area at the end of the cul-de-sac. On the way in, I noticed the for-sale sign out front of this place and, on my way out, stopped to look at it. Something about the place appealed to me straight off, so I called the number on the sign and arranged for an inspection the following day. That's all it took. I bought myself a new home."

"Right, then there was a further delay while the work you wanted was carried out. How long after James' disappeared was it before you moved out of the big house and into this one?"

"Uhmm, about eighteen months or so; maybe a bit longer by

the time I bought all the new furniture and white goods."

"…And you didn't receive any of these strange letters while you were still living in the big house?"

"No, but mail wasn't delivered to that house. I had a post box at the post office near work. The grounds were gated. Nobody could get in to reach the house to leave an envelope. There were no letters before the first one which arrived at the start of work on this place."

"What about James' phone, computer – that sort of equipment? I assume all that came to you as well as all his other possessions?"

"Y-e-s, but now you mention…." My mobile phone chirped, interrupting what had been an intense question and answer session. I intended checking who it was and calling them back later. " Oh… it's my production manager. I had better take the call. It must be something serious for him to call me at home."

Chapter 4

"Is everything all right?" Jo asked as I wandered back to her with my mobile phone still in my hand. "It was a brief call, so I assume it wasn't anything too serious."

"I'm not sure about that. Something is not right, but I don't know what it is. He's asked to see me – privately – and stressed the rest of the workforce shouldn't know about our meeting. I've invited him to come here. I hope you don't mind the intrusion. Having him come here is against my rule of separating work from home, but I felt it might be the best way to deal with whatever he wants to talk about. He will call in on his way home from work."

"It won't be a problem. I'll get on with preparing dinner while you deal with your manager."

"Earlier you said you had a couple of questions regarding the letters. I think we dealt with one of them. What was the other one?"

"I doubt it is relevant. I was wondering about the things you found to occupy you now you are not at work full-time."

"You're right. They are not relevant. I volunteer with a couple of charity organisations, and I joined a writing group. Each of those takes up one morning a month on a different week. I also joined a book club. It seemed like forever since I last sat down to read a book. We have a set book to read each month and are encouraged to read at least one other of our own choosing. We discuss the set book and our own-choice one at our monthly afternoon meeting on the last Wednesday of the month. And, if I'm going to belong to a writing group, I need to find an occasional bit of time to actually write something."

"Okay, I agree. None of those seems likely to cause threatening letters to arrive. There was something else I wanted to follow-up with you. It was about something you said earlier. I made a note of it."

Jo took a couple of moments to look through entries in her notebook. "Ah yes, here it is. When I asked you about James' computer, phone, etc., your answer was tentative, and I think you were going to say more. Was there more to add?"

"I'm not sure this is relevant either, but it struck me as odd at the time. James had a company laptop which he took with him wherever he went, but he also had a personal machine. When they drew up the inventory of his estate, the company's laptop was not at home."

"Did he have it on the boat with him? Don't they sometimes use a computer during a race to check or set their course or something?"

"Not on the short races we did. When I noticed the computer wasn't at home, I checked the boat. I wanted to make sure it went back to the company and didn't get caught up in James' estate. It wasn't on the boat. I received a shock when I went to talk to our IT department about it. They had the machine. James' secretary had handed it back the day after he disappeared."

"I don't see anything odd about that. Isn't that what you're expected to do?"

"Under normal circumstances, yes, I would expect her to hand it in if it were still on his desk at work. But, there is an anomaly about the time it went back to the IT department. They keep a register of all the machines, and record all movement of each of them during the life the machine. I checked the register. She handed in James' machine first thing the morning after he disappeared."

"Okay, so she is efficient. Why does it bother you?"

"James disappeared late in the evening, and it wasn't until quite late the next day word of his disappearance leaked out. It was as though she knew he wasn't coming back before she arrived that morning, and took the laptop back to the IT department soon after she came in."

"Did you question her about it?"

"No, I never mentioned it. I suppose, while I thought it was odd, I still was in such a befuddled state, I didn't follow up once I knew the laptop wasn't missing."

"Did James' personal computer ever turn up?"

"No …and not for the want of searching. So, do you see why I thought the matter of the laptops was a bit odd?"

"When we first started discussing James' disappearance, I asked you if there were any signs, or anything to indicate what happened. Might the absence of the laptops be some indication of something amiss with the man-overboard assumption? Was there anything else struck you as odd about his disappearance?"

Now here's the hard part. I'm not sure how to answer Jo's question without looking a fool. Jo lost patience with me when I took so long to answer.

"What seems to be the problem? Is there something you don't understand about the question, or is it something you don't want to talk about? If it is the latter, just say so. We don't have to discuss anything you don't feel comfortable about."

"It's nothing to do with any of that; it's just… Argh, what the hell… It's just that I'm not sure whether there was something odd, or whether I imagined it. It was when I searched the boat for the laptops. The lifejacket locker didn't seem to be stuffed as full as it usually was. I suppose someone could have tidied up. Packing them in neatly might have freed up a bit of room."

"Were you wearing lifejackets at the time?"

"We do during races if it's a bit rough or squally, but we weren't wearing them on the run home that night. It was beautiful calm sailing; no need for lifejackets. But as I said, I'm not sure what was missing, and it was sometime after the event when I checked the locker."

"It's worth keeping in mind. You never know, it might slot into the puzzle one day. I was going to ask you about James' mobile phone. Was it the company's or personal?"

"Personal; while he bought it, he used it for everything. Just as I do with mine. The company paid him a set amount every month to compensate for its use on company business."

"I don't suppose anyone checked the calls log after his disappearance…?"

"Not that I am aware of, but the police might have done so in the course of their investigation. Do you think it could be important?"

"I don't think they would bother for all cases, but circumstances surrounding this one might have prompted them to take a look. I don't know if it's important, but it might be worthwhile finding out."

Lunchtime had well and truly rolled past. It was two o'clock and, feeling a little peckish, I was keen to take a lunch break. This morning's session was mentally exhausting, and perhaps a bit emotionally draining as well. Jo didn't argue about stopping for lunch. We managed to drag out our break until almost four o'clock. After that, I had a couple of things to do and Jo went off to sort out the notes she took during the morning. I expected Gordon Grimshaw, my production manager, to arrive sometime soon after six o'clock.

Just before six o'clock, Jo decided she needed extra ingredients for the dish she was preparing for dinner and went off to the shops. She had only been gone a few minutes when Gordon arrived. I took him through to the lounge room. After the usual ritual of offering him coffee or a drink – both of which he refused – we got down to the reason for our meeting.

He dithered about getting on with it and commented several times about not being sure he wasn't imagining things. With a bit of encouragement, he finally told me of his concerns. A précis of those concerns was, in his opinion, figures were not adding up. I argued the company was doing well. He agreed, but insisted things didn't look right. Part way through our discussion, I heard Jo return from the shops. As what Gordon alluded to appeared to relate to possible cash flow anomalies, I wanted Jo to hear what he had to say. While hesitant at first, Gordon agreed to go over everything with Jo present.

"Jo, thanks for joining us. This is Gordon Grimshaw, my production manager. He has concerns regarding some aspects of the company's business. I'd like you to hear what he has to say, and perhaps give me your opinion later."

Once Gordon began his story, it rolled on uninterrupted for the next few minutes.

"I know it's going to sound ridiculous, but I do feel concerned about it, and thought it worthwhile bringing it to Miss McCarthy's attention. Miss McCarthy and I both agree the company is doing well. While orders are keeping us busy, we haven't had to resort to overtime to fill them. I've checked our costings. We're not under-charging anyone for the work we do, and we are applying the appropriate profit margins. We've been so busy, we seem to be ordering supplies just about every second day. Yes, I know it is a good sign. It means our production rate is high and, therefore, our profits also should be healthy. I've checked the accounts… I know the accounts aren't my responsibility, but I had a feeling something wasn't right, so I checked them. They are healthy. There's plenty of cash in them but…"

Gordon shook his head and appeared at a loss as to how to continue his story. Jo was miles ahead of me with interpreting what he said so far. She jumped in to help him continue his story.

"If I understand you correctly, you're saying production is high and all the appropriate costings have been applied. But, I think your concern is about the level of those accounts you mentioned. Do you think something doesn't add up there?"

"Yes, that's it in a nutshell. Everything says we should be rolling in cash. While the accounts are flush, to my way of thinking, they should be higher than they are. There should be more cash in them than there is. I tried reasoning it out in my mind to reassure myself everything was okay, but I can't shake the feeling that it's not."

About five minutes later, after Jo had asked several more questions and I had thanked Gordon for bringing it to our attention, the meeting ended. Before he left, Gordon reiterated he didn't want anyone at work aware of our meeting. I was able to reassure him he had no cause for concern. After he left, Jo and I adjourned to the kitchen where we combined the final preparations for dinner with the review of Gordon's information.

The chicken pot pie Jo produced for dinner was delicious, and coupled with a couple of glasses of Chardonnay, had us feeling quite relaxed and mellow afterwards. We retired to the lounge room, where I knew Jo would revisit Gordon's concerns.

"Over dinner, I thought about Gordon's comments. Has he been with the company long?"

"Oh yes, I think it's been about forty years. If he says he has concerns, I'm prepared to be worried as well. He knows how the place works as well as I do – probably better. I trust his judgement and, if his instinct says something is not quite right, I'm damn well going to look into it."

"He seems an astute operator. I agree his concerns are worth looking into. It's up to you what you do about it, but I'd be willing to have a bit of a poke around to see what I can find. If I'm going to do that, I suggest it's best if the staff and employees aren't aware of it. Not in the first instance anyway; not until we're sure something is amiss."

"Thanks. I'd feel a lot happier if we did that, and I agree it's best kept under wraps initially. I imagine you'll want to poke around in recent business transactions. The best time to do that might be Saturday night. Only the security guard would be on site then, and I think I could get you in without alerting him to your presence. Tomorrow is Friday. I plan to go in for a couple of hours first thing in the morning. I won't have a chance to do much poking around then, but we will have the rest of Friday and all day Saturday to work out our game plan."

It wasn't a late night, but it was a restless one for me. I couldn't help feeling I had taken my finger off the pulse some-where along the line and the consequences were now coming back to bite me. If I'm honest, I knew from the outset when I made Gordon manager, his role and responsibilities were unreasonable. But, I was so busy feeling sorry for myself, all I was focused on was creating an easy life, instead of thinking about the welfare of the company. I know now, just as I should have known then, I have to pick up my responsibilities and return to occupying my office full-time.

*****

This morning found me struggling to be ready for work on time. I wanted to be there before the rest of the workforce. I had become slack about running the company. In appointing Gordon Grimshaw manager, I never intended he should shoulder any more responsibility than the production side of operations. Running the company was my responsibility. I had become negligent, only spending a couple of hours in my office since Jo's arrival.

As I peered out from behind the pile of paperwork on my desk, a procession of surprised faces greeted me as the office staff passed my open door on their way in to start the day. 'Surprised' does not describe the look on Krista Thomas' face when she saw me there. Krista was James' secretary. There were occasions when I wondered if she might be more than that, but there was never any evidence to support my suspicions.

Majella Franks had been my father's secretary and then mine when I took over. Soon after I appointed James managing director, Majella resigned to accompany her husband when his company transferred him overseas. Her resignation left me without a secretary but, as I was withdrawing from the day to day running of the place, I didn't need a replacement. Prior to Majella's resigning, James had appointed Krista as his secretary. My return to work after losing James was not warmly welcomed by Krista. It was obvious from day one we were not going to get along.

Not wanting to precipitate an unpleasant situation, I allowed her position to continue following my appointment of Gordon Grimshaw as manager and my subsequent partial withdrawal from running of the company. What she did to fill in her time remained a mystery to me. On the few occasions I asked some of the senior staff about what she did, their comments, while not derogatory, suggested she was not well liked. How she filled in her day was a mystery to them also, but they found her particularly officious while she went about it.

By the end of my Friday morning's stint in the office, it was obvious the matter of Krista as my secretary would need to be resolved in the near future. Not only was she unhelpful and rude, on one occasion she was openly obstructive. As a consequence, my few stern words about it sent her off somewhere to sulk for the rest of the time I was in the office. In spite of her absence, my morning was quite productive. It took me twice as long as I intended, but I cleared the paperwork from my desk and put in place a couple of things in preparation for our covert visit on Saturday night.

Jo and I took in a show in the afternoon and dined at a little bistro before returning home. Over coffee and port in the lounge room, we discussed plans for our visit to the company's office the following night. The matter of the security guard still bothered Jo.

"You keep telling me it will be okay, but it will defeat our purpose if the security guard gets wind of our visit or, worse still, records it in his log. For this to work – and for possible future visits – everyone must be kept unaware of it. I don't see how you can do that in regard to the security guard."

"It won't be as difficult as you think. In any case, Jim, the guard on duty tomorrow night, has a long connection with the family, and had a special connection to my father. If I asked him not to see, record, or talk about what happens tomorrow night, that's how it would be. Rather than put him in such a position, I checked on the guard's circuit for tomorrow night. Their patrols through and around the property change every night. The key check points remain unchanged. It's just the route the patrol takes each night changes, and they are set by the head of security only a couple of nights in advance."

"Okay, that's a sound security measure, but I'm not sure how it's supposed to make me feel any more comfortable about our plan."

"Something I've never bothered about in the past, I did today. When the head of security left at lunchtime, I had a quick look at the guard's circuit for tomorrow night. Timing will be crucial, but I'm positive we can pull it off without alerting Jim to your presence. Anyway, this morning, I took the precaution of telling him I might come into the office sometime tomorrow evening to catch up on some work. I told him it was his decision but, if he saw me there, he shouldn't be concerned and I didn't think there was any need to log my visit."

"Good thinking. You said timing would be crucial. I presume that has something to do with spiriting me into the place unseen. How complicated will it be?"

"At precisely seven o'clock tomorrow night, Jim is scheduled to enter one of the storage buildings at the rear of the plant. Ten minutes later he should key in at the security point at the far end of the building before making his way out again. It gives us a total of twenty minutes from when he enters the building until he exits it. We'll have twenty minutes to enter the building and have you discreetly set up in my office."

"Is that tight timing for what we need to achieve?"

"Not at all; we should do it comfortably in about half that time."

With Jo's concerns put to rest, at least for the moment, we moved on to other topics before saying good night about half an hour later.

A seething mass of mixed emotions, I had trouble falling asleep. If there was something amiss with the way the business of the company was being conducted, I wanted to know about it. I hoped it would be nothing more than a nervous twitch on Gordon Grimshaw's part and that, on investigation, everything would prove to be okay. Then, there was the question of what to do, and how to go about it, if things proved not as I hoped.

Chapter 5

If I had plans for today, they were nothing more than wishful thinking. Jo had other ideas. She spent most of the day learning about the company's operations, the senior staff and their various responsibilities. Late in the afternoon, we took time to go over every step of tonight's visit in fine detail. While I was quite confident we could pull it off without any problems, Jo remained sceptical.

Our timing was impeccable. It was exactly seven o'clock when I let us into the building. We went straight to my office where I introduced Jo to her workstation. A small alcove off the front wall of my office ran behind the secretary's area out front. I don't know what its intended use was, but tonight the alcove suited our purpose. During my time in the office yesterday, I set up a small table and computer in the alcove in readiness for Jo.

My first priority was to call the guard to let him know I was in my office and would be there for some time. While he knew I was coming in, it was a courtesy to advise him of my presence on site. As was my normal practice, I left my office door open. Should the security guard happen to come by to check on me, he would not see Jo at her workstation tucked back in the alcove.

After logging Jo on and giving her a quick tour of the system, I left her to get on with whatever it is she does while I settled in behind my desk. There was no chance I would become bored because I had nothing to do. For some time, several production reports had remained unmolested in my in-tray. By nine o'clock, having spent the best part of two hours poring over facts and figures, I was in danger of collapsing headfirst onto my desk. In a bid to wake myself up, I checked my emails and surfed the web with no particular purpose in mind.

A few times during the hours we were there, I wandered over to see what Jo was doing. Each time, she was working on a different account. Her open notebook beside her was filling fast with scribble relating to each of the accounts as she worked through them. The short walks to and from Jo helped keep me awake. After last night's poor sleep, staying awake and focused tonight proved a challenge. Our arrangement was, Jo would tell me when she had done enough or wanted to leave. I would check the guard's route to determine the best time to depart without attracting his attention. It soon became obvious, Jo was so involved in what she was doing, she was unlikely to want to leave before midnight.

At around eleven o'clock, Jim, the guard, came towards my office. I dropped a stapler on my desk to make a noise to attract Jo's attention, and then signalled a warning about the approaching guard. The faint clack of her keyboard ceased. By the time Jim knocked on my door, I was flipping through a pile of paper spread out on my desk.

"Begging your pardon, Miss McCarthy, I was just checking you were okay. Apologies if I interrupted you. I thought I should let you know I'm due to come off duty in about half an hour. Stan is to take over from me and will arrive in about twenty minutes. I have one more circuit of the grounds at the back of the property to complete before I come back to wait in the lobby for Stan's arrival."

"Thanks, Jim. I was just about to leave. As soon as I manage to pile these papers up again, I'll be out of here. I won't be here to bother Stan when he comes on duty. Good night, and stay safe."

I glanced across at Jo as Jim disappeared from sight. She nodded to indicate she had heard and understood we needed to be on our way within a few minutes. With the papers I deliberately strew on my desk now back in a folder, I went across to Jo and logged her out of the system. A quick check on the timings of Jim's patrol indicated our best time to leave was in about five minutes. We waited the five minutes before wasting no time making our way out to my car.

During our exodus, I handed Jo my car key. As soon as I opened the door, she slipped out and raced to the car, unlocking it as she went. By the time I'd locked the door behind me and was sauntering across to the vehicle, Jo was curled up on the back seat and invisible. I obeyed all the speed signs as I drove out of the parking lot, and used my remote to time to perfection my opening the huge wrought iron gates to exit the property without the slightest delay. As I turned onto the highway, I caught a glimpse in the rearview mirror of the gates sliding closed behind us.

A few metres further along the highway, I broke the heavy silence in the car. "It's safe to sit up now. We are on our way home. Traffic is light at this hour tonight. We should be in the kitchen fixing ourselves hot drinks in under fifteen minutes."

That was the only conversation during the trip home. Then, we were in my kitchen with Jo parked on a stool at the breakfast bar watching me at the stove making hot chocolate. We took several long swigs of our drinks before conversation intruded the quietness of the kitchen.

"That must be the noisiest clock I have ever heard," Jo said as she glared at the clock high on the wall above the kitchen benches. "Doesn't it bother you … and should a battery-operated clock make so much noise?"

"No, it doesn't bother me because I don't notice it anymore. There's nothing wrong with the clock. What you hear is the second hand clunking off the seconds as it makes its way around the clock face. In the interest of preserving your sensitive ears, perhaps we should adjourn to the lounge room."

Once settled with what remained of our hot drinks, conversation flowed freely. And, there was only one topic of conversation: what Jo found in the accounts.

"I give Gordon top marks for alerting us to his concerns. He was right when he said business had been good. I did a quick check. Production this year is up on that of the previous two years by quite a bit. Pricing appears to have increased a little this year, but it is in line with the CPI increase. Overall, the cost of contractor supplied components has increased by a similar percentage. A couple of contractors haven't increased their costs. I suspect they are bound by the conditions of pre-existing aged contracts."

"I checked some figures while you worked. The volume of materials coming into the works suggests the place must be working at close to capacity. So, it seems we are agreed business is good. Why do I feel there is a BUT about to come?"

"Well, there might be when I know a bit more. Apart from a healthy volume of sales, there appears to be plenty of orders waiting to be filled. I suspect the wait time on orders is starting to increase. If, as you say, the place is running at close to capacity, the volume of orders arriving might be exceeding manageable levels. I don't know what options are available to you, but you might have to look at what's needed to ensure an acceptable turnaround on all orders. I have to admit to being a bit curious about what prompted Gordon to start digging into the accounts. From what I can see, it's not something he does regularly."

"That's correct. He receives regular financial reports, so is happier to spend his time on the factory floor ensuring every-thing goes smoothly there rather than poring over a computer looking at accounts. In the part of our meeting before you joined us, he explained his reason for checking on the state of the accounts. Part of his job is to ensure the ongoing maintenance and continued operation of the plant. He is aware we have been operating at full capacity for quite some time now, and the load on some of the machinery is a concern."

"Does that mean a breakdown of some sort is imminent? If he's worried about the condition of some of the machinery because it might impact on options available to increase throughput?"

"All or any of that is a real possibility. At about this time ev-ery year Gordon draws up a maintenance plan for the factory for the coming twelve months. It includes all the usual stuff: which machinery needs major overhauls and those items which require nothing more than an inspection and maybe a bit of fresh oil or grease. But, it also includes recommendations regarding capital expenditure. Major replacements or upgrades are highlighted in his recommendations. In the report he intended presenting to management at the end of this month, he thought to include the replacement of two major pieces of equipment. He decided to establish the viability of such replacements by checking the accounts before including the recommendations in his report, rather than have management reject them out of hand later on."

"Is that the way it usually works? I mean, does management simply look at the account balances and say yay or nay based on the cash available? Even if indications are failure to spend the money on maintenance or replacement might result in a major breakdown and a greater loss due to production downtime?"

"In my time – and my father's before me – that was not the case. I'm not saying cash flow wasn't a consideration but, whether to spend the money or not was based on much more than the accounts' bottom lines. James did not favour our approach, and often made decisions involving major expenditure unilaterally. We argued many times over his refusal to spend money when it was clearly essential, and to make decisions without the input of the management team. I assure you, as I also assured Gordon, it is not the way we will do business in the future. There will be a return to the old ways – my way – of doing things."

"Good to hear. I wouldn't mind a brief explanation of how each of the accounts is intended to be used. If it's too complicated, we could leave it until tomorrow."

"It is a bit complicated, so perhaps we should leave it for now. I suppose, what I'm particularly interested in is your opinion of the state of the accounts. After all, that's what caused Gordon some degree of indigestion in the first place."

"Well, as Gordon did, I checked all the costings – in and out – and checked the relevant profit margins have been applied, as well as the various taxes. The accounts all have healthy balances – *very* healthy balances – but I don't believe they are quite as healthy as they should be. Given the increased rate of production and higher volume of sales, I would expect to see more in those accounts than I saw tonight. I don't want to send you into a tailspin. There may be perfectly good reasons why the balances sit as they do. Until, and unless, I explore the situation further, I'm not really in a position to give you a definite answer about the state of your accounts."

"Yeah, I hear what you're saying, and it tends to agree with Gordon's assessment of the situation. It's getting late, and I think I need a clear head to discuss things further. Perhaps we should leave it for tonight and continue this tomorrow."

Jo agreed. She wanted some time to look over her notes and sort out a few things before further discussions. I knew it was going to be another restless night. My gut instinct was telling me I had a major problem. Tonight only served to confirm what it had been trying to tell me for the last couple of days.

*****

Neither of us surfaced early this morning. It was after one o'clock when I headed for bed last night. When two o'clock rolled by, I was still awake and stewing over what might be happening within my company. I suppose I fell asleep sometime after that but, late though it was when I surfaced, this morning seemed to arrive much too soon.

With a thick head and feeling sluggish, I forced myself out of bed and made my way down to the kitchen, half expecting to find Jo halfway through breakfast by then. She didn't arrive in the kitchen until a minute or so after me. While she seemed brighter than I felt, the dark circles under her eyes suggested her night wasn't any better than mine. There was no conversation; just exchanged wan smiles by way of a good-morning greeting. For me, conversation was out of the question. It took all my concentration to work the coffee machine.

Our intention was to make an early morning visit to the Sunday markets on the pretence of stocking up on fresh fruit and vegetables. In truth, our visit would be simply to have a poke about … and probably to come home with nothing, which is what usually happens when I go there. It was too late for the early visit required to be at the markets for the best pick of the fresh produce when the stalls began trading. Apart from that, there wasn't a hint of interest in the Sunday markets to be found at 10 Minstrel Court this morning.

While I made coffee and set out the usual breakfast fare, Jo set the table.

"Please make the biggest pot of strong coffee possible this morning." Having made her request, Jo flopped down heavily onto her chair at the table.

I sat opposite her and we ate in silence. Neither of us had the strength for conversation. A second mug of coffee did manage to breathe some life into us. With our dishes added to the dishwasher, and a fresh pot of coffee brewed, we took ourselves and the coffee pot out into the garden. Perhaps a little fresh air might get the juices flowing again, I thought as I struggled to adjust to the bright morning light. After a short while, I risked a few words to Jo as she intently studied her coffee mug.

"…Sleep well last night? You look a lot brighter than I feel."

"Me… sleep well? You must be joking. By the time I sorted out my notes from our visit to your office, it was after three o'clock. I piled into bed ready to crash for what was left of the night. My mind had other ideas. It kept going over 'what-if' scenarios to explain possible anomalies in your accounts. I must have fallen asleep at some point while it was still dark, but I don't think it was much before I woke up again. We do need to revitalise ourselves though. There's plenty still to discuss about the potential situation within your company."

Jo was right. I had a plethora of questions to ask, even though some of them I knew she wasn't in a position to answer yet. Most of all, I wanted to hear her ideas on how we should proceed with investigating the matter. I was about to explain that to her when she interrupted my thinking.

"The problem with sorting out and organising my notes last night was it allowed me to see where I lacked information about the company's operations, about the various accounts, and a host of other issues, some of them quite inconsequential perhaps. Last night, we said we would discuss today what the various accounts are used for. I still want to do that but, as a result of all my thinking last night, I now have other questions to add to the list, questions I hadn't thought of until the wee hours of this morning."

"Well, it sounds like it will be a gabby sort of day, because I'm feeling a bit the same way."

"Okay … do you think we might go inside away from all this bright light before we begin?"

We avoided the lounge. The chairs in there are far too comfortable and constitute a danger this morning – a danger of falling asleep in them. Instead, we opted for the harder, straight-backed chairs at the kitchen table. A short delay ensued while I poured long glasses of orange juice and Jo flapped about organising her file and her notebook.

First came the easy bit: what was the purpose of each of the accounts Jo looked at last night. Explaining the accounts didn't require too much effort or hard thinking on my part. Then came the embarrassment, and it continued for some time: who had authority to operate each of the accounts? Who dealt with what part of the paper trail associated with invoicing customers? Who maintained the ledgers? Who did the bank reconciliations? ...And on, and on it went. To almost all the questions, my answers were rapid fire and succinct: dunno!

How could I have become so totally removed from those processes? Jo's frown as she studied me from across the table did nothing to make me feel any better. I tried convincing myself it was okay for me not to know. Such matters were James' responsibilities, and no doubt he made changes during his time at the helm. It didn't work. James had been gone for nearly two years. For those two years, I was supposed to be running the company. Being made aware of my shortcomings – my *negligence* – was not the most pleasant experience.

"You don't need to say anything. The look on your face says it all. Thank you for the wake-up call so effectively delivered.

One thing already to come out of this is my definite decision to return to running the company full-time. While I neglected my duty, my father probably endured a frustrating time lying in his grave watching me ruin his company."

"There's no point in beating yourself up about it. Now is for discussing how we are to proceed to remedy the situation."

"I'm guessing you have some thoughts on the matter."

"The only way to get to the bottom of it is with a full forensic investigation, starting with a forensic audit of the books. I see one major problem with that: how to do it."

"That should be easy. I'll announce I am looking to overhaul and update systems and procedure, with a view to moving to modern technology where possible."

"No. That won't work. It must be done covertly if we are to find the source of the problem … A-n-d, we still have to establish there is a problem.

"Why does it have to be covert?"

"If you go rushing in with all guns blazing so to speak, the culprit, if there is one, will go to ground, and the trail we need to follow will come to a dead end."

Why is nothing ever easy? The lunch we planned to have at the marina went the same way as the visit to the Sunday markets. We settled for cold cuts and salad at the table where we worked. The rest of the day was spent discussing the company's operations, interspersed with more question and answer sessions. It came as something of a relief when I called a halt to it so I could prepare dinner.

By the time I went to bed on Sunday night, the only thing resolved was the need for a proper covert forensic audit. How to pull off such an undertaking will occupy my thinking most of tomorrow. Just as well I managed to almost clear my desk while we were there last night. I fear I will be a tad preoccupied tomorrow.

Chapter 6

Sitting here in my office in a silent brooding building on this Monday morning, I keep reminding myself of Jo's parting words this morning: *act normal, don't do or say anything out of the ordinary.* It was a tall order given my current state of mind about what might be going on under my nose within my company.

"So far so good," I murmured as I smiled and nodded at the passing cavalcade of workers traipsing past my door on their way to their desks. The real challenge will be when Krista arrives … and responds to my cheery 'good morning' with her usual sour scowl. In keeping with her established routine, my secretary was late again this morning. Do I challenge her about her timekeeping, or do I heed Jo's words and pretend I hadn't noticed? I decided to ignore it today. After all, she was only half an hour late!

After making a mental note to suffer Krista's hostile attitude until the end of the week before tackling the matter head on, I moved to thinking about my first task for today. With a major management meeting tomorrow, I needed to talk to Gordon Grimshaw about his presentation at the meeting. He would be expected to present his works program for the coming twelve months. I intended postponing his presentation until the next month's management meeting. I needed the right words when I advised Gordon of this. There was no need to dance around the topic, I told myself, just tell him about your plan. I keyed in Gordon's number.

"Gordon, do you have a minute to talk about tomorrow's management meeting? … Good … No, don't worry about having your report ready in time. That's why I called. When we reach your report on the agenda, I intend to apologise to the meeting for its absence. My line will be something like this: I haven't been around much and you haven't had a chance to discuss issues with me as you did with James prior to compiling your report. Therefore, I have deferred the presentation of your report until the next meeting... How does that sound to you? If you would prefer to present your report as it stands, please say so, and we will proceed accordingly. On the other hand, if you are happy for me to defer it so we can discuss it in the interim, you may don your best disgusted look when I make the announcement."

While remaining his polite self, his surprise at my proposed move was evident. He asked the anticipated questions. I didn't want to answer over the phone. Then, I saw Krista leave her desk to fetch her usual cup of coffee. Now I could say things I didn't want her to hear.

"Gordon, do you have any plans for after work this evening? … Oh, that's good … I would like a meeting to discuss a couple of issues from our previous meeting. I suggest you have dinner with Mrs Grimshaw, and return here afterwards. How does that suit you? … Great; suggest a time … Okay, eight o'clock tonight here in my office. Thanks, Gordon ... And nobody needs to know about this except us."

After Krista's return to her desk, I embarked on what I hoped would appear a normal day. "Krista, do you have my copies of the meeting papers for tomorrow's meeting? They don't seem to be on my desk, and I plan to spend much of today going through them in preparation for tomorrow."

"Did you look on the system? They're probably there some-where."

"Yes, I am aware at they will be on the system – somewhere. And we're both aware your job is to print them off, arrange them in a folder, and have them on my desk by this morning at the latest. Now, I can understand perhaps that's not how James did things, but it is how I always did it … And, I expect it to continue that way. I expect the folder to be on my desk within the next hour, thank you Krista."

I anticipated some form of retaliation for my rebuke, but perhaps she thought better of it. For the next half hour or so, a passer-by might be forgiven for thinking a demolition crew was at work in my front office as Krista slammed and banged things about, taking out her displeasure on her desk and everything on it. With teeth clenched tight, I ignored the performance, even when the folder of meeting papers was thrown onto my desk and skidded across it to almost land in my lap. I held grave doubts about being able to endure matters until the end of the week.

A number of issues cropped up, delaying my start on the meeting papers until about eleven o'clock. I barely opened the folder when the next disaster struck. A large part of a complex where the company's property is situated was plunged into darkness when a transformer supplying power to the area blew up. We have a large diesel generator we can bring online in such instances to keep the production line flowing, but it can't generate enough power to supply all our operations' needs.

Any services not essential to production were shut down. It meant the office staff had a half day off – including me. I picked up my bag and my folder of meeting papers and was on my way out of the office when an idea occurred to me. I dug my phone out of my bag and keyed in Gordon Grimshaw's mobile number.

"Apologies Gordon, I know you're flat out trying to keep the place running, so this is brief. I've changed our meeting venue. The time remains unchanged, but it is now at the same place as our previous meeting."

He indicated he understood the meeting would be in my lounge room 10 Minstrel Court. I dropped my phone back into my bag and continued out to the car park. After buying a few groceries on the way home, I surprised Jo by arriving in time for lunch. She was eager to know how my morning went. I don't know what she thought might have happened, but she seemed surprised when I had nothing untoward to report.

The rest of Monday was unremarkable. After lunch, I took my folder of papers out into the garden and started on the tedious task of reading reams of management lies. Having expended the best part of a red pen scribbling notes to myself all over them, I decided I'd earned a coffee break. Armed with coffee, I finished reading the last papers in the lounge room. I now had something else with which to shake up tomorrow's management meeting: the appalling standard of the reports submitted to the management meeting. I was shaking my head about the rubbish submitted when Jo came to see if I'd like another coffee.

"What's the time? Ah, so the sun should be down somewhere by now, making it time for something a little stronger than coffee I think."

Jo's leg of lamb roasting in the oven filled the house with the heady aroma of lamb, rosemary and garlic. I felt myself salivate the moment I entered the kitchen.

"I've just added the potatoes, so dinner is about an hour away; how about a glass of wine in the meantime?"

She waved an unopened bottle of cabernet at me. How could I refuse? "Definitely … but it will have to be just-the-one until after my meeting with Gordon this evening."

Typical Gordon, he arrived right on eight o'clock, and I took him through to the lounge room. Apart from offering him a drink first, there was no time wasted on preliminary niceties. He was here in his own time, and I didn't want to take up any more of it than needed. I went straight onto the business of the meeting.

"I'm not going to give you details of why I wanted the rest of the staff and employees to remain unaware of our meeting. Suffice to say, it has something to do with the reason our previous meeting happened as it did. I want you to prepare your works report in line with the production requirements as you see them. It should include any recommendation for capital expenditure you see necessary, and at least rough costings for such works. In other words, I want you to prepare your report as you did *in the old days.*

This means preparing your report honestly and as you see the work required to maintain the best interests of the company and its production. Then, again as was the practice, you will submit your report to me for discussion and comment. After that, make any adjustments in line with the outcome of our discussions, and prepare it for submission to the next management meeting. At our last meeting you mentioned a couple of improvements you thought worth considering. I hope to see those in the preliminary report for discussion. Does any of that need clarification?"

"No, Miss McCarthy, everything is quite clear. May just say one thing? It's good to have you back. It's unfortunate, but I think you might find it rough going for a while. Again, if I may make so bold, James – Mr Rothwell – established what you might call a 'mates' club' within the management team. Many of the old ways were dispensed with under the new order of things."

"Thank you for that. I was coming to that conclusion myself. Don't concern yourself about my having a rough time of it. You seem to have forgotten I'm very much my father's daughter. I'm not suggesting all the old ways remain valid today. What I am saying – only to you at this stage – is that I will be reviewing how we operate; how we do things throughout the company. So, yes, life is likely to become interesting before I'm done."

When I saw Gordon out to his car, I swear I saw a new spring in his step. It felt good to know I had at least one ally in the camp. I hoped there might be others. I have a feeling I'll be needing all the support I can get. Once Gordon left, I went to my small office in what I think was once a boxroom in a back corner of the house. I felt guilty about abandoning Jo, but I needed to sort a few things out in my mind before tomorrow's management meeting.

*****

I had attended management meetings while James was managing director, but my presence generally was ignored. Based on the way the meetings progressed, I developed a feeling everything about the meetings was rehearsed. Nothing about the decisions taken upset me. I felt the decisions were remarkable for the little discussion required to reach them. That's not how I remember the process from my time at the helm, or my father's for that matter. Still, I opted to become a virtual bystander. On many occasions, I had to remember, by sidelining myself, I didn't know enough about an item on the agenda to argue against it. Perhaps this was the 'mates' club' Gordon mentioned in action.

For the first time in several years, the meeting was scheduled to start at 8.30a.m. instead of the more recent practice of commencing at nine o'clock. The undisguised grumbling I heard about the early was one of the many other 'feathers' I intended to ruffle today. And, the first of those would be Krista's.

About five minutes before the meeting was to commence, I picked up my folder and started for the conference room. As I passed through my front office, Krista was conspicuous by her absence. "Not a problem," I muttered to myself, and took a detour to the financial manager's realm located along the corridor in the opposite direction to the conference room. The finance manager wasn't in his office, so I skipped that step of the process and went straight to the reason I was there.

"Majella, I wonder if I might borrow you for a while this morning? I would ask your boss' permission, but he seems to be out of his office. Anyway, I doubt he would object as he will be tied up at the management meeting for most of the morning."

"I don't have anything to do that can't wait, so how can I help?"

"Well, come with me now to the conference room to help me set up for the meeting. Then stay and take the minutes of the meeting. Bring whatever you need with you now."

"I don't need to bring anything. I'll record them straight onto the computer set up in the room for that purpose. I'm a bit concerned about doing this. Taking the minutes of management meetings is supposed to be Krista's job. I doubt she will be happy if I do it."

"She's not here, and the meeting is due to start in a couple of minutes. So, it isn't going to be a problem."

As we rushed past my office on our way to the conference room, I checked Krista's desk. It remained undisturbed from the previous day. If she was trying to make a point, she probably won't arrive until shortly before nine o'clock, the time James commenced his meetings. By the time I settled in my chair at the head of the table to await the arrival of the others, the decision was made. I wasn't going to wait until the end of the week. Krista and I would have words tomorrow.

Only Gordon Grimshaw arrived on time for the scheduled start. One more arrived about a minute after Gordon, a couple of the others were five minutes late, and the last one managed to stroll in about ten minutes late. As soon as I had the first two seated at the table, I opened the meeting and started working down the agenda. The two attendees endorsed the minutes of the previous meeting and I moved onto the next item on the agenda. No doubt, this item's vexatious title of 'Information' probably upset a few people … as it was designed to do. It replaced what used to appear on the agenda as 'Managing Director's Address'.

Those who arrived five minutes late came in as I finished explaining the change. Later arrivals came in some way into the business to be covered by this item. I struck my first blow for the day.

"Thank you for gracing us with your presence, gentlemen; the stuff you've missed you'll have to find out about from others. Now, moving on with the information to the management team, the next item on my list is timekeeping ... and it would appear appropriate today. Staff members have developed a lax approach to the time they arrive at work and when they leave. Such behaviour will not be tolerated in future, particularly on the part of senior staff – such as yourselves. You set the example for junior staff and employees. Timekeeping within those ranks cannot be policed with credibility if they are merely imitating the practice of senior staff. And, that brings me to the next notice I bring to your attention today: the *Three Strikes Rule.*"

My Three Strikes Rule generated predictable reaction from around the table. Amidst the guffaws and openly rude comments, only Gordon and one other sat silent and grim faced. While I was prepared to allow the others their moment to express their derision, I wasn't about to let it run on.

"Gentlemen – if I may call you that – if you would come to order please, I will explain the rule to you. It is important you understand it and how it is to be – and will be – applied. Those employed by this company appear to suffer no consequences for their actions. There must be consequences, or there is something approaching anarchy within its operation. This new rule allows for three warnings for misdemeanours or worse. In the case of an event constituting a third misdemeanour, the offending staff member or employee will have their employment with this company terminated. In case you hadn't guessed, it's the old 'three strikes and you're out' routine. Many misdemeanours I have witnessed on a daily basis probably merit only one 'strike'. Others of a more significant nature will incur at least two demerit points. Punctuality is important at all levels of employment within this company. It shows commitment, or a lack thereof. So, arriving at work late or sloping off early will incur penalties. The rule comes into force from tomorrow. Relevant officers responsible for record keeping under the rule will be instructed on its application later today."

I paused to gauge reaction and to take a breath before continuing with the bombshells I intended dropping today. After receiving no response to my request for any questions, I took up from where I left off.

"The next notice I bring to your attention relates to my own visibility within this company. As from today, I will be returning to running my company full-time. I'm sure that news does not thrill some of you, and my next news item probably will thrill you less."

A particularly obnoxious manager snorted and demanded, "Well really, what next…?" His outburst was supported by snorts and derision from some of the others around the table.

I chanced a quick scan of those seated before me. Apart from some uncomfortable shuffling when subjected to my searing scrutiny, silence descended over the table. Gordon and one other attempted to hide their embarrassment by focusing on their folders. Now I had thrust in the knife, I might as well twist it.

"I would take a moment to point out, gentlemen, your late arrival for this meeting and the poor behaviour during this meeting – by some more than others – would be sufficient to earn you multiple warnings … if the three strikes rule were in place today. It might be to your advantage to keep that in mind. Now, unless there is anything requiring clarification on the rule and its application, I will move on to the next notice."

No one broke the silence, so I made a show of consulting my notebook before clearing my throat and launching into the next item on my list of 'information'. This one I suspected might well strike fear into the very hearts of some of those assembled before me.

"One last piece of information I would share with you at this time has to do with an overhaul of the company's operations. Many of the current processes and systems have been in place for some time. My plan is for a complete review of all aspects of our operations with a view to streamlining and updating wherever possible. Mindful of the current findings on climate change and carbon emissions, the review also will look at how we stack up in this regard. I perceive we are working at almost full capacity at present, and that leaves us vulnerable in the event of a stoppage or major breakdown. There is no Plan B to implement in such an event. It stands to reason then, we must think about our current plant, equipment and technology. It may be that upgrades – perhaps significant – are required to ensure a trouble-free future. The proposed review will not happen overnight. It will be thorough, measured and considered, and as such, may take some time to complete. There will be more on this as the proposal take shape and a start is made."

The personnel manager, his face a bright red round balloon, made no attempt to hide the vitriol in the comment he spat at me "So, you're barely back in the place and you are going to implement cost-cutting initiatives. What are you really telling us … or not telling us?"

"This is not a cost-cutting measure, but it is possible initiatives put in place as a result of the review might result in long-term cost reduction. There is no hidden agenda, and there is no more I can tell you at this time as the basis for the review and how it should proceed are yet to be drawn up. You will be kept informed as the matter progresses."

Then it was the safety manager's turn to vent some spleen. "If you're so interested in climate change and our carbon emissions, take a look out the window at the sea of employee vehicles in the car park. How much must they contribute on their daily commute to and from work?"

"Surely you're not suggesting only those prepared to ride a bicycle to work be employed on this site? Now I think on it though, it might be a health initiative to benefit all staff and employees. And, we do have an obligation to be mindful of our employees' well-being."

Before any further nonsense could be thrown at me, I moved quickly onto the reports. After again reiterating the reason there was no Works report, I spoke in general terms regarding the other reports submitted.

"Before I close this meeting I would like to make comment on the reports received. To put it bluntly, they are a pile of crap. They say nothing and are of no value whatsoever. Perhaps they are what sufficed as monthly reports in the past, but they are a waste of everyone's time. Reports of the same standard will not be accepted in future. Your reports are supposed to indicate what is happening, or has happened, in your department during the preceding month and include some indication of what is likely to occur in the coming month. Instead of the annihilation of so many trees in the production of so many pages of useless reports, it is expected future reports will exceed no more than two or three pages."

While everyone was still spluttering and muttering about my comments on the reports, I closed the meeting. It was almost eleven o'clock. Future management meetings will not run for so long. The managers wasted no time in exiting the conference room. I made my way across to Majella to ask about the minutes.

"Will you be able to finalise the minutes without compromising your own work?"

"It won't be a problem. There is nothing on my desk requiring immediate attention and my boss won't be in this afternoon. The minutes don't need much tidying up. I should have a draft to you by close of business today."

"Your boss won't be here this afternoon…?"

"No-o, I heard him arranging to meet someone for lunch. That usually means he won't be back this afternoon."

Majella removed a memory stick from the computer and left. A minute or so later when I followed her out of the conference room, I encountered the finance manager making his way back to his office with a steaming mug of coffee in hand. I had a few words with him in the corridor.

"Apologies for borrowing your secretary this morning. It was an emergency. I did try to ask your permission before the meeting began, but you weren't around,.."

"I was probably on my way to the meeting already."

"Hmmm … I think not. You arrived late."

With that, I left him staring after me as I swept off to my office aglow with self-righteousness and basking in the view from the higher moral ground.

The morning's battles were not yet over. The next would be waiting for me when I arrived at my office.

Chapter 7

Krista Thomas' face was not a happy one. As soon as I entered my front office, she challenged me about why she was replaced as the minute secretary for the management meeting. Good; it gave me the opportunity to air a few grievances.

"You weren't here. You were late – AGAIN. This company does not wait for the pleasure of your company before it gets on with business. So, the simple answer is: The meeting was to start at 8.30; you weren't here, so someone else had to stand in for you."

"What do you mean about the meeting starting at 8.30? Management meetings start at nine o'clock. They always have. If there was a change, why wasn't I told?"

"Well, you did know. You sent out the notice of meeting which clearly stated the meeting would start at 8.30. Just so there is no misunderstanding in future, regardless of past practice, this is not the past. Management meetings will start when I say they will … with or without you. Oh, you should read the draft minutes when they arrive. Pay particular attention to the bit about the Three Strikes Rule."

All I managed to achieve by lunchtime was to eliminate any hope of support from most of the senior staff, and opened the first skirmish with my secretary. Not a bad effort if you're into masochism I suppose!

Coward that I am, I spent the afternoon hunkered down in my office battling a lack of concentration as I dealt with an influx of papers that arrived during the morning. As promised, Majella sent through the draft meeting minutes late in the afternoon. As usual, I left them on the system for Krista to print out and bring into my office with the mail tomorrow morning. I left for home not long after the last of the other cars left the parking lot.

Jo was busy organising dinner when I arrived home. Her greeting was fairly accurate.

"Welcome home. A-a-h, I see you haven't made many friends today. Pour us glasses of wine, and then let's adjourn to the lounge where you can tell me why your face is so long this evening."

It didn't take long to fill her in on the day's activities. Soon after I started, she started giggling. It turned into a full bodied chuckle by the time I ended my report.

"Oh, you did have one of those days. Is there repair work required, or will you let the situation run its course?"

"There is nothing to be done other than to follow through on the promises – or threats depending on your view – delivered this morning. If I had any doubts about a mates' club, my exposure to it confirmed it is alive and well. And, the war with Krista is about to escalate. The only positive thing about it is that it will be short lived. One way or the other, she will not be my secretary come the end of the week. Now, whether that's of my doing or her choosing remains to be seen. Anyway, enough about me; what did you today?"

"…Nothing exciting or taxing. There were a few domestic chores, caught up on my emails and other correspondence, went for a long walk, picked up the paper on way home, and generally lazed away the rest of the day. After the kind of day you had, I don't imagine you feel much like discussing either of your *other* problems this evening."

"Maybe after a shower and dinner, I'll feel more inclined to do so. I really do want to talk through those issues and possibly formulate plans on how we go about resolving them."

A steaming shower followed by cold rinse brought some life back, and Jo's chicken pasta with ice cold white wine finished the job. By the time the dishwasher was loaded and the kitchen tidied, I was more than ready to delve into how we might solve the problems of the mysterious letters and whatever was going on at the company. Jo decided to tackle the matter of the letters first.

"At the risk of stating the bleeding obvious, sorting this one out is going nowhere. We've nothing to suggest the letters will stop arriving. If we stick with that for the moment, when might we expect the next letter to arrive?"

"Much as I hate to think about it, if it follows the previous pattern, the next letter is likely to arrive on the anniversary of James' disappearance. If that were the case, a fourth letter will arrive in about three and a half months' time."

"Well, it gives us time to investigate what is happening and implement preventative measures to eliminate the likelihood of another letter."

While I agreed, I hoped she had a definite plan, or at least some thoughts on what we should do next. There wasn't time to pursue the matter with her, before she moved on to the company issue.

"Sorting out the company thing is going to be difficult. Under other circumstances, a full-on forensic investigation would be initiated. Even then, it would take some time to get to the bottom of what was happening and who might be responsible. Trying to run a covert investigation is going to be nigh on impossible. I suspect short stretches of time here and there won't achieve much, but would increase the risk of our activities being discovered. If you really want to sort it out, there has to be a full-time investigation. While you know how your company operates and its personnel better than I do, I don't think you've come up with any ideas on how to achieve that. Nevertheless, something you said tonight about putting your staff on notice about your planned review of operations might be useful. Maybe, once such a review begins, there might be opportunity to bring me in as an outsider hired to review the accounting system."

"Y-e-s; that might be a possibility. While I do intend such a review should take place, I haven't given it much thought yet. It's a long way from happening, and I think bringing you in before anything else happens might look a bit obvious. But I agree with you about the limited possibilities open to us at the moment. We can't always pick a shift when Jim is on duty, and

I don't want to put him in a difficult position if what we are doing becomes common knowledge. I know a few hours here and there aren't enough."

It wasn't a late night but, in many ways, it was disappointing. Perhaps naïvely, I hoped, by some miracle, Jo might have thought of ways to attack my problems, or at least one of them. It wasn't to be and, after the day I had, the disappointment was in keeping with the rest of it. Sleep didn't come quickly, but the night wasn't as restless as the previous few had been.

*****

Something akin to a feeling of dread settled over me as I prepared for work this morning. Jo sensed my mood and allowed a silent breakfast. There were few words before we said goodbye and I headed off. As I drove into the company's parking area, I realised I hadn't even asked Jo about her plans for the day. The last thing I want is for her to become bored and decide to move on. I need her here with me, not only to help sort out my problems, but also for her company to help keep me sane.

All morning, I was distracted and achieved little. My mind was preoccupied with trying to work out how I might manage to have Jo here full-time conducting the forensic investigation we now considered a necessity. Only one brief meeting with Gordon Grimshaw constituted my contribution to the company's operations of the morning. Its intrusion lasted no more than five minutes. Once he left my office, I forced myself to look at this morning's mail. The draft minutes of yesterday's meeting were there. Majella did an excellent job. I found nothing to correct or alter, and sent them out for printing and distribution.

In spite of achieving very little all morning, by the time I decided I felt peckish, it was well after my normal lunch hour. So much the better, there would be no queue at the cafeteria … And not much to choose from either. I settled for the last piece of quiche and a fruit juice and took them back to my office. After one bite of my quiche, my lunch was interrupted.

Fate stepped in to lend a hand. Claude Dietrich, a long-time chief accountant came to see me. Having received the bad news this morning, he came to tell me he was resigning due to ill health. Due to the nature of his illness, and in spite of the problems it might cause, he asked to leave at the end of the week. I felt shattered for the man. He had been a fixture here since my father's time, was astute and one of the best workers in the whole place.

He was right about it being inconvenient timing. We were in the middle of the usual flurry of activity associated with end of financial year and preparing tax returns. Still, that was of no consequence at a time like this. His request to leave at the end of the week was approved on the spot, but with a heavy heart. He shared the fact that he didn't need to think about what he might do after leaving here as the time he had left to fill-in would be very short. Nevertheless, his concern about leaving the company in the lurch at such time persisted.

"Thank you for your concern, Claude, it's no more than I would expect from you after all the years of service you've given this place, but it's not for you to worry about. We will muddle through somehow. Something just occurred to me. I do know someone who would be ideal for the job and who I think might be available for an immediate start. I'm sure she will agree to come in, even if it's only for a few months to get through this period of the year. So there, you have nothing to worry about as far as the company is concerned. Take it easy for these last few days, and know that I will be sorry to see you go, and particularly under such distressing circumstances."

Stunned, after Claude left my office, I sat thinking back on my many encounters with him over all the years he worked for the company. My earliest memories of Claude were as a small child who accompanied her father into work on occasions. Dad sometimes handed me over to Claude to look after while he was busy with other business. Claude always had sweets in his desk drawer. I think they were the best sweets I ever tasted.

It was late in the afternoon before I dragged myself away from melancholy thoughts and tried to focus on something else. After shuffling paper around on my desk without actually achieving anything, it was time to go home. I think I might need something stronger than a glass of wine tonight. Claude's news hit me harder than I expected. It was while I was driving home, I remembered the comment I made to Claude about knowing someone who might possibly take over the reins from him.

Of course, it was Jo I alluded to. Not only would she be more than capable of doing the job, it was the opportunity we needed for our investigation to proceed. This evening, I almost skipped into the kitchen. Jo noticed the difference.

"That's an improvement on yesterday. So, come on, share with me whatever it was that brightened your day."

"In a way, it was a sad event, but it has a silver lining. My chief accountant is retiring on Friday due to ill health. There will be an opening for an accountant-type person. You don't happen to know anyone who might be interested?"

"It will give us the perfect opportunity to delve into the company's operations without drawing attention to what we're doing. As a new staff member, I would need to familiarise myself with all aspects of the accounting system and how it is handled. When would I start work?"

"Not as soon as I would like. I undertook not to mention Claude's departure to anyone until after he was gone. He doesn't want any fuss, and it's the least I can do for him after all he's given to the company over so many decades. But, it means I can't do anything about a replacement until the start of next week. I did check the security guards' roster before I left my office this evening. It seems Jim is on duty on Friday night and will have the same patrol circuit as he had last Saturday night. Tomorrow, think about whether you want another covert visit, or if you would prefer to wait until you're officially installed in the place."

Conversation for the remainder of the night was far more upbeat than on the previous night, and afterwards I had my best night's sleep in a week.

*****

As I drove into work this morning, I remembered something I saw yesterday afternoon. It didn't register properly at the time, probably because I was so preoccupied with other matters. Remembering it this morning brought on an angry reaction. It looked as though today would be another day that didn't get off to a good start. At nine o'clock, the day's outlook became even worse.

Soon after eight o'clock, I took myself off to the finance manager's office. Majella informed me he had not arrived yet. Seething, I returned to my office and created the documents I would require sometime later. Yesterday, at five minutes past three o'clock, I noticed the finance manager's car drive out of the carpark. He was about to become the first person to score a strike under the new Three Strikes Rule. To fill in time until said gentleman might choose to honour us with his presence, I dealt with the morning's mail.

The only significant item amongst it was a capital application for the purchase of replacement computers. Under the company's replacement policy, six machines were due for replacement about three months ago. Justification for the expenditure basically echoed the policy. It was the costings, especially the depreciation and rate of return figures which caught my eye. "They can't be right," I muttered aloud, "and those quotes are far too high to be realistic."

After a couple of phone calls to obtain ballpark figures for the purchase of new computers, I spent some time using those costs to calculate the associated figures required on the application form. A quick call to Majella confirmed no quotes for the supply of computers had been received in recent months. My next call was to Claude. A few moments later he was in my office.

"Claude, I have here a capital application form. I assume you didn't complete it?

"No, Miss McCarthy. Only the finance manager prepares those."

"Please take a moment to look at its figures and tell me what you think."

As Claude ran his finger down the table of figures, I watched his eyebrows draw in together until they almost met across the bridge of his nose. When he reached the bottom of the page, he returned to the top and repeated the exercise before looking up at me.

"I'm not sure what to make of this. The prices shown here for the purchase of the new machines is outlandish. As far as I can see, they are comparable with our standard models – newer versions of course – but nothing out of the ordinary in terms of make or capability. But, apart from the price shown, the calculations are strange. Based on those figures, we shouldn't spend the money. Instead, we should run the existing machines into the ground and then go back to using pens and paper. Would you like me to rework the application?"

"Thanks, Claude. No, that won't be necessary. I would appreciate it though if you have a quick look at these other figures I've drawn up. Do they look more realistic?"

"Yes, the prices are closer to what I would expect, and the calculations look about right. Is there anything else I can do for you?"

"No thanks, Claude. You've been helpful, but I suggest you don't mention this episode to anyone." He gave me a knowing look, and turned and left the office.

Is this part of the problem we are hoping to uncover, I asked myself. There is no way I can convince myself this rubbish was an accidental error. It looks like something someone who knows nothing about accounting might produce. That thought set my mind off in a different direction. I reached for the phone to call the personnel section, but stopped myself. A recollection slammed in from left field. There was something strange in one of the filing cabinets in my office. I saw it while checking what was in each of its drawers. I didn't examine in detail the files in that drawer, but something now suggested they would not normally be kept in this office. I bounded across to the filing cabinet and yanked open drawer.

As I walked my fingers across the top of the files, I chanted the labels as I went. These were the personnel files for all of the management team. "Interesting … and convenient for my present needs," I murmured as I pulled out the finance manager's file. "Now, let's see what we know about you."

It turned out we didn't know a great deal about him at all. The file contained the usual contact and next of kin details, but his education record interested me. The photocopied documents tell the story: started a psychology degree; changed to accounting after one year; changed to economics after the first year of accounting; failed all subjects at the end of first year and was sent down. There was no evidence he ever undertook any further education.

"That explains the ridiculous figures on the capital application form. He has no idea what he's doing." The empty room I spoke to had no opinion on the matter.

Just before nine o'clock, having finished with it, I returned the finance manager's personnel file to the filing cabinet, and took the now dealt with mail folder out to Krista's desk. As I walked back to my desk, I noticed a vehicle enter the property's main gate. I watched it park, and the finance manager alight and saunter into the building. Oh dear, I fear the day is about to become difficult, but I waited about fifteen minutes before initiating it.

Armed with a folder containing the rubbish capital application form, and the two documents relating to his misdemeanours, I went to visit the finance manager. Again, he wasn't in his office. Majella confirmed he had arrived, but she thought he went for coffee and would be back soon. I asked her to tell him I wanted to see him as soon as he returned to his office.

Suffice to say the meeting did not go well. The finance manager took offence at being rebuked for bunking off yesterday afternoon and arriving late again this morning. I pointed out he had now incurred two strikes, and handed him the documents confirming the fact. The next couple of minutes involved shouting and bad language on his part. I waited for him to calm down before moving on to the next item I wished to bring to his attention.

I slapped his attempt at a capital application form on the desk in front of him and demanded to know how he came by his prices for the machines, before turning to his calculations and telling him they were rubbish. Then, the meeting moved to the really interesting stage.

"I have found no evidence of your qualifications to hold the position you do within this company. Your poor attempt at this capital application form confirms you have neither the skills nor the knowledge to perform the duties associated with such position. I have no option but, for the integrity of the company and its financial dealings with its many customers and clients, to remove you from your present position."

"You think you're going to terminate me…"

"No; that isn't my intention. It so happens there is another vacancy in the accounting department. One of the accounts clerks went on maternity leave this week. She will be gone for twelve months and isn't sure whether she will return at all. I'm offering you the opportunity to fill the vacancy."

My offer did not meet with his approval. It produced another spate of bad language and abuse, before he got around to telling me what I could do with my company and the job. Couldn't have worked out better; I called the security guard to my office. The ranting and abuse continued until the guard arrived. In the presence of Stan, the security guard, I delivered the final blow in this particular battle.

"As I said earlier, it was not my intention to terminate you. However, you have made it clear you no longer wish to work here. You have one hour in which to clear your desk and vacate the property. You will take only that which is yours with you. You will not remove any objects, files, documents, or anything else belonging to this company. Jason, another security guard, will monitor that process, and will then escort you to your vehicle. Your services are no longer required by this company, and you should not enter onto the property again. Thank you, Stan, please escort the former finance manager to his office and hand him over to Jason."

Chapter 8

Still somewhat shaken by my day at work when I arrived home, last night turned into a subdued and early night. Jo was wise enough not to press me about the matter. It wasn't as though I hadn't terminated employees before. It's something that comes with the territory. But, there hadn't been many, and none were as rough as yesterday's. It wasn't because I dreaded going into work today that I dawdled about, and ended up having to rushing to avoid arriving late. The underlying problem was I felt deflated. So flat in fact, I would rather stay home today. I can't remember ever feeling that way before, and I'm not sure why this feeling, bordering on foreboding, hangs over me.

It was as if people sensed my mood. There were no cheery 'good mornings' from others as they straggled past my office. No one came to my door for most of the morning. Then, late in the morning, Claude tapped lightly on my door. Crafty old fox he is, he waited until he saw Krista leave her office before coming to see me. If Krista were still at her desk, he would never have made it to the door. She seems to have developed the notion only managers are allowed access to me.

"Come on in, Claude, what can I do for you?"

"Er, well, Miss McCarthy, I may well be speaking out of turn here, but I thought it best to talk to you. This morning, I heard a bit of a whisper in the finance department that our manager was no longer with us. My departure this afternoon will make things difficult for the department. I'm not suggesting I'm management material, but I do know the ropes better than the others. I'm prepared to stay on for a while, albeit a short while, if it helps with the situation. Of course, all that is on the premise there is some truth to the rumour I heard."

"That's a noble gesture. Thank you, Claude, but you should proceed as planned … unless you want to stay on."

"No, Miss, that wasn't my motivation for coming to see you. My situation remains unchanged I'm afraid."

"Well, for your information only, Claude, this time the rumour is true. As of yesterday afternoon, the finance manager is no longer employed by this company. I won't be saying anything official about it until Monday, so please keep it to yourself."

"I know nothing about it." He dropped me a nod of approval. "Congratulations; you're well rid of that one, if you don't mind me saying so."

I slipped away to do a quick spot of shopping during my lunch hour, and then spent the afternoon trying to psyche myself up to face farewelling Claude at the end of the day. I called and asked him to hang back and come to my office after the others left for the weekend.

My mood didn't improve much as the day progressed. I was pleased Jo rejected the suggestion of another covert poke about in the files tonight. The afternoon seemed to drag on. While a couple of reports to read remained on my desk, I wasn't in the least bit interested. Instead, I found myself thinking about future staffing arrangements. With both the chief accountant and the finance manager gone, opportunity presented itself to combine the two positions. I could move the best of the clerks up to a new position of senior clerk. It would create a vacancy in the ranks for a clerk, but it shouldn't be too hard to fill if it were deemed necessary.

Pleased with my thinking on streamlining the finance section, I let my mind roam until it settled on the personnel section. For some time before James took over the reins, I felt there was something wrong with the arrangement of this section. While mentally listing the functions carried out by the section, the first question arose. Why was payroll lumped in with the personnel function? Shouldn't it be a part of finance? Maybe there were accounting implications involved. I should ask Jo about it tonight.

Taking the time to just sit and think was paying off. I could see other possibilities for change within the personnel section. With my mind in hyperdrive, I didn't notice the afternoon slip away. The sight of people traipsing past my office on their way home for the weekend jolted me back to reality. After only a few more minutes, Claude would appear at my door. I tidied my desk and organised the couple things I would need. About five minutes later, as I sat watching vehicles exiting the property's main gates, Claude tapped on my door.

"Excuse me, Miss McCarthy, but you asked me to see you after everyone left."

"Come in, come in. I wanted to say thank you and goodbye. If only your leaving were under different circumstances, maybe this would not be such a sad and heartbreaking occasion. I just wanted to say a few words before you left. If my father is looking down, I know he would want me to include him in those words. I don't think either of us can handle much more than what I am about say. My heartfelt thanks to you for all you have done for this company over the decades; for your commitment, your effort, your loyalty … and for the most wonderful sweets you always had on hand for a small child. It seems so little after so long, but this comes from me personally. And, I'm sure it has my father's approval."

I handed him a small gift wrapped parcel containing the best gold watch I could find. There was a brief pause while both of us composed ourselves again before Claude croaked his thanks. Then it was my turn again. "I know Mrs Dietrich is fond of French bubbles, and you are not averse to them yourself. I hope you both enjoy this, and maybe it will help recall a fond memory or two of this place as you share a glass."

There was a slight tremble in his hand as he accepted the bottle of French champagne. He swallowed hard – as did I – before he thanked me and said he had more than enough memories to see out the bottle. With that, he turned and strode out of my office without a backward glance. As I watched him drive out of the carpark for the last time, I felt the tears trickle down my cheeks. "There goes one of the best this company ever employed," I told the empty office.

After taking a couple of minutes to pull myself together again, I too headed home. While I was a bit down after fare-welling Claude, I was in a better frame of mind than I had been the previous two nights. Tonight, I was looking forward to discussing my preliminary thoughts on restructuring the way we do things.

On arriving home, I was greeted by the sound of thunderous hacking. The sight to greet me when I reached the kitchen was enough to make my blood run cold. It brought me to an abrupt halt at the door. With my big meat cleaver in hand, Jo carried out a vicious attack on the body of a chicken already partially dismembered on the chopping block.

"Is it safe to enter?" I had to yell to be heard above her feverish onslaught.

"Only if you promise to pour us something long and cold to drink. We're having stir fry for dinner. That is, if I ever finish hacking this bird to pieces. It is cooked, so it should come apart easily. Apparently it has other ideas, and sees some benefit in resistance."

"Maybe your problem is not so much chicken's resistance as blunt cleaver. I haven't used that one in years. On the other hand, the smaller one is dangerously sharp."

"Now you tell me. Pity you weren't here earlier. Anyway, it's all but done now, so I can leave it while we have a drink and you tell me about your day."

"Happy to have a drink with you so long as it's a quick one. I missed lunch today, and I've now discovered I'm starving."

Twenty minutes later, Jo was battling the large gas wok burner on my stove as she tried to persuade it to provide just the degree of heat she wanted and for it not to burn the house down. She shot me a withering look when I couldn't resist an obvious comment. "That is a vicious burner. Be careful it doesn't cremate everything, including you."

Once dinner was over, we moved to the comfort of the lounge room. We were barely settled into our chairs before Jo asked about the finance manager's departure.

"How did today end? You didn't feel it necessary to sack anyone else today, did you?"

"Not today, but saying goodbye to a favourite long-term staff member was quite gut-wrenching. And, that brings us to something I wanted your opinion about."

After explaining how the finance section was now without its two top-ranking staff, I outlined my thoughts on the opportunity it suggested.

"Since we discussed installing you as the replacement chief accountant, the finance manager's position also has become vacant. My thinking was to combine the two positions. I don't believe the now ex-finance manager contributed much to the department. He didn't have the qualifications or the knowledge to do so. As a result, the chief accountant became lumbered with responsibility for the operation of the whole section. What are your thoughts on combining those two positions?"

"From my superficial knowledge your systems, I think it would provide a more efficient approach to running the finance department. The possible downside might be a gap in the supervisory aspect of the chief accountant's role after it's eliminated. Having one chief with only a tribe of slaves beneath her might lead to poor supervision of day-to-day operations. There needs to be someone with a little more seniority as a buffer between the manager and the others."

"Thank you; that fits well with my thoughts on the subject. One of the clerks has been with us for years and has proved to be a good unit. Some time ago he began a business degree, but family and financial circumstances forced him to abandon it. Still, his studies combined with what he has learned on the job make him a valuable member of the team. In my opinion, he would make an excellent senior clerk. While he would retain most of the same responsibilities he has now, the new position would take on supervision of the other clerks employed in section. Is that likely to work?"

"Sounds like an excellent idea to me. I take it your plan is for me to become the finance manager. If that is the case, I would leave promoting said clerk in abeyance until I've had the opportunity to scrutinise his work and ability. The position of finance manager would allow me to poke around in any and all files relating to financial transactions of the company. There's been no mention of when I might be required to take up my new position. Should I prepare myself to begin work on Monday?"

"No, you have another day or two of holidays ahead of you. Officially, the management team are unaware of the loss of the two staff from the finance department. I plan an emergency meeting of the team for first thing Monday morning to advise them of those developments. That's when I'll tell them how fortunate I was in finding a replacement at such short notice. I'll take the opportunity to share my plans to restructure the positions. I wish I was further advanced with similar thinking regarding other sections. It would make for a great shakeup on Monday morning. I think I might enjoy that."

Jo's support for my restructuring ideas so far spurred me on to think about obvious changes to other sections which would benefit the company's operations. Having had some preliminary thoughts about the personnel section, it was no surprise my mind wanted to continue in that direction. On Saturday, after Jo and I had our mid-morning coffee in the garden, I got down to work. Realising I wanted to work, Jo collected our mugs and disappeared inside, leaving me alone with my thoughts and a pad to record them.

Many sketched charts filled the first few pages of my pad before my thinking gained traction and became more coherent. I remained convinced payroll was a function for the finance section and should be removed from personnel. In my mind, the personnel section should deal with employee information, orientation and induction matters, scheduling various training sessions the company runs and recording who attends, but it left me wondering about such functions as security and safety. At the moment, and for some time now, those two functions have come under the responsibility of the personnel section. Was that the appropriate place for them. Perhaps that's something else seeking Jo's opinion on might be beneficial.

Maybe I was expecting too much when I broached the subject with Jo. She needed me to explain who did what and the various functions currently the responsibility of the personnel section. After making copious notes as I endeavoured to provide the information she required, she took her notebook off to her room to formulate her thoughts on the matter. Again, I was surprised when she didn't come back to me with her thoughts until Sunday morning.

"I don't know whether my thoughts on restructuring the personnel department will be helpful or not. I can tell you, from the outset, I agreed with your suggestion to move payroll to the finance section. Beyond that, it became more complicated. Nevertheless, I do have some suggestions."

"Any thoughts would be welcome. I'm sure they will generate the discussion necessary to develop draft plans."

"Okay, first on my list is security. I have some thoughts on that, but we should leave discussing it until a bit later. While safety was more problematic, it was clear from our discussions yesterday, you do not need a safety manager and a safety officer. After kicking it around for a while, my suggestion is to downsize to only a safety officer, and to locate him in the personnel section. … HOWEVER … there might be another option open to you, but it is dependent on something else happening."

"I just know this is going to be complicated. Come on, lay it on me. What else has to happen?"

"Now, please don't react too violently, but my suggestion is to create a new section or department – whatever you want to call it. Its role would be to take care of all those odd functions no one is quite sure where responsibility for them should reside. I see it including such functions as security, PR … and maybe safety if it doesn't fit with personnel. I know creating yet another department won't thrill you when you are in streamlining mode, but it's worth thinking about."

Our discussions occupied my mind for the remainder of Sunday until Jo commented on my preoccupation over dinner that night. She succeeded in making me feel guilty, and I apologised for being such poor company.

"You're right. This is not something I should bring home from work with me. I should shut my office door and focus on it while I'm at work."

"True; but, going back to work and having to think about restructuring, has managed to take your mind off those upsetting letters you received."

"I haven't forgotten about them. I just need to get the work thing settled down and running the way I want before I devote any more energy to trying to get to the bottom of what the letters are about."

"Well, that brings me to something else I hoped to talk to you about this weekend. In whatever time I have before you want me to start work, I thought I might do some digging around in relation to those letters. I still think it's possible they are meant for someone else, possibly the previous occupant of this address. It's worth finding out who that was before we dismiss the possibility. There are a couple of people I know who could help in establishing who was living here before you. More details of the police investigation into James' disappearance also might be useful. An old friend of mine is a detective here. I might have a chat to him."

"No! We've been over this before. The police gave me a rough time of it while they conducted their investigation, and they were none too receptive when I went to see them about the letters. I told you before. We need hard evidence before I am prepared to talk to the police again. The last thing I need is you stirring up people's interest at this time in either me or what happened to James. It's not that I don't trust the police or those other people you know, but I also know what I have experienced in the past. No, I do not want you digging around in the letters or James' disappearance. Let's sort out the situation at the company first, and then we will think about how to proceed with the other. I don't want an argument about it, Jo. I'm telling you to leave everything else about my life alone. Confine yourself to what is going on in my company."

Jo flounced off to her room in anger. The truth is, I was pleased she did. I was so angry with her, if she hadn't gone off, our situation might have degenerated into a full scale row. She knew how I felt. I made it quite clear on more than one occasion in the past. In the end, I too went to bed early and had a terrible sleepless night.

*****

Things remained tense at breakfast this morning. Jo didn't come down until shortly before I was ready to leave for work. We exchanged nothing more than stiff 'good mornings' before I marched out of the house. All the way to work, I questioned whether bringing Jo into work in the company was the right decision. She might have strong argument for what she wants to do about investigating the letters – and now James' disappearance as well but, if she is going to work for me, things will have to be done my way. She is strong willed, especially when she thinks she knows best. Maybe she is about to learn a hard lesson about me and how I do things.

Wouldn't you know it? Just when I'm dealing with a full head of steam and a major load of bad temper, things only get worse. I suppose it was to be expected after I landed an extraordinary management team meeting on them as soon as the day began. My outlook on life darkened further when a couple of them arrived late for the meeting ... And the meeting was further delayed while they experienced the full force of my bad mood. Nevertheless, it eventually did get underway.

"While I'm sure you are all aware of what I wanted to share with you today, it's important you hear about it from me. At the end of last week, two senior members of staff, the finance manager and the chief accountant, severed their connection with this company. Their departure has opened the door to begin restructuring. To this end, I have sourced a replacement for the finance manager. The chief account's position will cease to exist. Instead, I propose promoting one of the existing clerks in the finance section to the position of senior clerk. All this might require a day or two before it comes into effect. Please be mindful of the situation in the meantime if you are dealing with the finance section."

"Are we to know something of this finance manager's replacement you came by at such short notice?" the personnel managed demanded.

His tone combined with the way in which he worded the question only served to make me more bloody minded. His section most definitely would be restructured – and soon. I barked my response to his question.

"Jo Ballard has postgraduate qualifications and an impressive past work history. Both of which make her an admirable replacement for the finance manager. She will take up her position at a time still to be decided, but during this week."

"Her…? You propose filling a manager's position with a female? I would remind you, managers in this company are male."

The personnel manager must have had a bad weekend too. It gave me some satisfaction to think I'd just made his day worse.

"And, I would remind you I own this company. Your opinion is of no consequence in this matter. You are not a board of directors able to influence or dictate what will or won't be done. You are employees of my company, as are the other members of the workforce. Nevertheless, I will address your comment. Gender bias has existed in the company far too long. This is the twenty-first century, not the horse and buggy days. My father was a man of his time. The gender bias he endorsed is a relic of those times. There is no room for it in the company any longer … and I will employ whoever I see as the best person for the job. Before any of you decide to argue this point further, you should take on board my final words on this subject: This is how it will be. Like it and work with it, or … I think the phrase is … *hit the road,* because there is no longer room for such bias in this company."

After closing the meeting and dismissing them, I remained in the conference room for a minute or two after they left. Yes, I was being a coward, but I had vented my spleen. I had run out of venom and did not want to be bailed up by one of them on my way out.

The rest of my day was spent locked in my office working on how to restructure the personnel section.

Chapter 9

Jo: a covert operation

"Another day of marking time," I grumbled aloud to the empty house. "This is not how I like to do things. I know Mel's had a rough time of it since James disappeared, and that includes her treatment by the police, but we need to do something about those letters before the next one is due to arrive."

So, is this what Jo Ballard is reduced to these days, I asked myself; sitting alone in a kitchen talking to myself. It might be Mel's problem and Mel's life, but I would be less than a good friend if I didn't get off my backside and do something to help. To hell with all her do-it-my-way stuff from last night. Doesn't the old adage say something about *what the eye don't see?* She is unlikely to see or know anything about what I get up to while she is at work. And I won't be mentioning it to her unless and until I have some of that 'solid evidence' she keeps banging on about.

"Hello, Sydney. Good to see you are still where I hoped to find you. Since it's been so long since we last spoke, this is Jo Ballard in case you've forgotten me."

"Jo Ballard … You're right. It has been a while. Are you home again?"

"Yeah, for a while anyway. I thought we might catch up for lunch or a drink."

"Oh yes, and what is it you want me to do for you? I'll bet it is something not quite kosher. When did you have in mind for us to meet?"

"Uhmm … Today if possible; time is in short supply on this one."

"So happens it's supposed to be my day off, but I came in to tidy some paperwork. I could manage lunch. Name the time and place."

It was after nine o'clock by the time our brief call ended. I had a couple of hours to prepare for my meeting with Syd Hartley at a quiet pub where we shared many a drink in the past. Syd was not one to suffer fools lightly, and would not tolerate wasting time. If I wanted Syd to help, I needed to be succinct when I gave him the facts; no unnecessary words or chatter. Maybe the best approach would be to record all the facts as dot points in a document he could take away with him after our meeting; a sort of *aid to memoire*.

The next time I checked my watch, it was eleven o'clock. I needed to be on my way in half an hour at the latest. While it took only minutes for me to gather up all I intended taking with me, freshen up and be on my way, Syd already was seated at a table when I arrived. I ordered a drink on my way past the bar.

"Thanks for this, Syd. I don't doubt your life is as busy as it ever was."

"Yeah," he sighed. "Crime doesn't go away. It just gets worse, and there is more of it these days."

"I hope the food here is as good as it used to be."

"It is. I often drop in here for a meal. So, shall we order? And then you can get on with telling me why we are here. Are you working a case?"

"Oh good, straight down to business; anyone would think you weren't pleased to see me again, and after such a long time too. Since you ask, I'm supposed to be on holidays and staying with a friend."

"That would be Melissa McCarthy I imagine."

"Yes, I am staying with Mel. She got rid of the big house and now lives in Minstrel Court. My unit is still leased out. I haven't been here long, but I now have two investigations to take care of."

"Are they linked?"

"I didn't find out about them at the same time. While at first glance they appear two separate cases, my gut instinct is telling me they might be linked. The first major hurdle I've encountered goes back to a couple of years or so ago. To eliminate some possibilities in regard to the first investigation, I need to find out more about that earlier event. It might prove to have no relevance to the present matter but, without more information I can't eliminate it from my thinking."

At that point, our meals arrived causing the usual interruption to discussions. Conversation didn't resume until we had almost cleaned our plates. Syd posed the first question signifying it was time to get back to the reason we were there.

"Okay, let's start with the first incident you want to investigate. Why do you need my help with it, and what is it about?"

After explaining about the arrival of the mysterious notes, I reiterated Mel's comments regarding her experiences with the police. I told him how, as a result, she was reluctant to approach the police again without more evidence.

"Sounds like a pretty straightforward case of mistaken identity. Maybe the notes are meant for someone else, probably the previous occupant of the house."

"That was my first reaction as well, but the timing of the arrival of the notes tends to negate that idea and push the possibility of coincidence a tad too far."

With the aid of my notes I detailed how the three envelopes all arrived on significant dates, dates relating to Mel's husband, James.

"If the pattern runs true to form, it's likely a fourth envelope will arrive in about seven or eight weeks' time. I don't have the exact date, but it will be on or about the second anniversary of James' disappearance. As neither of us is a fan of coincidence, you will understand why I need to go back and investigate James Rothwell's supposed drowning. Those notes have to be connected to James in some way, don't they?"

"Hmm, I agree it's worth taking a closer look at James' disappearance. I guess Mel gave you a detailed account of what happened, and there will be considerable information out there in the public domain. So, what is it you think I might help you with?"

"I suppose I'm interested in what the police investigation into James' disappearance turned up. In the course of our conversations on the matter, Mel mentioned two things she believes were missing at the time the police conducted their investigation: James' personal laptop, and a lifejacket from the boat. It was sometime after they carried out the inventory of James' estate for probate purposes that she realised the laptop was missing. I suggested it was possible the police had removed it in the course of their investigation. She claims she asked them about it when she realised it was missing. They assured her they didn't have it and, had it been there at the time, they most certainly would have taken it."

"It won't be too hard to look into that one. I'll do a bit of surreptitious digging around. What else?"

"I don't know how to put this. I can imagine your response, but my gut is telling me James' phone records from around that time could be useful. Mel believes the police took the phone. If they investigated the calls log, they didn't discuss it with Mel. I find it hard to believe they would confiscate the phone and not request the records."

"You're right about that. It would be routine procedure in a case such as this. I'll add it to the list of things to keep an eye out for while I'm doing my digging around. Now, you mentioned something about a lifejacket. What's the story there?"

"As you might imagine, in the early stages of the investigation into James' disappearance the police searched the boat from top to bottom, and dragged Mel around with them. They asked her if anything was missing. She hadn't noticed anything out of place at the time. It wasn't until sometime later – I don't know how long –something about the lifejacket locker niggled her. She went back to check it, and found there seemed to be a lot more spare room in the locker than normal. The lifejackets usually were a jumbled mess, jammed in and occupying every bit space in the locker. The last one usually took superhuman efforts to shove it in. On the occasion she went back to check the locker, the thing that struck her was the way the lifejackets were neatly folded and stacked, leaving quite a bit of vacant space. Realising what the implications of her discovery might be, she took it to the police. Well…"

"Yeah, I can imagine how that went. If I were conducting the investigation and she turned up some time after the event to change her story, I would want to know why she was trying to shift the focus in a different direction."

"You weren't involved with that investigation. It surprised me a bit. I thought you would have been in the thick of it."

"Had I been here, there is a fair chance I would have been involved. It all happened about twelve months after I lost Linda. I thought I was okay and battled on for almost a year before I realised I was a long way from okay. Granted three months leave, I took myself off to the Maldives for a couple of months. After returning, I spent the next month visiting family and friends all over the place. It wasn't until I returned to work I found out about James' disappearance. By then, the investigation had gone quiet. I didn't follow up on it."

"It sounds like the police were convinced James' disappearance was suspicious, and had Mel earmarked as their prime suspect. I suppose it's not hard to see why she hasn't got a lot of respect for or trust in the police after all that."

"Okay, I'm going to see if I can find anything on the laptop and the log of his phone calls. I'll spend some time going through the case notes, and anything else there is. You never know, something might jump out at me. What about these mysterious notes and the possibility they weren't meant for Mel?"

"I'm going to talk to another acquaintance, one I've often used in the course of my official investigations. I'm hoping to gain some background information into the house in Minstrel Court, and it's more recent occupants. Again, it's about eliminating possibilities, and not necessarily about finding answers."

"You said there was a second situation you are investigating. What's that all about?"

"To say I am investigating it is something of an overstatement. Last week, our attention was drawn to the suggestion something 'fishy' might be happening at Mel's company. So far, I've only had opportunity to spend about four hours poking around in their files. It might be premature, but I found enough to suggest misappropriation. Fate has worked in our favour on this one. As a consequence of a sequence of events, Mel intends installing me in her finance section, probably in the next day or two. I'm trying to do what I can before I start full-time work for her company. Something I should mention, Mel is unaware I'm talking to you or my other acquaintance about either or both of these investigations. It would be best for the situation to remain that way."

"There can be nothing she can read into old friends meeting up for a meal or a drink on the odd occasion. After all, you and Linda were close friends, and you were her bridesmaid when we married. After the wedding, I think you spent as much time at our place as you did at your own flat. It's only natural for us to want to rekindle the friendship."

"That's something else I missed out on when I was overseas and, as with James' disappearance, I didn't hear about Linda's death until sometime later."

We didn't linger much longer. That's how Syd is. Once the business is done, there are other things to do and other places to be. Today, I was happy enough about his approach to life. I too needed to be elsewhere for a meeting with someone else. As I left the pub, I realised I had about half an hour to fill in before my meeting downtown with Craig Newman.

It came as something of a surprise when Craig suggested a three o'clock meeting. Unlike Syd Hartley, Craig tended to be chatty. A solicitor, Craig's preference was for meetings outside of work hours, unless whatever I wanted to talk about was on-the-books. In the latter case, it often was hard to keep him focused on the business in hand, and stop him wandering off onto totally unrelated topics. If I were less generous, I might consider it a ploy to boost his billable hours.

This time, I arrived at the coffee shop well ahead of my scheduled meeting. Craig arrived about five minutes late; not bad for him. Running late for meetings was his standard practice. This afternoon, I didn't mind. It gave me time to get my head around what to tell him, and what to ask him to do. After the usual greetings, it was obvious Craig was in one of his chatty moods. I checked he wasn't billing me for the meeting.

"No, of course not; why do you ask?"

"You seem prepared to settle in and chat … and our meeting is during work hours."

"Ah, my world is a different place these days. My mentor and long-time owner of the firm wanted out, so I bought it. I now have my own legal practice, and it's doing quite well. Hence, I am able to spare some time for an old friend."

"Well, I don't have too much time before I need to be home again. Would you mind if we got down to business?"

He gave me a surprised look and gestured for me to begin. My abridged story of the letters was all he needed to begin searching for the information I wanted. "Okay, so it's 10 Minstrel Court we are interested in, and there is nothing illegal involved in what I am going to look into for you?" I nodded. "Shouldn't take much trouble to identify the previous owner from the Title Deeds held by the Titles Office. Nothing more than a routine property search involved. If it was a rental property, I would need to track down the property manager to obtain the information you require. I might have something for you by tomorrow, or the following day at the latest."

Craig wanted to stay and chat. I wanted to be home and with dinner preparations happening before Mel arrived. By the time she came home, the lamb chops were marinating and the vegetables were organised. I had psyched myself up for the nothing-happening-here performance I needed to produce once she arrived. She didn't seem to notice anything different, so maybe I'm a better actor than I thought. It would be just as well if it were true. I might have to maintain the façade for a few days yet.

*****

True to his word, Craig Newman called me late the following afternoon. I was relieved to hear from him then as there was some suggestion I might be starting work tomorrow. His news was both helpful and disappointing at the same time.

"I managed to track down the previous owner of the Minstrel Court property. It was owned by a company, so I contacted the person whose signature was on the documents relating to its sale. She turned out to be a secretary or PA, but not the actual owner. The former owner, a woman, was away and not expected back until later tonight. I asked for the woman's name with a view to contacting her tomorrow. The woman I spoke to refused to provide the name. She told me calling the same number I called this morning would put me in contact with the appropriate person."

"Well, that's a good start. I suppose there's nothing to do except wait for whatever tomorrow brings."

"Ah yes, tomorrow … there's a bit of a problem there. I've now got a court appearance for most of tomorrow, so there are two ways we might progress for here. Either you could leave it until I find another few minutes of spare time to call the woman, or I give you the information and you call the woman. I suppose it comes down to whether the information is urgent or not."

"With my own situation likely to change at any time, I think it wise if I follow-up with the woman to progress the matter as far as possible while I can."

Craig provided me with the number to ring and the name of the person he spoke to earlier today. He also gave me the name of the company under which name the property was held. There was little more I could do tonight, but I could run a search on the company to see what turned up. I was about to go up to my room to search the internet when Mel arrived home.

She looked tired, but not as stressed as in the previous few days. There was no hurry for dinner, so we sat and chatted over a drink. I nudged the conversation in the direction of the company by asking if there were any new developments today.

"No, thank goodness, nothing new today. Of course, there is still a fair bit of tension through the place. I imagine it will continue for a while before settling down. I've given a lot more thought to restructuring the personnel section. Your opinion on some of my proposals would be most welcome – but not tonight. Perhaps it would be best to let my thinking on the matter rest for a day or two before I trot it out to discuss with you. You never know, leaving it alone for a day or two might allow it to clarify further."

"I'll be interested to hear about it whenever you're ready. Speaking of work, I was wondering if you made any decisions about when I should join the workforce. It doesn't make a lot of difference to me I suppose, but I do feel we are wasting time if I can't access the files in the meantime."

"Yeah, I've had similar thoughts. My thinking is, next Monday would be a good day for you to start. In the meantime, there might be an opportunity for you to be on-site officially. As the new staff member to start next Monday, it would be logical for you to be given a tour of the site, and to have a longish orientation and pre-employment session with me … in my office. It would be quite aboveboard, and would ensure we weren't interrupted. What do you think?"

"I think it's a brilliant suggestion. When might this orientation session occur?"

"How about Saturday afternoon…? I checked the rosters and the security guard on duty will be Jim. Not that it would be a problem whoever was on duty, but I just prefer it was Jim rather than any of the others. So, unless you have something else on, we could have lunch somewhere and then go into work afterwards. There would be no time restrictions as this was official company business I was conducting."

Her suggestion couldn't have worked out better. I assured her Saturday afternoon was fine with me. What I didn't mention was the fact that I was pleased I wasn't starting work until next week. It gave me a few more days – starting with tomorrow morning – in which to continue my covert investigation into those matters Mel had told me to leave alone.

*****

This morning found me anxious for Mel to be off to work. Then there was the small matter of waiting until a suitable hour before I tried calling the number Craig Newman gave me yesterday afternoon. As I still hadn't found out anything about the company that was the registered owner before Mel purchased the place, I filled in the time until my phone call by searching the internet for whatever it might provide.

There was scant information on the particular company, but I did discover it was a subsidiary of a larger entity. This particular subsidiary appeared to have been established specifically for dabbling in the property market.

Chapter 10

Jo: a covert operation continues

The same woman Craig spoke to yesterday answered my call. She seemed none too pleased I interrupted her morning. It took a few firm words before she relented and went to fetch the woman I needed. In the few moments it took for the woman to come to the phone, I tried to compose what I would say. My thoughts hadn't untangled themselves when a woman's voice rattled off a name I didn't catch. After the usual apology for interrupting her morning, and for the vague nature of my enquiry, I launched into my spiel. So far, this woman appeared more willing to talk to me than the other one.

"I believe you – or your company, that is – previously owned the property at 10 Minstrel Court."

"About twelve months ago now it was sold. What is your interest in the property?"

"A letter arrived at that address. There was no return address on the envelope, so we marked that one 'not at this address' and sent it back to the post office. Now, another letter has arrived. We felt obliged to try re-addressing it to the intended recipient. Our problem is, we haven't been able to make out the name on the envelope, and so we haven't been able to trace the person to whom it was intended. I'm assuming, as the previous owner, the letters were intended for you. I'm sorry, I didn't catch your name but, if you give me your name and address, we will send it on."

She laughed. "There'd be no point in sending them to me. I never lived there. It was a rental property, along with a couple of others in one of my portfolios. They weren't perform-ing particularly well, so I decided to divest myself of them and invest in something else. If the letters were meant for the last tenant, I'm not surprised you couldn't decipher the name on the envelope. I believe she had a foreign name. My property manager would be able to help you with that one. But, I don't know about forwarding them onto her. Maybe you would need to hand them into the police."

"The police…?" I didn't expect that comment.

"I don't know all the details; didn't want or need to know. I think it had something to do with drugs but turned into something more serious. All I can tell you is that my property manager was pleased to see the last of her. Some months earlier, I told them to put the property on the market. They argued the market was flat at that moment, and it might be better to continue renting the property. I said no but, when the place hadn't sold after some time, I was about to rethink that decision. Anyway, I happened to be in the neighbourhood one day and decided to drive past the property. A woman was applying a SOLD sticker to the for sale sign out the front of number 10. I was pleased to see it gone; didn't think any more about it. I'm sorry I can't help you with your problem of the letters, but my property manager might be of more assistance. If they're reluctant to talk to you, tell them you've already spoken to me."

She gave me both her details, and the property manager's contact information. I felt excitement stirring. Her reference to the tenant falling afoul of the law might explain a few things. Could it be so easy to find the information Mel needed to go back to the police? My gut told me not to get ahead of myself. In reality, I was a long way from proving anything. I called the property manager.

"Yes, I managed the property at 10 Minstrel Court until it was sold about a year ago now. What was it you wanted to know about the property?"

"The previous owner gave me your contact details and suggested you might help with my enquiries." I spun her the same story about letters turning up without a return address and an indecipherable recipient's name. "We returned the first one to the post office. When the next one turned up, we felt we should attempt to forwarded on to its rightful recipient, but we didn't have a name or a current address. We wondered if you might be able to help with that."

"I can give you her name. It's foreign has a complicated spelling. You have a pen ready I'll spell it out for you in just a moment." I heard the cracking of a keyboard for a few moments before she spoke again. "Right, I have the file open. Here is the name you wanted. Now, about the current address; I can't be definite. You need to address it to a prison, but I'm not sure whether it's one here or overseas somewhere. It was an interesting period before we finally had her out of the house."

"Might I inquire what was interesting about it? The mention of prison has me intrigued."

"She was about three months behind on the rent. We did think about calling in the bailiffs in case she did a midnight flit and left us no chance of recovering the rent arrears. There had been any number of complaints from the neighbourhood about noisy parties, loud arguments, vehicles coming and going at all hours of the night. You name it. Everything that upsets neighbours went on there. Then, one of the neighbours rang to say the police had just carted her off. Judicious enquiries revealed she was arrested on various drug charges. I don't remember the case going to court, but a bit later I heard she was extradited to the continent for some serious crime committed over there. That's about as much as I can tell you. If you're determined to forward mail onto her, I suggest you talk to the police. Maybe they can provide you with more details."

Oh, I did like the sound of that tenant. She sounds like the right sort of person to be the intended target of the mysterious notes delivered to Mel's address. I still needed to do a bit more digging before I discussed it with Mel. Perhaps I need another conversation with Detective Inspector Syd Hartley. If it's as simple as it sounds, we might be able to close this investigation quite soon.

By the time I had tidied and added today's notes to my file it was lunchtime. I was hungry, but the morning's phone calls had me hyped and eager to press forward with the investigation. Syd Hartley was probably at work, and probably up to his ears in a case. Somehow, I managed to hold off calling him until after I had lunch. Expecting my call to go through to voicemail, I was surprised when he answered almost on the first ring.

"Syd, tell me if I'm interrupting something and I'll call back later."

He cackled as he responded. "How considerate of you. I don't remember it being a part of your repertoire in the past. No, this is a good time to talk. I'm sitting here keeping my desk company in an otherwise empty squad room. I was going to call you today but I wasn't sure what your situation might be … Didn't want to create a problem by ringing at the wrong time."

"Today is fine. It looks as though I might not start work until next week. If you are going to call me, does it mean you found something of interest?"

"Well, I had a preliminary dig around and I have something you might find interesting. But, I'm more interested in why you called me."

"I've been doing some digging too, but in a different direction and on a different matter. It produced some odd information which I'd like to run past you as soon as possible."

"Is this in relation to the other investigation which may or may not be linked to the one I'm looking into?"

"Yeah, that's the one. I'm not sure what to make of what I found."

"I just need to finish something I'm doing at the moment. What say we meet at our coffee shop in about an hour?"

Things were going much better than I dared hope for today. I calculated I had about half an hour in which to organise my thoughts, and my notes, before heading out to meet with Syd. The coffee shop was deserted and I was early for our meeting, so I had my pick of the tables. I selected one in the corner furthest away from the counter. Syd arrived about ten minutes later and, as usual, we were straight down to business as soon as we ordered our coffee and Danish pastries.

Passing on to Syd information gathered from my phone calls this morning took little time, and I gave him a copy of my notes from the calls. After a few moments of thought, he recalled the case involving the tenant from Minstrel Court.

"Yeah, my recollections are a bit hazy, but I do remember the woman was a nasty piece of work. She was in trouble here but, when we were processing her information, we found outstanding warrants for her arrest from somewhere overseas. I'm not sure about the details, but I seem to remember her overseas crime being of a more serious nature than the ones she was charged with here. Am I to assume you now believe those mysterious notes Mel received were intended for that other woman, the tenant?"

"She seems a good fit for the contents of the notes, but I don't have anything concrete to tie them to her. I would be interested in details of the crimes she was involved in, and possibly where she ended up. I don't intend talking to Mel until I'm more confident it is just a case of mistaken identity, and the letters are meant for the other woman. Now, what do you have to tell me about your digging into James' disappearance?"

"Don't get too excited just yet. I haven't found anything too monumental at this stage, but it's early days. James' mobile phone was in with other evidence. I checked the file to see if the investigation obtained a record of his calls around the time of the incident. I couldn't find one, and it doesn't appear there was a request for one. While I wasn't sure I'd be able to get one after so much time had elapsed, I decided to give it a go anyway. A friend in the right department did me a couple of favours. It was worth taking a punt in my opinion."

"The calls log produced something relevant…?"

"As I said, it's early days. Having said that, there was some interesting stuff going on at the time, and had been for a while from what I can see. I still have to check a couple of numbers before I know who or what was running up his phone bill. Something occurred to me while I was talking to my friend about obtaining the report, and I decided to stretch our friendship a little further. First, the obvious question was whether the phone was used at around the time James supposedly fell overboard. The second question that came to mind was whether there were any other phones registered in James' name."

"Oh, I do like the sound of those questions. Please tell me the answers you received are just as exciting."

"Ah well, I don't have all the answers yet. But I was able to confirm something my friend told me once I had the report. At around the estimated time James was busy disappearing, there were calls to and from his mobile phone. Both calls involved the same 'other' number. Before you ask, I haven't yet been able to identify who owns the other phone."

Bugger. Syd had me sitting on the edge of my seat until then. What a letdown... Still, my instinct told me it was important, and I'm sure Syd thought so too. After complimenting him on what he dug up so far, I asked if anything else came to light in the course of his digging into the case.

"The only other definite thing I have to share with you is that there is no laptop amongst the evidence collected at the time of the investigation. The records make no mention of one having been found. I'm not sure we can read anything into that yet, but it does smell a bit off. And, there is no mention of a lifejacket being missing, or of Mel coming forward after the event to suggest one had disappeared."

Syd had nothing more to offer. I had a myriad of questions. I just didn't know what they were at that precise moment. The only thing I was sure of was Syd's information was both interesting and tantalising. I wanted to know more, but Syd indicated there was no point in lingering longer. He had nothing more to tell me and would be in touch when that situation changed.

On my way back to my car, as I passed a butchers shop, I realised I had nothing planned for dinner. I backtracked and went in hoping inspiration would strike as I waited for the butcher to serve the woman ahead of me. If I had nothing prepared for dinner when Mel arrived home this evening, I imagined difficult question would be asked about what I had done all day to not have time to think about dinner. As I fronted up to be served, the sight of some fine T-bone steaks in the glass fronted counter were all the inspiration I needed.

As coincidence would have it, for the first time in days, Mel did ask how I'd filled in my day.

"Not with anything very exciting… I went for a walk and picked up a couple of steaks for dinner. But, apart from that, I have nothing to show for a lazy day at home."

"What happened to all the writing you were going to do? You claimed your intention was to spend your holidays rekindling your love of writing. Have you done any at all since you've been here?"

"Well, you can't write until you've thought about something to write. I've had a couple of ideas but, when I started mapping out their storylines, they didn't have the substance to go far. Today's walk might prove worthwhile in this regard. The beginnings of an idea came to me as I walked the street to the butchers. I'll devote some time to developing it tomorrow."

Maybe it wasn't the truth, but it wasn't untrue. I did go for a walk – along the street from my car to the coffee shop and back again. An idea for a story did occur to me, but it was as I was driving home. Regardless, I do think it has potential and I will explore it further … in between the other important stuff I'm doing at the moment. The unfortunate thing is, the moment I admit to having put words to paper, Mel will demand to read it. It's a long time since I've had time or opportunity to indulge in what used to be my spare time hobby. I'm not sure I want anyone reading what are bound to be poor efforts after such a long time away from it.

Nothing of any import happened after dinner. Mel claimed nothing interesting or upsetting happened in an otherwise boring day, and I was careful not to mention anything likely to reignite her interest in my day. After watching part of a movie on TV – by about halfway through, we were both nodding off – we settled for an early night. The only thing worthy of note occurred on our way up to our rooms: Mel confirmed everything was in place for me to commence work at the company on Monday, and she had set it up for us to spend Saturday afternoon in her office.

At last I would be able to get on with investigating the anomalies I identified earlier in her company's operations. While I welcomed the opportunity to get stuck into that investigation, it meant I had only a day or two left in which to continue looking into those mysterious notes.

*****

The prospect of starting work with Mel on Monday spurred on my thinking last night. While I might have retired to my room early enough, it was a long while before I welcomed sleep. With such short time at my disposal to come up with the 'solid evidence' Mel required before she would consider going back to the police about the notes she received, I needed to be focused and have a definite plan for the time available. Such thinking was heavy going and ran well into the night, leaving me thick-headed from lack of sleep this morning.

As soon a Mel was on her way to work, I fetched my laptop and attacked Google with a vengeance. Armed with the name of the previous tenant, I was determined to find out as much as I could without having to rely on Syd Hartley finding with something. No doubt, he would find details of the crimes involved but, in the meantime, I would discover as much as I could. Syd was a busy man. Who knows how much time he will have, or how long it will take him, to look into everything we've talked about?

While I searched Google, I kept reminding myself my first task this morning was to contact Craig Newman to thank him for his assistance and tell him of the progress I made as a result of it. I didn't want him wasting time going over ground I already covered. As there wasn't much else I could think of for Craig to help me with, it was best he knew now I wouldn't be annoying him again unless something needing his input arose in the future.

Little was added to my file as the day dragged on. By mid-afternoon, I held a desperate hope Syd Hartley might call before the end of the day. Once Friday ended, it would become difficult for me to slip away from either Mel or work to meet with Syd. I tried telling myself it didn't matter if I didn't hear from him anytime soon. From tomorrow, I envisioned myself so immersed in the anomalies in Mel's company's accounts, I would have little headspace left to deal with whatever Syd might produce.

Everything uncovered so far tended to indicate the former tenant is the intended recipient of the hand-delivered notes. It should be more than enough to tell Mel about and to take to the police. But, something held me back from even broaching the subject with her. The whole thing seemed tied up nicely … until you thought about the dates. Arrival of the notes on those specific dates, and only then, goes beyond the bounds of coincidence. And, the moment I remembered the significance of those dates, I knew we were nowhere near sorting out this mystery.

Friday came to a disappointing end. Syd didn't call. Craig was out of the office all day, so I contented myself with sending him a text message. Mel seemed keen to go out for dinner. The suggestion held less appeal for me. I was in a flat mood after my lack of progress today … but I didn't feel inclined to cook dinner either.

Our meals in a little Italian restaurant were excellent, unlike conversation which was stilted and in short supply. Mel asked several times if I was okay.

"Of course I'm okay. My brain is a bit fog-bound tonight, that's all. I spent the day preparing for the investigation I'll carry out from tomorrow afternoon and for who knows how long after that. I'm probably a bit mentally exhausted; nothing more."

It might not be the whole truth, but there were grains of truth in it. Anyway, what's wrong with a white lie if it saves a good night out from destruction?

<h1 style="text-align:center">Chapter 11</h1>

Saturday dawned clear and bright before changing its mind and exchanging blue skies for dark threatening ones. By ten o'clock, the heavens had opened. The rain showed no intention of going away, and continued to bucket down at lunchtime. I wondered whether this might be an omen of some kind about the operation we were to set in motion. The only good thing about such a horrible morning was it allowed Jo and me to sit in the comfort of the lounge room while discussing how our investigation should progress.

"The first thing I'll need to do when you arrive at the plant this afternoon is introduce you to Jim, the security guard. While our intention is to cloister ourselves in my office so you can use the computer to start digging into files, it's important we are seen doing normal orientation things. My usual approach is to show new staff members around the place before taking them to my office. That way, the new employees don't spend the first day looking for the toilet, or the canteen, or anywhere else they might need to go."

"Yep, I support that. It would be useful to see where I will be located and where, in relation to my office, those working for me are located. I'll make a list of names and who sits where. Nothing impresses the plebs like the boss' knowing who they are by name from the moment they sit down to begin work."

"Right; your work area will be the last thing I'll show you. Your office is just along the corridor from mine so, when we finish in there, we can come back to my office to get on with the real stuff we came to do."

"What about access to the computer systems. I won't need it this afternoon. You can log in for me as you did last time we were here, but I will need to be given access first thing Monday morning. Is that likely to be complicated or time consuming."

"No. I've arranged for one of the IT team to come to your office soon after your arrival. He will introduce you to our systems ... Please look like it's all new to you while he goes about it ... I think they have created you as a user on the system, but he will sort out passwords and login protocols while he is with you."

"Okay, that's good. Between now and two o'clock I'll decide which files to attack first."

"Well, do it quickly, so you've sorted it out before we go for lunch. I thought we might eat at that little bistro down by the river and go into work from there afterwards. If we leave the house at eleven o'clock and indulge in a long, lazy lunch, I'll be able to fill you in on a lot of the company's history and significant events that happened during its time."

It was one o'clock when I checked the time. "Let's order a fresh coffee and then head off. I'll leave first. That way I can be there before you, and will have Jim handy to introduce you to him when you arrive. Don't be surprised if he dashes to open the door for you. He's a bit of an old-world gentleman is Jim."

I was right about Jim opening the door. He opened the main gates in readiness, before joining me in the reception area to await Jo's arrival. As soon as Jo climbed out of her car after parking in front of the entrance, Jim rushed over and threw open the door for her. The introductions were carried out as soon as she was over the threshold and Jim had closed the door behind her. Then, after giving him an overview of what we would be doing, I led Jo upstairs to the office area.

"First port of call probably should be your new empire ... Here we are. Welcome to your area. This is where Majella Franks, your secretary, sits. Your office is through that door, and out in front is where the clerks do their thing."

"I'll check out my office later if there is time. I would like to look over the clerks' area. Tell me the name of the person who sits at each of the desks. People think you are superhuman if you can address them by name on your first day. I'd like to establish something akin to that situation if possible first thing Monday morning."

Jo wanted to know the duties of each of the clerks. She struck out. I didn't have a clue who did what. After sticking her head into her new office, she was ready to move on.

"Right, where to from here? We need to have this tour of the place done with as soon as possible so I can start on the real reason we're here."

The rest of our tour included the toilets, canteen, meeting room and as far as the platform overlooking the factory floor. With the tour over, it was time to settle into my office for the remainder of our time here. As soon as we entered my office, I grabbed several documents off my desk and brandished them at Jo.

"These need to be signed. It doesn't have to be right now, but it should be done before we leave today."

"I'll just set the computer to boot up and then I'll come and sign them."

Within a couple of minutes, the computer was up and running and I'd logged Jo onto the system. The new employee forms were signed and ready for despatch to the personnel section for processing. I sealed the documents in a large envelope and scrawled *To Personnel* across the front of it. Didn't I trust my own staff with confidential information? Maybe … but something urged me to put them in a sealed envelope. If I'm honest, it's probably only Krista I don't trust. Not an ideal situation between a boss and her secretary! I need to devote some thought to how to fix it.

Before leaving work yesterday, I had all but cleared my in-tray. It left me with little to entertain myself with today. After dealing with the remaining couple of documents, I sat twiddling my thumbs for a few moments while listening to the sounds coming from Jo in the computer alcove. I couldn't judge whether things were going well for her or not as she mumbled to herself.

"Damn! …. Where is it? … Why is that here? … That's interesting … O-o-h no! I don't think so …"

Not being able to interpret Jo's mumblings gnawed at me. Now I didn't have any work of my own to occupy me, I wanted to know what she was finding in the various accounts. To ease the suspense, I broke the prevailing silence of the room.

"Jo, would you like a coffee or something? Maybe take a break for a few minutes?"

She asked for a coffee, so I took myself off to the small kitchenette to do battle with the recently installed coffee machine. Surprise, surprise! A small amount of milk remained in the fridge. Determination accompanied by copious swearing eventually had me heading back to my office with two mugs of frothy cappuccino. Thankfully, Jo opted to take a break while she drank hers. It gave me an opportunity to ask questions without interrupting her work.

"How is your digging about in the files going? From where I sit, it sounds interesting."

"I'm not sure 'interesting' is the word I would use. In layman's terms, I have come across a few 'funnies'. They aren't ringing alarm bells yet. I need to dig a bit deeper before I know whether to be concerned or not."

"I think you are saying there are a few things of concern, but you need to do more work before you confirm it. Is that an accurate translation?"

"Pretty much. Even at this early stage, I think it is safe to say there is something rotten in your accounts. I'm picking up a bad smell. While I know uninterrupted slabs of time like this won't be available after Monday, I still think it possible I'll have a definite report for you by mid-week. As a new kid on the block, it wouldn't look out of place if I chose to work back on one or two nights. Might not need to but, after today, I'll have a better idea of how much time it's likely to require."

"At the risk of sounding ludicrous, is there anything I can do to help?"

"Actually, there is. I've got a short list of companies who are supposed to be suppliers. It would help if you checked them out and identified what they supply and how regularly those supplies might be ordered."

While not sure what I was required to do, anything was better than sitting here doing nothing. Jo fetched the list I was to work on and explained what she wanted me to do. It didn't sound daunting. I started on it before she made it back to her computer. I wasn't sure if two computers logged onto the system at the same time using my login would raise any flags on the system, but I felt I had a plausible explanation if the IT guys queried it.

By the time I'd researched every possible avenue and made copious notes about each of the companies for Jo, I was surprised to see it was almost five o'clock. While I didn't want to rush Jo, or stop her if she was in the middle of something important, I was concerned it would look a little odd if we stayed too much beyond five o'clock. I took the outcome of my research across to her.

She was leaned over close to the screen and pounding the keyboard as she murmured, "Come on, come on!"

"Would it help if you asked nicely?"

"What…?"

"I wonder whether saying 'please' instead of just snarling 'come on' at it might encourage a better response. Here's the information on those companies you wanted." She cast no more than a cursory glance at the sheet I held out to her.

"Hmm … yeah, thanks. I'll look at it later."

"While I appreciate how much fun you're having, we should call it a day very soon. I see you are going to need a new writing pad. There are only a couple of pages left in that one."

"Okay … Just give me five minutes to finish this bit, and then I'll be ready to go. Yeah, I'll have to try to pick up another pad sometime tomorrow."

"That's not necessary. Ask Majella to fetch you a pack from the stationery room."

To fill in time, I tidied my desk and then returned our coffee mugs to the kitchenette. By the time I returned to my office, Jo had abandoned the computer and stood stretching her back.

"I'm all done for today. If you shut down, we can be on our way. I don't have anything prepared for dinner. What are your taste buds suggesting?"

"They haven't kicked in yet, so there is no suggestion so far. Don't worry about it. I'll pick up some chicken on the way home."

Five minutes later, on our way to the door, we said good night to Stan, who had taken over from Jim. He opened the main gates from his desk, and I allowed Jo to depart first. I waited until she had turned onto the main street before following her out the gate.

On the way home, I picked up a pack of fried chicken with all the trimmings. The chicken went into the oven to keep warm while we both freshened up for dinner. It was after dinner, while sitting in the lounge room with our drinks, that conversation turned to the success or otherwise of our afternoon in my office.

"I'm pleased we went in. From my point of view it was a successful few hours. I think I will stay late on Monday night. It's the scent of the chase, you see. I'm itching to get on with the stuff I started looking at just before we left this afternoon. Not to pre-empt anything but, if I spend a couple of hours on it on Monday night – and all goes well – I might have some preliminary info for you after that." Jo appeared mentally exhausted. An early night seemed like a good idea.

While I spent Sunday doing various domestic chores around the house, Jo spent most of the day going through her notes from yesterday and identifying what she wanted to do next.

*****

Over breakfast, I made some inane remark about today being Jo's 'big day'. She shot me a look I couldn't interpret, but I understood enough to leave the subject alone. As is my usual practice, I left home early to be at my desk by no later than 7.45a.m. Jo, wanting to create the right impression on her first day arrived about five minutes later. I called out to Majella as she was on her way past my office.

99

"I'll walk along with you. Your new manager has arrived, and I'd like to introduce you and the others in the section first thing. I think you'll find this one a bit different to work for." She raised an eyebrow at me, but didn't comment.

After introducing Jo to Majella, we stood at the front of the clerks' area and I made a general introduction to the gathering. Jo thanked me and said hello, before announcing she would be coming to speak to each of them individually. Majella retired to her desk, but I hung back for a few moments to gauge Jo's reception from the clerks. Even in the short time I watched, it was obvious she had won them over. On my way out, I stopped by Majella desk. "When you get a spare moment, please fetch a pack of writing pads for Jo's office."

"No problems; I'll do it now while she is busy getting to know the clerks."

When I returned to my office, Krista was not at her desk. She was now twenty-five minutes late. From my window, I checked the carpark for her little blue sports car, and was in time to see it driving through the main gate. She was late, and it would probably take her another several minutes before she was seated behind her desk. I watched her park and climb out of her car.

"What do we pay secretaries these days? It's obviously too much if she can afford a car like that." I must stop talking to myself like this. It's not a good look. Before I know it a rumour that the boss is losing the plot would be circulating.

Today, Krista and I will have a few hard words. I don't doubt this is how she behaved when James was in charge. I'm just beginning to realise how foolish I'd been letting him run the place. Regardless, Krista seemed determined to continue as she did when James was here. There had been one conversation about her lax timekeeping. Her efforts today will earn her a second strike, and I will again remind her of the 'three strikes and you're out' rule. I won't have that conversation with her yet. Best I leave it until later when some of my anger has subsided.

The first thing I did at my desk this morning was send a message to the management team inviting them to an informal meeting at 8.30. I intended having coffee with the team and its new member. Jo was aware I planned to do this but, when I spoke to her about it, I didn't have a definite time in mind. And, having sent the message out to the other members of the team, I forgot to tell Jo the time. They all would be traipsing into the conference room in a few minutes and, so far, nothing was organised. I went along the corridor to Jo's office to tell her the time of the meeting and, while I was there, asked Majella to set up coffee for everyone.

As anticipated, the meeting was stilted. I introduced Jo and suggested she would catch up with each of them individually to familiarise herself with how the place operated. Gordon Grimshaw, wonderful old man that he is, played his part to perfection. He rushed forward and warmly welcomed her on board while shaking her hand with some enthusiasm. He betrayed nothing of having met her previously, and Jo responded in kind. Her welcome from the others was lukewarm at best. Nevertheless, having followed all appropriate and polite protocols in holding the meeting, I felt entitled to take the higher moral ground.

When ten o'clock rolled around, I realised I still hadn't spoken to Krista. Was now the right time? Was there ever a right time? As I sat pondering the question, I saw Majella go past on her regular morning trek to the mailroom to collect recently arrived invoices and orders. The sight of her passing my office reminded me I needed to talk to Jo about the appointment of a senior clerk. I should do that now and, on my way back from Jo's office, I would stop at Krista's desk and invite her for a 'chat'.

Krista wasn't at her desk when I left my office. Heaven knows where she'd gone this time. I'd barely laid eyes on her all morning. As I neared Jo's office, I thought I could hear raised voices. No, one raised voice; Krista's voice. I hesitated, not sure whether to interfere or allow Jo to deal with it. Then, I heard Jo's quiet but firm voice respond. I knew the confrontation was over when I heard Jo say, "You're way out of line, Krista. Go back to your own office and worry about your own work."

Not wanting to be seen eavesdropping in the corridor, I ducked across the corridor and into the stationery room. By leaving the door slightly ajar, I caught a glimpse of Krista as she thundered past towards her office. Seething, I waited a minute or so before exiting the stationery room. All thoughts of speaking to Jo abandoned for the moment, I started back along the corridor towards my office.

Not again! This time Krista's raised voice assailed my ears from somewhere in the vicinity of her desk. "…She is busy, and doesn't need to be bothered by the likes of you. If you've something so important to speak to her about, make an appointment. Now, shove off back to where you belong."

Stunned I was frozen to the spot. With my feet finally mobile again, I hurried towards my office, but was still some way along the corridor when Gordon Grimshaw rushed out and along the corridor ahead of me. He turned the corner and continued in the direction of his office on the factory floor. He didn't see me, and I was too shocked to call out to him … but not so shocked as to remain ineffective for more than a moment. The red mist descended. With a full head of steam building inside me, I strode the remaining few metres and into to my front office.

"My office, please," I growled at Krista as I passed her desk. She blinked in dismay a couple of times, and hesitated as if making ready to defy me. "NOW…! And close the door behind you."

Chapter 12

Krista gave me a defiant look, but grudgingly shoved her chair back from her desk and followed me in, closing the door with a good deal more vigour than required. It didn't help cool my mood. And, the way she stood just inside the door and glared at me did nothing to help her cause. I launched into what I had to say. The red mist was all the way down, and I'm sure my blood pressure was all the way up.

"I'm not sure what you think your position in this company's operation is, Krista, but I'm here to tell you your behaviour would be unacceptable even if you were the manager. You seem to think timekeeping is something for other 'lesser' mortals to worry about, and you can swan in and out whenever you choose. I don't know or care what arrangements were in place when James was managing director but, in case you hadn't noticed, he is no longer running the place … And he will not be coming back."

When I stopped for breath, Krista gave me a dismissive toss of her head and continued standing tight-lipped and rigid just in front of the door. I wasn't sitting, and I certainly didn't feel inclined to offer her a seat. She offered no comment, so I continued.

"You were late arriving again this morning. This is not the first time I've spoken to you about being late, and it is the second time since the 'three strikes rule' came into practice. In case you are not quite sure how it applies to you, it means you now have two strikes against you. One more misdemeanour and you are out on your ear."

No toss of her head this time when I paused. Instead, she glared hard at me and her top lip curled up on one side in a snarl. Right, so no misunderstanding about how she feels about me or our current conversation. As I was about to resume my commentary on her behaviour, she deigned to honour me with a response.

"I wasn't late. There are things I do first thing in the morning. And, no, they don't include coming into your office and bowing before you to let you know I have arrived. But, for your information and the benefit of this 'conversation' I was here at eight o'clock."

The word 'conversation' was spat at me with enough venom to almost bowl me over. I parked the matter of her tardiness for the moment, with the intention of returning to it later.

"Let's move on to your behaviour and, in particular, your complete lack of respect for senior staff. The way in which you treat senior staff is clear indication you have an inflated opinion of your importance around here. So we both understand what your position is, I'll explain: a secretary is no more than a member of the office pool who has been give different responsibilities and answers to a different supervisor.

Perhaps you were allowed to assume some elevated importance under James but, in reality, it doesn't exist. To put it bluntly, if it were allowed before, such an arrangement also disappeared along with James. Members of my management team are important and busy senior members of this company. You do not have the right to yell at them or abuse them. You do not have the right to prevent them from seeing me at any time, unless I am engaged with someone else."

"I have no idea what you are on about. I hardly see members of the management team these days – unlike when James was here. His door was always open to them, and they often dropped in to speak to him. Now, no one comes near this office. They seem to prefer not to. So, I can't see how I could possibly be guilty of the things you accuse me of doing. Perhaps it's not that I'm doing anything wrong; perhaps the problem lies with you … and your jealousy of the working relationship I had with James – and with the other senior staff."

"You deny yelling at the new manager – hurling abuse at her – and you deny preventing the production manager from meeting with me? …And, in the latter case, using totally unacceptable workplace language?"

"Are you deaf or something? I already told you I have no idea of what you are on about. Not guilty, Ma'am. So, what are you going to about that now? It's your word against mine. I think the senior staff you are on about are more likely to support me than you."

Oh, I do like a challenge. When this is over, I must speak to a few people to find out exactly what things were like in this office when James was here. I wonder if Gordon Grimshaw might like to drop by for a drink one evening after work. But, right now, it is time to rise to the challenge she's thrown out, and to establish my position and authority around here.

"Krista, not only do you disregard timekeeping rules, are disrespectful to senior staff, and seem to think your position far superior to mine in this company, but you LIE … bold-faced, openly lie. There is no…"

I didn't get to continue. Krista let out a yelp and started advancing towards my desk, eyes blazing and abuse pouring from her mouth now screwed up in a perpetual snarl. By the time she reached the desk, spittle had accumulated in the corners of her mouth. Much of what she hurled at me went by without me taking it on board, but her final words, delivered as she thumped on my desk, did register with me.

"…So, oh so high and mighty lady, you are going to have to prove your accusations when I take action against you. I've been wrongly accused; slandered. And, I intend to seek compensation and justice. So, now, what are you going to do about that? You got some more fancy words you want use?"

"Before I address your questions, I would like to point out your recourse to action against me is pretty limited. You don't belong to a union, and a civil court trial would be lengthy and expensive – for you, that is. My insurance would cover the cost of the best legal minds around. … BUT, neither of us need concern ourselves about that.

Now, to address your questions, or should I say 'challenge'… I don't have any fancy words to use, but I do have all the words I need."

At last, as I reached into my partially opened desk drawer, I noticed a hint of uncertainty about her. I brought out my mobile phone and showed her the screen so she could see it was set to record. I rewound, tapped PLAY and then fast forwarded to her comments about being on time this morning. I played that portion of the recorded conversation. I saw her swallow hard a couple of times before her chin resumed its defiant angle.

"That's inadmissible. You didn't tell me beforehand you were recording our meeting."

"As one of the participants, I didn't need to. I also didn't need to tell you because the circular explaining the Three Strikes Rule that went out to all employees and staff explained that any meeting associated with a misdemeanour under that Rule would be recorded. You should have read the circular.

"Where was I? Oh yes, I remember." I rewound and replayed the bit about her being here on time.

"The fact you didn't see me doesn't mean I wasn't here." Some of the sting had gone out of her.

"That would be true, but I did see you. I saw you drive in twenty-five minutes late, park your car and get out of it. I don't know what you did after that, but you still were not at your desk ten minutes later when I went past on my way to the conference room for coffee with the management team. So… you lied. How much does one of those sports cars cost anyway?"

I couldn't help the final barb. It was out before I could stop it. It was petty and uncalled for, and I lost a little of the high ground because of it, but not enough to lose the battle. She seemed struck dumb by my question about the car. Shock registered on her face when I asked it. So, while I appeared to have something of an offensive advantage, I pushed on.

"If you prefer, I could ask the finance manager and the production manager to join us before we revisit the matter of your responses to your disrespect for senior staff. Should I make the calls, or should we proceed without them?"

When I looked up at her, Krista was nibbling a thumbnail. The fire appeared to have gone out of her. She stopped annoying the nail and shook her head.

"That won't be necessary. Are you firing me? If that's what your plan is, get it over and done with."

"No, I wouldn't want to make life so rough for you. We all have commitments. Finding yourself suddenly out of a job makes meeting those commitments a concern. But, you cannot continue in your present position. There is a vacancy in the office pool since one of the women went on maternity leave last week. That position is available if you want it. The woman is likely to return to work after twelve months. In which case, it gives you time to find something else in the meantime."

"The office pool...! Go out there and be just one of the clerk typists? I don't think so."

"It's all I have available to offer you at the present time. If you don't take that position, your only other option is to sever your employment with this company."

"I'd sooner leave than end up out there with that lot."

"Okay, it's your choice. Collect your bag and any personal items, and be off the premises within the next half hour."

Under other circumstances, her stunned look would have been worth capturing. It's unclear whether her reaction was stunned or disbelief, but she continued to stand there just staring at me. There was no way I was backing down. I strode out from behind my desk, marched past her and flung open my office door. She still didn't move.

"Krista, you need to be out of those main gates within half an hour."

To emphasise the situation, I called the security desk and asked the guard on duty to come up to my office. Peter, the guard on duty today, arrived a couple of minutes later. I met him near Krista's desk. Krista finally had come out of my office but still hadn't moved to her desk.

"Peter, Krista is leaving us. She has been given half an hour to collect her personal items and be off the premises. She is not to return here in the future. Please oversee collection of her belongings and escort her to her car. Ensure she leaves the property."

The deed done, I returned to my office and shut the door. About ten minutes later, I watched Krista, with her bag over her shoulder and carrying a small box, make her way to her little blue sports car. Peter accompanied her and held the box for her while she opened the car door and climbed in. From our different vantage points, Peter and I stood and watched her drive out through the main gates.

There was no victory – no real satisfaction – in what happened this morning. In my mind, there was no question. Krista could not remain as my secretary, and I doubted she was fit to be anyone's secretary. I suspected how she was could be attributed to her time working for James. While I don't know what their relationship was, it's part of something which concerns me. Every day I see more evidence of James' poor management during his time in charge. The worry is how deep the rot developed during his time has penetrated the company's operations. No doubt, over the next weeks, months and years, that will become evident. One thing is certain: I have a difficult road ahead of me.

My first difficulty to overcome is the lack of a secretary. For a few brief moments, I pondered whether I needed to replace her. Lord knows what she did to fill in her days. I certainly didn't. Most days I hardly laid eyes on her. Much of the work I would normally send out front to be done, I've done myself. It's not a good arrangement, but do I really need a secretary? Should I continue to manage as I have been, at least for a while anyway, until I prove the need for a secretary one way or the other?

One concern I had about not having a secretary was what to do on those occasions when situations arose that I couldn't take care of myself. There were a couple of occasions in the last few days when I had to call on Majella to fill in for Krista who was missing. It would be unfair for such practice to continue, not only for Majella, who already has her own workload to content with, but also for Jo, who is being robbed of her secretary's time. Perhaps I need to talk to Jo. In any case, my befuddled mind could benefit from input of her wisdom.

A meeting with Jo would have to wait. She has scheduled a meeting with her whole team about now, so it's unlikely she'll be free before lunch. As no one had collected my morning mail, and for something 'mind in neutral' to do, I took a stroll to the mailroom. The surprised look on faces there when I entered was hilarious, and the only bright spot of my morning.

With nothing of major import in today's mail, it was opened, recorded and flicked through in about half an hour. I decided an early lunch might be worthwhile, since I couldn't settle to do anything else. Rescheduling the personnel section still awaited my attention, but my mind was not inclined to that today. A visit to the canteen held more appeal. The place was empty, so I had my pick of everything on offer and opted to eat at one of the tables instead of taking it back to my office as I usually did.

All good things must come to an end and, as I'm hammering people about timekeeping at the moment, it would not be good to be seen lingering longer than the allocated lunch break time. I took a large coffee to my office with me. After placing it on my desk, I wandered along the corridor to see if Jo's meeting was still happening. I ran into Majella on her way to the stationery room.

"If you are roaming the corridor, I'm guessing Jo's meeting is over. Is she still in her office and free to see me?"

"Yep, meeting is over and it went down well with the others. I think they appreciated the initiative. She is free if you want to go in."

Jo greeted me warmly. I think she was happy with the outcome of her meeting. "I was wondering if I might borrow you for a while for some wisdom and words. But, I noticed it's lunchtime. Are you available after lunch?"

"Why don't I get lunch and eat it while we talk. You're looking a bit haggard. Is everything all right?

"I don't know. That's why I need to talk to someone more intelligent than I am at the moment."

While I waited for Jo to appear, I tried sorting my thoughts out so I would have something to use as a starting point for planning for the future. Just as I was starting to make sense of what happened this morning, my phone brought the process to an abrupt end. The meek little voice on the other end wasn't recognisable at first.

"I'm sorry. I'm sorry. I know I'm interrupting you, but please may I speak to you for a moment?"

"Krista…? Is that you, Krista? Yes, I have a few minutes. What did you want to speak to me about?"

Was this the same woman who left my office only a few hours ago?. It certainly didn't sound like her. Then caution stepped in. Why would she ring me after this morning's episode? There was only one way to find out: let her tell me. Something about the call had a wave of sympathy running through me.

"Are you still there, Krista? I'm listening if you want to talk to me."

"I'm sorry for the way I was this morning; for the way I've been since you came back. I don't know why it happened. I suppose, somewhere deep down, I kept hoping James would come back. When you returned, I had to accept the truth. He was never coming back no matter how much I wished it was otherwise."

"I understand his disappearance was hard to understand, harder still to accept. But, was there something in particular you wanted to talk to me about?"

"Thank you. I know I don't have the right to ask, but I was wondering if you might forgive my earlier performance and offer me the position in the office pool again. I would be happy to work there, even though I know it's only until the other woman comes back. Would you at least think about it, please?"

"I see. Well, I would need to give it some consideration … and there would need to be conditions. Leave it with me. I have a meeting in a couple of minutes. Can I call you back later?"

Jo arrived to find me studying the note of Krista's phone number I scribbled before the call ended.

"I brought you a coffee too. You looked as though you could do with one when I saw you before. If anything, you look worse now. What's happened?"

After giving Jo a blow by blow description of my session with Krista this morning, I ended with the latest development. "She just called to apologise for her behaviour, not only this morning but since I came back to work, and to ask if the offer of a position in the office pool might still be open to her."

Jo's eyebrows, which had slowly crawled up her forehead as I outlined this morning's confrontation, now almost came together across the bridge of her nose

"What are your thoughts on maybe extending an olive branch and agreeing to her coming back to work here?"

"To be honest, I'm not sure. From my first day back here full-time, because of her attitude, I didn't want her as my secretary. Since then, the situation has worsened, not improved. In spite of this morning, I was prepared for her to keep working here but not as my secretary. I suppose I should have felt some degree of relief when she opted to quit. But, my problem is, all along, something has been telling me I need to keep her here at the company. It's as though I need to keep an eye on her; to know what she is doing. It doesn't make any sense does it? Why would I want to know what she is up to?"

"I can't give you a straight answer to that one, but I can tell you I think your instinct might be spot-on."

"Has your investigation turned up something about her?"

"No-o, not really, but there were a couple of things that had me asking WHO and HOW. No evidence pointed to Krista, but she did come to mind as one person who might be worth a look as we dig further into things. It's up to you but, if your instinct says you should offer her the job, I suggest you run with it …

for the moment at least. We could keep a close eye on her and take whatever action seems appropriate in the future. In the meantime, what are you going to do about a secretary? Don't tell me you don't need one. Let's leave it for now and discuss it tonight … after whatever time I leave here."

"You do whatever you plan to do after everyone leaves. I'm planning to stay behind to work for a while as well. I'll organise something for dinner and we can eat here."

With tonight organised, and Jo back in her own office, I called Krista at the number she gave me to explain some changes were being introduced, and it would be a few days before I knew if the vacancy still remained. I didn't know why, but instinct prevented me offering her a job. I think she was disappointed, but she didn't say so.

My mind couldn't focus well on anything for the remainder of the afternoon. There were too many doubts and questions hammering it. It wasn't until after everyone left that I managed my first productive efforts for the day.

Chapter 13

By the close of business on Wednesday, I was feeling a bit ragged around the edges. Formulating a new streamlined structure for the personnel section was proving more difficult than I imagined. So far, the only thing I had decided was moving the payroll function to the finance section where it always belonged. Jo worked late on Monday and Tuesday nights, and said she might be late again tonight. I don't want to intrude on her day at work, but I needed her around to help brainstorm this restructuring I'm trying to do.

While Jo worked back until about eleven o'clock on both nights, I only worked until about nine o'clock on Monday night. In spite of my best efforts to find out how her investigation was progressing, she was noncommittal, saying nothing more than it was 'going okay'. An added frustration is that people have realised I am here. Work has poured in – and now I don't have a secretary to help deal with it.

First thing Thursday morning, I rang Jo's office to ask her to have coffee with me. It gave me about two hours to sort out what I wanted to ask her about, and what my questions might be. Busy coming to grips with her new position as finance manager, she looked a bit tired as a result of three late nights in a row. The last thing I wanted was for her to burn out.

She arrived in my office at ten o'clock with two large cappuccinos in hand. "I didn't know what you planned but, whatever it was, I thought we probably would need fortification, so I brought these with me."

I started with small talk. "How are you settling in to the new job?"

"It's going well, and no surprises so far. Everyone knows what they are doing, so it hasn't been too challenging. There are a couple of changes I want to make, and soon I think. At the moment, one person deals with the entire paper trail for each invoice, from when an order is received through to processing the payment for it. It's the same with the company's purchases. From when we place an order for goods, through until we pay the invoice for its supply, one person deals with every step of the transaction. This is not sound accounting practice. I will make changes to those processes, but I'm thinking it will be after I finish digging in the files. It's likely my investigation will show the present practice has allowed something rotten to sneak in."

"It's up to you to make the changes you consider necessary, particularly in the light of whatever your investigation turns up. Speaking of which, how is the poking about in files going? You are starting to look tired. I want to uncover whatever is going on, but I don't want to kill you in the process. Perhaps, instead of working late nights, leave it and come in on the weekend for a few hours."

"Hmm… yeah, I'll see how things go tonight. I do want to work on again tonight, but I don't think it will be a late one. If it goes as expected, I might need to talk to you tomorrow about how to progress. Was there anything in particular you wanted to talk to me about this morning, apart from the investigation I mean?"

"There is. I wanted your thoughts on something. While I doubt Krista did much while she was here, my workload is increasing and I'm beginning to think I do need a secretary. Should I wait to appoint someone until after I've developed my restructuring plan? I don't want to go ahead and recruit some-one only to find soon after an alternative approach opens up for me. Any thoughts on the subject…?"

"Possibly… but it will depend on how you might feel about what I'm going to suggest. Majella is very capable, and I don't keep her busy. Yesterday, I found her tidying the stationery room for something to do. Perhaps we could share a secretary. You would have an idea what workload you could create for her. Together, we might provide her with something more fulfilling than at present. Of course, the question of where to locate her might render the suggestion impracticable."

"Oh, I like the idea but, as you say, how do we manage her physical location? Leave it with me to think on for a bit. I take it you still plan to work back tonight?" She nodded. "Okay, I think I might do so too for a while."

There wasn't anything on my desk that couldn't wait until tomorrow, but I wanted to stay on for a while in the quiet after everyone left. While I thought I would try to make some progress on what was beginning to feel like a fanciful idea of restructuring the personnel section, Jo's suggestion to share a secretary gave me something more interesting– and more immediate – to sort out. Besides, it would be something positive to help take my mind off Jo's investigation.

While we both have no doubts her investigation will reveal the likelihood of misappropriation of funds, I am growing impatient to verify it and act on it. Who knows how long whatever it is has been going on? It's possible it has been happening for years. I suppose that might make it more difficult to confirm and prove beyond any doubt. While I know and accept that, it doesn't stop me wanting results … and wanting them now.

At a bit after eight o'clock, we dined on an acceptable but unexciting curry from the canteen reheated in our kitchenette. Instead of returning to my office with our dinners, I decided we could eat at Jo's desk. She looked brighter tonight than when I spoke to her earlier today. In fact, I thought I detected a hint of excitement about her.

"Perhaps we might dine at a different venue tonight," I said as I plonked the food down in front of her. "You seem to have gained a burst of energy since this morning. I'm beginning to wilt and you are looking as bright as I've seen you. O-o-h … Am I sensing you might have found something interesting? Come on, don't just sit there looking smug. What have you found?"

"I wasn't looking smug; a bit elated maybe, but not smug. Yeah, I have something. It might prove only a part of what we are looking for, but it is a start. Actually, you found it. Remember the list of companies whose information I asked you to dig up for me? I discovered one of them was a shelf company. The long, convoluted track back to its origins – its owner – has taken me some time. About five minutes ago, I hit pay dirt. It's all a front. There is no parent company as such, and certainly isn't one which supplies the materials we have been paying for on the shelf company's invoices."

"So, this is a bit like when you have a ghost employee on the payroll being paid every week? But, in this case, it's a company of sorts receiving money via dummy invoices for goods supplied?"

"Thank you for mentioning a dummy employee. Maybe payroll should be the next account I subject to a bit of poking about. But, yes, your analogy is correct. I'm almost one hundred percent sure significant money is being syphoned off in that way. By the time I leave here tonight, I should have all the evidence I need."

"Well, don't stay too late trying to find it. Is it too soon for me to ask whether you've identified if a significant amount is disappearing?"

"Again, everything is on a 'to be confirmed' basis but, yes, from what I have found so far, it is significant and it is on a regular basis."

I was stunned. "Who… How is it possible … and how long has it been happening?"

"If you go away and let me get on with it, I might be able to answer some of that by the time I come home tonight."

Never slow to take a hint, especially when offered so succinctly, I left Jo humming to herself as she peered at her screen. The frisson of excitement rippling through me made sure I couldn't concentrate on anything once I returned to my office. Just go home, I told myself, there's nothing you can do here. Heeding my own advice, I grabbed my bag, said good night to Jo as I passed her office, and was on my way home a few minutes later.

TV couldn't hold my attention and, after about fifteen minutes of minor domestic chores, they didn't interest me either. I desperately wanted to stay awake until Jo came home, but it wasn't to be. A bit after ten o'clock I gave in and went to bed. I did not hear Jo come home.

*****

Jo's phone rang early this morning while I was in the kitchen preparing breakfast. I couldn't hear what was said from where I was downstairs, but the call didn't seem to last long. Soon after, she joined me in the kitchen.

"What time did you finally come home last night?"

While dealing with her mouth full of toast and marmalade, Jo seemed to ponder my question before attempting an answer. "You're beginning to sound like Mother. I don't know what time it was, but it wasn't too late. Can I leave you to clean up? I want to slip in a bit early this morning. There are a couple of things I want to look at before the day gets going."

With that, she picked up what was left of her toast, snagged her bag off the chair back where she hung it earlier, and was out the door. Maybe I was out of line asking her what time she came home, but I didn't think I was, and I didn't mean anything by the question. Me thinks something is afoot and I'm not being included in whatever it is. Now that is a worry. Why not? What am I not being told? Perhaps today will require some careful conversations.

Soon after I arrived at work, I ambled along the corridor to Jo's office. Jo's door was closed. Majella was out front with the clerks and I didn't want to disturb her. With no other options open to me, I headed back to my own office. About ten minutes later, Majella stuck her head around my door.

"I saw you come to the office before. Is there something I can help you with, or did you need to see Jo?"

"Well, I was going to talk to Jo about something, but it can wait. Maybe there is something you can help me with. What can you tell me about that small room between my office and Jo's? It's locked and none of my keys open it."

"I don't know that I can tell you much about it at all. I think it was locked soon after James took over running the place. If

117

you remember, you and I both left the place about the same time. I've never seen it open, or seen anyone going in or out of it, since I've come back. I suppose James might have been using it for some purpose, and could access it via the interconnecting door in his office – in your office. If that were the case, it would explain why the entrance from the corridor is kept locked; to keep people out."

"None of my keys open that door either, not even my master key. If you get a moment, please ring downstairs and see if there is a key for that room, or maybe there's a new master key since mine."

I expected her to go back to her own office and make the calls from there, but she simply went to Krista's desk to use the phone. Within moments, she was back in my office and looking a little concerned.

"There isn't a specific key for either of the doors to that room, but they are bringing up a master key to compare with yours in case your key has been superseded. Ah, this sounds like the security guard coming now. I'll bring him in to you."

Within a couple of minutes she was back in my office with the security guard in tow. "We need to try the key in the door in here. It doesn't open the one from the corridor."

As Majella spoke, the security guard already was rattling the handle and jiggling the key in the lock.

"Sorry, Miss McCarthy, our master key won't unlock either of the doors to that room. While I'm here though, may I check your key to make sure it is the latest version of the master?" I handed over my key. He placed it against his master, and held them both up at eye level to compare the teeth. "No problems there; your key is up-to-date, so it won't open those doors either. Is there something you'd like me to do about it?"

"Thank you for going to all that trouble but, no, I'll deal with it."

Despite knowing it would not unlock the door, denial insisted I try my key again. Having confirmed the situation, I was more determined than ever to see inside the room.

"Majella, I don't know if the company deals with a particular locksmith or not but, would you please find a locksmith and asked them to come to unlock those two doors. I suspect the wisest thing will be to change the locks."

"I don't need to go outside for a locksmith. We employ one these days. Shall I ask him to come and deal with the doors?"

"How come we employ a locksmith? I don't remember us ever needing to employ one in the past."

"It was when we started manufacturing those doors. You know we manufacture both internal and fancy-looking front doors?" I nodded and she continued. "They all required handles and locks fitted, and then customers – or even the builders when they were installing the doors – started losing the keys. Mr Grimshaw somehow obtained approval to employ a locksmith. The man's been employed here for a couple of years now, and he seems to be kept busy."

"Good to hear he's kept busy, but please see if he can spare a couple of minutes to come up here and do something about these doors."

Just as I was about to go for a coffee, Majella arrived with a middle-aged bloke in work clothes trailing behind her.

"Miss McCarthy, this is Phil the locksmith. Is it okay if he tries those doors now?"

Coffee was my priority, so I left Majella supervising Phil as he fiddled with the doors. When I returned to my office, they were both waiting with long faces. Majella broke the good news.

"Sorry, Miss McCarthy, we had no luck. Phil says he needs to change the locks, are you okay with him going ahead with that?"

Rather than have the poor man feeling I was peering over his shoulder, I took the document I was reading and sat at Krista's desk. A few minutes later, on his way past, Phil stopped to give me a progress report.

"I don't know who installed that lock on the door in your office, but they did a shonky job of it. I've taken the lock out, so you can enter the room via the connecting door from your office if you want. Now I'm going to remove the lock from the other door in the corridor. I'll return later with replacement locks."

Not wanting to succumb to the indignity of rushing back into my office to burst into the room next door, I continued reading my document at Krista's desk until I heard Phil leave. Then, in a flash, I was out from behind the desk and into my office. I hesitated at the interconnecting door. There is nothing in there to attack you, I told myself. Open the bloody door and find out what's in there before Phil returns to replace the lock.

With unexpected trepidation, I pushed open the door and stepped inside. After a moment of scrabbling around on the wall, I found the light switch. The scene revealed by the dimmed lights stunned mw. I was unable to move for a few moments. The, coherent thought returned, and I once more found the light switch; a dimmer switch. I screwed the knob around to the brightest setting, and almost regretted it.

This was the stuff of B-grade movies. James had established his own entertainment area. Anyone entering from the corridor would find themselves in a lounge area of sorts. There were three expensive but comfortable-looking chairs and two sofas. Closer inspection revealed the sofas converted to futon type beds. The other end of the room beyond the lounge area was set up as something resembling a cosy boudoir.

The central highlighted area was an enormous round bed with an animal print cover over what looked like black satin sheets. I found myself marvelling at the fact you could buy round satin sheets to suit such a bed. A silver tray holding two champagne glasses sat on one of the ornate bedside tables. Perhaps the most impressive part of the room was the vast area of mirrored ceiling above the bed.

Soon, Phil would return to replace the locks. No matter how much I didn't want him to see the interior of the room, I couldn't see how to prevent it. At least if I turned the lights off, some of the sordid details might remain hidden. I rushed to the door and then stopped. Before I turned the lights off, I wanted to see what else was in the room. While standing adjacent to the light switch, I cast my eyes slowly over the room. A bar fridge, temperature-controlled wine cabinet, small stereo set up, a cocktail cabinet complete with an array of various glassware and bottles of liquor were strategically located around the room.

One swift flick of the switch and the room was plunged into darkness. I stood in my office just outside the doorway into the room to check how much of the room's interior was visible. Still too much, I decided. Then, after turning off the lights in my office, I checked again. I felt reassured. There would be enough light for Phil to see what he was doing, but it was sufficiently dark in the room for the furnishings to remain a mystery.

While it minimised the risk associated with the interconnecting door from my office, I could hardly apply the same strategy to the door from the corridor. As I stood chewing my lip and pondering what to do about it, a flash of inspiration occurred. I dashed back into the room and flicked on the lights again.

"Yes, I thought I'd seen a screen in here," I murmured as I marched to the other side of the room. There, folded and propped up against the wall, was an oriental looking screen. In a feverish feat of willpower and effort, I pushed the heavy screen through the lounge area to just inside the corridor doorway. Once it was unfolded, it probably screened most of the room from anyone who didn't venture beyond the doorway. I dashed back to the light switch, flicked the lights off, and rushed out to resume my seat at Krista's desk only a few moments before I heard Phil whistling as he came along the corridor.

At last, Phil returned to his workshop. I was back in my office, and keys to the secret room's two doors were on my desk. My problem now was how to dismantle and remove what appears to have been James' pleasure palace. The strategy will be to have as few people as possible involved and, therefore, aware of what was to be removed. Perhaps the most critical aspect of it all was how to remove that bed without having the eyebrows of everyone involved reaching for the ceiling.

In thinking about how to remove the bed as covertly as possible, I inadvertently allowed my mind to stray to somewhere I did not want it to go. That bloody bed…! I didn't need to be a member of Mensa to work out James set the room up as his love nest. This was a place where his trysts could remain hidden from the rest of the place, and from me at home. But the room was set up for more than just James and a paramour. Others had availed themselves of the comforts offered by that room. Did they have free access whenever they felt so inclined, or were they there only on James' invitation? And, was the full range of pleasures on offer there available to all and sundry, or were some of them reserved for James alone?

With my mind in such a whirl from all I discovered, in spite of my best efforts, I was unable to think of any way of emptying the room without its contents becoming common knowledge. By mid-afternoon, I gave up trying to devise a suitable strategy and decided to leave it in abeyance until I discussed it with Jo. Having decided, I wandered down to Jo's office to ask her about her plans for tonight.

"Jo, I hope you're not going to work back again tonight. I really don't want you to. Please take it easy. I don't want you having a breakdown. What are your plans? Should I prepare dinner for two?"

"Sorry, Mel, you might be dining alone again tonight. An old colleague called this morning. We've arranged to meet up for a drink after work at a favourite pub where a group of us often congregated of an evening. I don't imagine it'll be a late night, but it's likely we will indulge in a pub meal while we are there. You don't mind do you?"

"No, of course I don't mind. I'm pleased you're going to indulge in a spot of social life instead of working back here."

It's true, I didn't mind … But I was curious about an old friend contacting her out of the blue like that.

Chapter 14

Jo: more questions

"Sorry, Syd, my best intentions of leaving work on time today fell in a heap at the last minute. Thanks for waiting for me." It was nearly ten past six when I arrived for our six o'clock meeting. Syd already was installed at a corner table and intently studying tomorrow's racing form guide.

"I was reasonably confident you would arrive eventually. Anyway, I decided, seeing as I was here, I'd stay and have a meal even if you didn't turn up."

"Thanks for calling me this morning. I was beginning to think a lot of what I sent you to look into would turn out to be a wild goose chase and there was nothing to find about the house's previous occupant. The last thing I want is for you to invest a lot of work and possibly go out on a limb for something that is of no import. Your call had me counting down the hours all day. So, come on, don't keep me in suspense any longer. What have you managed to dig up for me?"

"Well, straight up, I can tell you your tenant is an interesting piece of work."

"She is not *my* tenant. I take it by 'interesting' you mean you found a file on the woman."

"Yeah, and the file is not closed yet. She has a long history of encounters with the law, dating back to her teenage years. In her early days, most of it was petty stuff, but her file shows her activities became more significant as she aged. Her latest exploits, and probably the reason she is no longer occupying the house, involve her lucrative business selling drugs. It took the police a while to catch up with her. Then, when they believed they had the evidence they needed to bring her to trial, she seemed to have disappeared off the face of the earth. Because of the business she was involved in, there was some concern she might have been made to disappear permanently."

"Okay, so the police began thinking she might have been done away with because it wasn't an uncommon end for people in her line of business. Was it the case?"

"No. It's probable things became a bit too hot for her around here, and she took herself off to somewhere she thought a bit safer: Europe. It's unclear exactly what she was doing, or where, but it managed to keep her overseas for at least twelve months. By sheer luck, she was spotted when she returned here. She was taken in for questioning."

"I wonder what brought her back here. Perhaps the cash ran out. Did the police have enough to charge her with anything, or were they restricted to just questioning her?"

"Why she returned remains unclear, but something in the later story suggests she left the continent for much the same reason she left here in the first place: things became a bit too hot for her. In the first instance, she was taken in for questioning but, as there was enough evidence against her, she was arrested and thrown in gaol. After all the usual delays, her case went to court. She was found guilty and looked like receiving a long sentence. Then, things became really interesting. Before her case was closed and sentence handed down, an application came in for her extradition to Europe."

"So she was 'gainfully employed' while she was abroad. What happened about the extradition, and what did they want her for?"

"We don't know for sure how she supported herself while she was overseas. The extradition request was for something more serious than her charges here. Their extradition request brought her original trial to a halt while various legal teams argued about whether she should be extradited straight away, or if she should serve whatever the sentence she was handed here before being extradited to face the music over there. The issue is still to be resolved."

"It sounds like everything remains in limbo for the moment. What happens to her while that's the case? Does she remain in gaol pending the outcome of all the legal wrangling, or did the original case progress to its logical end with the sentence handed down now being served?"

"Sort of … She was sentenced to a five-year stint in gaol for her drug dealing activities and was locked up, but the extradition application is still being argued in the courts. At some point in time, she will have to serve the five years she was given. What's still not clear is whether she will serve the five years first, and be extradited at the end of that time, or if she is extradited now. In the latter situation, her case would be heard in Europe and, whatever the sentence handed down, would be served there before she returned home to serve out her sentence here."

"What charges is she facing Europe? Are they the same as the ones she was charged with here?"

"Oh no, her European endeavours are much more interesting than her activities here. She faces a murder trial in Europe … But there's a twist to it. Don't get excited. I'll put you out of your misery and tell you about it. The files I was able to sneak a look at here are a bit sketchy. Well, they would be. It's not our case, so anything in the files is only for the sake of interest. I haven't been able to find out yet where the crime was committed. But, the authorities there believe her responsible for a body they hold in their morgue. His … it was a male … His face was so badly smashed, they haven't been able to identify him. Even his dental work was almost pulverised in the frenzied attack. Based on the initial evidence found, they believed the body to be that of her husband. Since then, for whatever reason, the thinking has shifted. They now think the body is that of an unidentified male with no obvious connection to the woman."

"As you said, it is very interesting. I take it the husband hasn't miraculously reappeared to prove it's not his body in the morgue?"

"As far as I know, nothing quite so helpful has occurred. The authorities, both here and over there, are still trying to establish whether she had a husband at all, or even a partner. DNA taken from the body doesn't match anyone on file. Without the identity of the husband, DNA matching over there is ruled out as well."

"I suppose the actual machinations of the various legal systems aren't of much interest to me. Everything you've told me so far tends to suggest those letters are meant for the tenant and are probably related in some way to her drug dealing activities. But… there are two aspects I can't reconcile with the information you've provided this evening. I know if I share what I know with Mel, she will argue the relevance of the dates on which the letters were received, and she would be right. It can't be a coincidence the letters arrive on key dates associated with James. The other thing now niggling me makes the tenant's involvement with the letters even more implausible. Surely her associates, colleagues, or whatever you call them, within the drug trade would be aware she is out of circulation, and has been banged up in gaol for some time. So, it doesn't make sense for them to be leaving her letters at her previous address."

"Hmm … Good point. What if they weren't meant for the woman? What if there is a husband – or a partner of some sort – and the letters are meant for that person? Perhaps the person sending the letters believes that other person was somehow involved in the tenant's operation."

"And, what if that other person continued to run the operation, at least for some period of time after the tenant was taken into custody? Syd, your information has been interesting, but I think we both know it has created more questions than we had at the outset. The only thing I'm sure about after talking to you, is that I won't be mentioning any of this to Mel … not yet anyway."

A short interruption occurred while we ordered our meals and glasses of wine to go with them. Then, we returned to our corner table and, while we waited for our meals, discussed what was happening with mutual friends. Our earlier conversation didn't resume until after we cleaned our plates. While I was eating, I thought of something else I needed to follow up with Syd.

"Did you have any joy with your search for James' laptop and phone?"

"Not the laptop; it is not included in the evidence gathered in association with James' disappearance. I found the phone. It wasn't recorded on the evidence register. It is a serious over-sight but, without its being recorded as part of the evidence, I don't suppose it caught anyone's attention. It doesn't appear a copy of the log of James' calls was requested or obtained."

"Bugger…! I harboured a tiny thought it might contain something useful. I don't know what I thought it might prove, but my gut instinct was telling me there was something interesting amongst his calls."

"Yeah, you managed to arouse my curiosity as well. After all this time – and when I hadn't been involved with the case – it was difficult to ask the tech boys to interrogate the phone, or to go to the relevant telco for the information without attracting a lot of difficult questions. As it wasn't registered as evidence, I quietly slipped in my pocket and took it home. Of course, by then it was flat. Its charger was nowhere to be found. If I saw a charger – anyone's charger – of the same make, I tried it to see if it would fit the phone. The exercise proved fruitless and I was seriously considering going to the tech boys for assistance when one last possibility occurred to me. My wife, Linda, bought a new phone right before 'the end'. When I checked it out, it was the same make and looked like the same model. Her charger had the phone charged up again in a matter of hours."

"I don't know how long the phone holds a record of its calls. Were you able to retrieve anything useful from it?"

Syd reached into the inside pocket of his jacket and produced a folded sheet of paper. He pushed it across the table to me, but kept his hand on it while he spoke. "Not being the most technically literate bloke around, it took me a while to work out how to get the records from the phone onto this piece of paper. Before you grab it and start devouring it, you should be aware it doesn't exist. I still have the phone at home but, when a suitable opportunity presents, it will go back into the evidence locker."

He removed his hand from the sheet of paper. I opened it out and glanced quickly at its contents. It was obvious Syd had resorted to typing up a copy of the calls logged on the phone. "Thanks, Syd. I'll study this in the privacy of my bedroom tonight. Before I do though, was there anything on this list which caught your attention?"

"While I don't know who the numbers he called belong to, there were some interesting aspects. I only managed to type this up last night, so there hasn't been time to study it in any detail, but I did identify interesting call patterns. Might be worth a look at some time... you might find this useful." He slid a memory stick across the table to me. "I saved my typed list on it for you."

It was time to change the subject. We reverted to discussing what some of our mutual friends were doing with their lives, and what Syd was doing with his and how he was coping without Linda. He talked about how he almost chucked his job after Linda's death, and how he first thought about it when she became so sick towards the end. I was grateful he hadn't done so, and I let him know. Investigating criminal cases was his whole life – apart from Linda. I suspect being a detective is what kept him going after she died.

We were winding up the evening, going through the usual good night routine and discussing when and if we should meet again when a thought slammed in from left field. "Where did that come from?" I thought aloud.

"Where did what come from? I didn't say anything. Did you hear something?"

"At the risk of sounding daft, I just had the strangest thought. If you can stay a few minutes longer, I'll run something past you. I'd appreciate your thoughts on the matter."

"It's my day off tomorrow, so it's only my beauty sleep I'm missing out on if I sit here and talk to you for a bit longer. Okay, let's have it. What's this thought of yours? I have no doubt it's going to mean more work for me."

"You might remember I said there were two issues I was investigating. The letters were one. The other was what I believed would prove to be misappropriation of funds from Mel's company. In the case of the latter, I have evidence to prove it, and I am now endeavouring to establish how it is being done – and by whom. In the last few days, there have been no less than three people leave the company. One of those was of his own choosing. Another had the option of accepting a lesser position or leaving. She chose to leave, but revisited her decision overnight, and has now asked to be allowed to accept the lesser position. Her situation is being considered and no decision has been made at this time. The third person, the finance manager, ended up getting himself fired. It appears he had no qualifications and, more importantly perhaps, no skills or understanding to carry out the job he was employed to do."

"Okay, so three people have left the company, and one of them has asked to be re-employed. So far, I haven't heard anything to suggest there is work for me involved in any of this. Perhaps it is your turn to put *me* out of *my* agony by telling me where this is heading."

"While it's still early stages of my investigation, to varying degrees, all three are possible suspects in my misappropriation investigation. Regardless, I do have a particular interest in how the hell the former finance manager was appointed to that position. Whispers overheard in the office have the former finance manager pegged as a great mate of James. I wondered whether it might be possible to look into his background without it becoming something of a mammoth undertaking."

"I could certainly take a quiet look to see if he features in any of the resources I have available. Your investigation is becoming more interesting by the moment. Give me the relevant details and I'll have a bit of a nose around when I'm back at work the day after tomorrow."

"Thanks, Syd. I don't want you wasting too much time on it, but I am a bit curious about him. Oh, and of course, at this stage, like everything else so far, it is for only us two to know about. If it proves to be relevant to the misappropriation investigation, I will share whatever you find with Mel but, unless and until then, I'd prefer she wasn't aware I was looking into his background."

After giving Syd the meagre information I had on the former finance manager, we walked out of the pub together and said our final good-nights in the car park. It was still early by comparison with my last few nights. I sat in the car for a few moments with the engine idling. The temptation was to go back to the office and do a bit more digging in the files. I knew if I started doing that, it would develop into another late night and Mel would become worried. Temptation overcome, I eased the car into gear and headed for home.

Mel had waited up for me. She sat in the lounge room reading a book. I suspected the book was just a prop and she hadn't been reading it at all. As expected, there was the usual attempt at subtle questions about how my night had been and how the meeting with my colleague went after not having seen him for so long. In themselves, there was nothing wrong with the questions. It was simply a case of my not wanting to discuss the evening … probably to avoid letting something slip that I shouldn't, and partly due to my guilt at what I was doing behind her back. Underpinning my antisocial frame of mind, was my desire to be alone to think about and analyse everything Syd gave me tonight, not the least of which was the calls log from James' phone. At this point in time, that is something I definitely do not want Mel to know about.

In the end, I claimed I had a headache, needed a long hot shower, and then bed. Mel looked disappointed but said she understood. With mug of hot chocolate in hand, I escaped to my bedroom. The chocolate was too hot to drink anyway, so the shower came first before I settled down with my chocolate and James' calls log. I don't know what I hoped to achieve by studying it at length, but something kept telling me some of the answers I needed were somewhere on that piece of paper.

Frustration does not make a good bedfellow. The calls log was unhelpful. The only calls I recognised were a couple to Mel's mobile phone. It didn't appear James ever called the house from this phone. There must've been occasions when he needed to ring home. Maybe he used his work mobile, or the phone on his desk if he was still in his office. I think I might need to go to work a little early again tomorrow. Perhaps the online register of staff phone numbers might prove helpful.

Sleep did not come easily or swiftly and, when it did choose to visit, it was restless and didn't stay long. I knew I would feel like death warmed up in the morning, but I also knew it was the thrill of the chase keeping me awake.

*****

I took my thick head off to my office via the kitchenette for my second cup of coffee this morning. The place was deathly quiet. My early arrival gave me about an hour and a half of solitude before the place came to life. I wanted to make a start on checking the phone numbers on James' calls log against the company's telephone book. But, this might have to be my last early start for a bit.

While I hate going behind Mel's back to investigate the issues I think are important, it's the only way I can do it without causing an almighty row. So far, it's been a successful covert operation. But Mel is becoming suspicious. This morning, she all but demanded to know what I had to do that required me to go into work so early. I know she is concerned I might be overdoing things; might be putting in too many hours working on her behalf.

She is concerned I might burn out or have a breakdown of some sort. What she doesn't realise is this is how I need to work in the course of my real job. Time is of the essence when I'm engaged on a forensic investigation of a company's or an individual's financial dealings. Depending on how my investigation progresses, I thought I would spend all day Saturday tracking those rogue transactions back to their originator. After her reaction to my early morning start today, that might not be a good idea.

It leaves me with two options: to have a hard talk to her about what I'm doing – without mentioning my covert investigation

– or, to kerb the amount of time spent poking about in the company's accounts. The latter is not my preferred option. Still, it is almost the end of the week. My investigation so far suggests those rogue transactions tend to occur twice a month, at the end of the second week and again at the end of the fourth week. In view of staff departures over the last few days, I am keen to see whether they continue. If they do, this being the fourth week of the month, another rogue transaction should occur on Friday.

Time slips away easily enough without wishing it gone but, in this instance, Friday can't arrive soon enough.

Chapter 15

Perhaps I'm becoming paranoid. I'm becoming convinced something is going on that I don't know about. Jo's behaviour lately has me concerned. I know she is putting a lot of effort into investigating the misappropriation of funds, but I have this feeling there's more to it. That she has another agenda. That she has something else happening at the same time. This morning only added fuel to that feeling. It wasn't her going into work so early I found unsettling. It was her refusal to tell me why that has me concerned.

All the way into work this morning I mulled over those unaccounted for incidents and why I'm finding them so unsettling. Put it out of your mind, Mel, I told myself. Nevertheless, I knew I would be insisting Jo and I have a long hard talk this evening. In the meantime, I need to put such stuff behind me. Now I'm at work this morning, there are bigger issues to deal with here … including *that* room and its interesting furnishings!

Jo wasn't in her office. She was out front doing her usual morning state-of-the-nation session with her clerks. I spoke to Majella instead.

"I don't want to interrupt Jo so, when she is free, would you ask her to come to my office as soon as she has some spare time. What I want to discuss might take some time."

Almost an hour later, Jo tapped on my door. "I had this mysterious message from Majella. You wanted to see me as soon as, and our business might take 'some time'. Okay, I'm here and I'm curious. Tell me what we're going to talk about."

"Well, my main objective is to show you something. Before I do, I think I should explain first so you know what it's all about. Earlier, we talked about a bit of restructuring of our own, which would involve sharing one secretary instead of employing two. Afterwards, I devoted some thought to the logistics of such a move, and where we might physically locate our shared secretary so all three of us would have easy access to one another."

"Yeah, I wondered about that myself. …Must admit I didn't come up with any ideas though."

"One vague idea did occur to me, and I decided to see how feasible it might be. There is quite a sizeable room between your office and mine. I decided to check it out, to see what it was used for in recent times. That's when I encountered the first hurdle. Both doors to the room were locked and no keys existed. Well, that's not really correct. There had to be keys. It was just that there were none here to unlock those doors."

"Uhmm … Are you suggesting they also disappeared along with James?"

"So far, I'm trying to avoid that conclusion, but without a lot of success I might add. Anyway, I got around that hurdle by having the locksmith replace the locks. Once he removed the old locks and went off to fetch replacements, I took a quick peek inside the room. I am still coming to terms with what's in there."

"What…? It can't be all that bad."

"Let's leave that for the moment. I wanted to tell you why the room figured so large in my thinking. I saw it as an ideal place to locate Majella as our secretary. The room is bigger than she really needs, but there would be room to put a couple of chairs in one corner to create a reception area for people waiting to see either of us. The area out front of my office where Krista was located could be turned into a small meeting room. I think it would be big enough to accommodate management team meetings. That way, the conference room would revert to its intended use for larger gatherings and as a training room."

"I must admit having management team meetings in that huge conference room is a bit daunting. Also, it allows people to spread out around it, instead of being a compact group. From my experience, such an arrangement is more difficult to manage than when participants are clustered together. Using a smaller room would be ideal."

"Okay, I know it's almost impossible for you to offer any further thoughts on the subject until you've seen the room. Let's take a look." With my hand resting on the door and handle, I paused before opening the door. "I don't how to prepare you for this. All I can recommend is to take a deep breath and prepare to be amazed."

Jo gave me a strange look, then shrugged and motioned for me to open the door. I allowed myself a moment to take a couple of deep breaths of my own before throwing open the door and reaching in to flick on the lights. I heard Jo gasp.

"Jesus…! Is there a red light hanging outside the corridor entrance to this room? If there isn't, there ought to be judging by the way it is furnished."

While Jo prowled around the room, I remained anchored just inside the door near the light switches. Every so often she glanced across at me and raised her eyebrows. At last, her survey of the room was done. She moved down to the 'sitting room' area and stood there, hands on hips and swivelling from the waist as she attempted to take in the vista before her. I saw her nod, more to herself than to me. Then, she looked up and beckoned me.

"There are very nice looking chairs here going to waste. Let's sit down and talk about it." I didn't argue, and collapsed into the chair facing her. As soon as I settled, she led off with her ideas. "Once you get over the initial shock, it's not too bad. I imagine you agree our first task is to remove the furniture so whatever other works we require in here can happen without shocking the daylights out of the tradesmen who come in to do it."

"Yes, that about sums it up. I don't how you can say it's not too bad. Look at it. What do we do with the furniture? How do we get rid of the stuff without the whole world knowing about it?"

"You're not thinking about it logically. Look at these lovely leather chairs we occupy. I wouldn't mind one of these in my office, and I think you could do with one in yours. There are times when you have large documents to read, and you would prefer to do it in comfort rather than sitting at your desk. I don't mean these chairs to be used for visitors. They're for our personal use and comfort. Those two bedside tables would be handy as well. We could take one each and set it beside the chair we move into our office. They would serve as nice side tables. You know… somewhere to put a mug of coffee or a notebook and pencil when we're working on something."

"Okay, I go along with all of that. It sounds great. But what about the rest of the stuff in here, what the hell are we supposed to do with that?"

"Well, for a start, those four framed works hanging on the wall need to go. I think they are only prints anyway. Nude females probably don't do much for either of us, so we can keep the frames and lose the 'artworks'. The coffee table here in this end of the room could stay. It could be located adjacent to those visitors' chairs you're going to place in a waiting area."

"I suppose that's a start, but there is so much other stuff to deal with… and it's all such good quality. I can't just get rid of it."

"If by 'good quality' you mean 'expensive', you're right. Everything in this room, including a bottle of very fine scotch and some eye-catching wines, are top-quality and expensive. It might help explain where some of the cash from company funds disappeared to. Sorry, I'm making light of something I know is upsetting you. So, let's look at what else there is in the room."

Jo bounced out of her chair and made another quick circuit of the room before settling back into the chair she just vacated.

"Right, that cocktail cabinet with all the glorious glassware in it might be okay tucked away in a corner of the conference room. If the glass doors on the upper part of the cabinet lock, it would ensure the glassware remained in situ and didn't walk out the place over a period of time. Of course, the grog in the cupboard would be removed before it was relocated. That small bar fridge might be handy in that little alcove off your office. I don't know what you'd keep in it, but that doesn't mean it wouldn't be handy on some occasions."

"Yes, I go along with that. Once it was there, I think we might find all sorts of things to keep in it. What about that temperature-controlled wine cabinet?"

"You don't want it at home? … No, I didn't think so. Perhaps, after emptying it, it might also be stored in a corner of the conference room, even if it's only as a temporary measure until we work out what to do with it."

"I absolutely love that lacquered Japanese screen. I've just the place at home for that."

"Good; it is beautiful and I was hoping you wouldn't suggest getting rid of it. It's a bit curious though. I would have expected to see it folded up and out of the way, not fully open and across the corridor entrance. I wonder what was behind having it there like that."

"It wasn't there. I found it folded up against that wall over there. I didn't want the locksmith seeing the contents of the room. With the lights turned off in here and in my office, it was dark enough for him not to be able to see into the room when replacing the lock on my interconnecting door. But, when replacing the lock in the corridor door, the light from out there would penetrate quite a way into here. I set the screen up like that to block his view."

"Top marks for good thinking. See, clearing out this room is not as difficult or insurmountable as you thought it would be. We've already worked out what to do with most of the stuff and, more importantly, we can do it all without involving anyone else. That only leaves the mirrors on the ceiling…"

"… And *that bed*!"

"Don't go all panicky on me now. I need to take a closer look, but I think those mirrors on the ceiling will be easy to remove, but will probably leave the ceiling a bit of a mess. As there is other work to be done in here, putting the ceiling to right again can be included. When we are ready to tackle the mirrors, we will need to ask Gordon Grimshaw to have his boys bring a couple of ladders up to your office. You don't get all wobbly on a ladder do you?"

"No, of course not. It would be a relief if they did come down easily. Okay, let's talk about the elephant in the room … The big fat, round elephant with the animal print cover and black satin sheets on it. I don't how I get that out – how anyone can get it out. Its diameter is greater than the height of the doors."

"I don't think it's the problem you imagine it to be. Give me a hand to get these covers and stuff off so we can have a look at what's underneath."

It took a bit of grunting and shoving, but soon the bed stood there in all its naked glory. I was surprised. "Oh, the mattress is just a big slab of foam rubber cut to shape. It's not a proper mattress with springs and things in it."

"It's not unlike what I expected, and getting rid of it won't present any major problems. That foam mattress can be cut up into bits and disposed of in one of the industrial bins on site. Right, let's pull it off the bed as far as we can so we can check the base."

"We are doing well so far, but I'm sure the base is going to bring our run of luck to an end."

Jo chuckled and motioned for me to grab hold of the mattress. "Prepare for another surprise. See … The base isn't one solid piece of anything."

"It seems to be all polystyrene. That can't be right can it?"

"Yes, that's how they made them. It's a bit like some of those old waterbeds you could buy. The base is comprised of walls of thick polystyrene that define the shape of the bed and hold what goes in the middle. In this case, the circular 'well' created by the wall is filled in with thick blocks of polystyrene, with a thin sheet of ply on top of the whole thing."

"It's not what I expected to find under all those bed clothes. Just because we now know what's under there doesn't make it any easier to remove it."

"How easy or difficult it will be depends on one question: do you own a saw?"

"A saw…? Yes, there is a number of saws of various types in my garden shed. What sort of saw do you want?"

"We'll have a look at what you have closer to when we need to use one. A chainsaw would be handy, but a decent reciprocating saw would do the job just as well."

"From memory, my garden shed runs to both of those."

"Well, I don't know about you, but I'm keen to get started on clearing out this room. …You have any plans for after work this evening? I thought we might at least deal with the chairs and the bedside tables. That shouldn't take long, and we would still be home at a reasonable hour for dinner."

Her enthusiasm was infectious. In my mind, I saw us taking care of more than the chairs and bedside tables before we went home this evening. After Jo went back to her office, the rest of the day seemed to drag on. To make it easy to move the bar fridge into the alcove off my office, I moved the small desk and chair Jo had used out of the way. Moving the fridge tonight wouldn't take more than another five minutes, so why wouldn't we do that while we were relocating other furniture?

At last, people were traipsing out of the place. I closed my office door and went into the adjoining room via the interconnecting door. Careful not to make too much noise until I was sure everyone on this floor had left for the day, I started moving furniture into my office. By pushing and shoving, I managed to slide one of the lounge chairs about halfway across my office when my door burst open, and Jo backed her way in dragging a large trolley with her.

"Is that the trolley I've seen parked in the stationery room?"

"Yes. I thought it would be useful for moving stuff about, but you seem to be managing just fine without it. I'll give you a hand. Where do you want this chair?"

I indicated a spot over against the far wall. With the two of us pushing, the chair slid easily across the floor to where I'd indicated. Jo stood back and looked at the chair now in position.

"Hmm … it works well there. Let's get the bedside table in here and parked beside it to see how it looks."

We loaded one of the bedside tables onto the trolley. While I wheeled it into the office and positioned it beside the lounge chair, Jo folded the Japanese screen and moved it out of the way. She ducked out into the corridor and trotted up and down it before returning.

"The place is deserted. Give me a hand to load one of these lounge chairs onto the trolley and I'll take it through to my office."

It proved more unwieldy than heavy, but we managed to load it onto the trolley. I steadied it as Jo dragged the trolley into her office. It fitted nicely in the front corner of her office and there was just enough room beside it to accommodate the other bedside table. A few minutes later, we both stood back and admired the two new additions to Jo's office.

"Okay Mel, what do you want to attack next?"

"I've cleared access into that alcove off my office. Perhaps we could move the bar fridge next. I suppose we better check what's in it first. I imagine an empty fridge will be heavy enough to manage without the additional weight if there is stuff in it."

"Well, would you like a drink before we progress any further?" Jo chirped as I opened the fridge and we stood staring at the contents.

Two bottles of champagne were well chilled, and the rest of the space on the shelves was filled with cans of beer and mixers; cans of two brands of beer, coke, tonic, soda water, and ginger ale. The small freezer compartment was packed with ice cube trays.

"Everything in there definitely has to come out before we try moving it. We need something to put it in." I looked around for something, even a rubbish bin would do, but I could see nothing suitable anywhere.

"I think I saw a couple of empty copy paper cartons in the stationery room. Hang on while I fetch them."

Jo jogged out into the corridor and returned moments later with two empty boxes. We filled both cartons with the cans and stacked the ice cube trays on top. Then the fridge went on to the trolley along with the two boxes of cans. Jo trundle the whole lot into my office as I trailed along behind carrying a bottle of champagne in each hand. Minutes later, the fridge was plugged in, turned on, and its contents reinstated.

Then, we faced the question of whether to deal with more of the contents of the room, or to call it a night and go home. I checked my watch. It was still early. If I'm honest, I wasn't ready to go home. I was still pumped up with the excitement of clearing stuff out of that room. "I don't feel like going home yet, Jo. What about those artworks on the wall? It shouldn't take us too long to deal with them. How about we do that?"

The four artworks were lifted down from their hooks and placed face down on the bed. We worked together opening the frames, lifting out the backing boards, and removing the prints. Then we reassembled the frames – minus artworks – and took them into the stationery room where we stacked them in a corner behind the cartons of copy paper.

Back in the room, I took a moment to survey what remained for removal. Jo came and stood beside me and, for a few moments, we stood side-by-side in silence. Jo spoke first.

"The next thing to think about moving is that cocktail cabinet. Using the trolley, the cabinet itself won't be too hard to move, but there's an awful lot of stuff to take out of it beforehand. We will need a couple of large cartons to pack all that glassware into as we remove it from the cabinet. All the bottles of grog can go into those couple of copy paper cartons we used before. Apart from packing the grog into the cartons, we can't do much more until we find ourselves a couple of large sturdy boxes to hold that glassware. So, I guess that means it's time to go home."

"Finding a couple of large cartons might not be a problem. A lot of the stuff they use on the production line arrives in boxes. The empty boxes are usually thrown in a heap next to the furnace for use as supplementary fuel. I'll have a look for a couple of suitable ones tomorrow. Yeah, I guess you're right. There's not much more we can do here tonight. Let's pack the grog into those two empty boxes before we leave."

In no time, the grog was removed from the cocktail cabinet and we were on our way to our cars. It was almost eight o'clock. The thought of having to go home and make dinner didn't excite me. I suggested we stop at a little bistro on the way home instead. Jo didn't argue.

Over dinner, Jo seemed unusually quiet, while I was still on a high of some sort. When Jo continued to be withdrawn, I became concerned.

"Jo, you've been very quiet all through dinner. Is everything all right?"

"Oh, yes, I'm fine. Against my principles, I've been thinking about work, and that includes clearing out remaining furniture in that room. Tomorrow is Friday. You'll need to see if Gordon can have his boys bring a couple of ladders up to your office, so we have them ready for us to attack the mirrors on the ceiling on Saturday. If you want to work back for a short while tomorrow night, and if you've found a couple of suitable cartons, we could move the cocktail cabinet into the conference room. That would leave only the wine cabinet, the mirrored ceiling and the bed to deal with over the weekend. I'll leave you to think about what you want to do. You can let me know tomorrow how we're going to proceed."

Neither of us was out of bed for long. Jo said she had a couple of things she wanted to do in her room, and I didn't feel like company. I didn't have to apply too much thought to how I wanted to proceed with clearing out the rest of that room. I knew we'd be working back, at least for a little while, tomorrow night. Sometime between now and Saturday morning we need to visit my garden shed to select the appropriate saws for our weekend demolition tasks.

Chapter 16

Jo startled me when she came into the kitchen for breakfast.

"Are you all right, Mel? You were deep in thought, and it didn't look like they were pleasant thoughts."

"Argh, I was thinking about that room…"

"Do you mean James' private social club, that room?" I nodded. "So, what's worrying you about it?"

"I'm not worried. I was wondering about where the keys might be and who else besides James might have a key to the *social club,* as you've named it."

"It doesn't matter now. You changed the locks, so now you hold all the keys to it. Why are you bothered about the keys?"

"I suppose I got to wondering about nobody having entered the social club since James disappeared. That begged the question: what if others had keys to the room. Had they continued to use it? I can't say I've noticed anyone showing any interest in the place since I've been back at work, but I don't suppose they'd want me to be aware of their interest."

"Maybe James gave particular managers each a key, or maybe all the management team had a key … No, Gordon Grimshaw wouldn't have one. He'd be appalled by what was in there. Nevertheless, you can't discount that others might hold keys. Maybe the key was on James' keyring, was handed in with the rest of his keys and nobody knew what the strange key opened. Regardless, it doesn't matter anymore! Stop worrying about it."

"I'm not worrying. You are right, but he would keep it on his personal keyring, not with his work keys. You know, I'm beginning to think no one else had a key. James was a control junkie. I knew it from the outset but, thanks to the separation of almost two years, I see it more clearly now. No, the social club was his and his alone. He needed the power to invite people in to join him there, or to exclude them. In everything, he had to be in control."

"Look, I've got to go. If this key thing keeps gnawing at you, go to security, or whoever looks after keys, and sort it out. But, do it first thing this morning. Otherwise your day will be wasted. You won't think clearly until you sort it out."

With that, Jo bounced up, grabbed her bag, and said, "See you later," over her shoulder as she headed for the door.

As usual, Jo was right. I would go down to the security first thing to check the register. Well, that was my intention as I drove into work. The world had other ideas. The phone on my desk was ringing itself out of its cradle as I let myself into my office. It was a long call from one of our suppliers and, as soon as the call ended, another call came in … And then Gordon Grimshaw wanted to discuss something with me. By the time I thought I might have a quick look at my emails, it was almost ten o'clock.

I remember debating with myself whether to for a coffee or go down to security first. Then Jo was rapping on my desk and looking concerned.

"All right, Mel, what is it this time?"

"What do you mean by that? What are you looking so concerned about?"

"You were sitting here like some great stone statue, unmoving and unseeing; just staring off into the distance. Are you still thinking about the keys? For God's sake, Mel, talk to me."

"If you are going for coffee, please bring one back for me too. Then, if you can spare a few minutes, have it here with me."

It seemed like only a couple of minutes later Jo was back with a large cappuccino in each hand. "Should I shut the door?" She asked as she deposited the coffees on my desk. After closing the door, she settled herself opposite me and fixed me with hard eyes. "Okay, now let's get whatever this is out in the open. I'm won't be fobbed off, Mel. Tell me what is behind all this."

"I don't know how it came to this. It started out as an idle thought this morning and festered into something worse as the day progressed. My thinking about that social club room led me to realise it was sitting there undisturbed for almost two years. That made me wonder about the keys; how many were there, who held one, where were they...”

“Yes, we covered all that at breakfast. You were to go to security to try to find answers to those questions. Have you done that yet?”

“No, and don’t nag. I was busy until about ten o’clock, and was trying to decide whether to it when you came along. Just before you arrived, something occurred to me. We talked about a key to the room being amongst James’ keys that were handed in. Were they handed in? ... By whom? … I didn’t hand them in. I’m sure of it. I know I wasn’t thinking straight for a while after James disappeared, but I wasn’t so far gone I couldn’t remember handing in his keys.”

“Okay … So, you didn’t hand in his keys. Then, they must have remained amongst his possessions and were packed up with everything else when you sold the house. They’re probably in one of the boxes stored in your basement.”

“If only I believed that. No, Jo, I didn’t hand in his keys because they weren’t there to hand in. His work keys weren’t in his office, or in his dressing room, or on the boat, or in his car. I wouldn’t have overlooked them, or ignored them. They were on one of the special keyrings, the ones with the enamelled company logo. It seems we have to add his bundle of work keys to the laptop, mobile phone and lifejacket that were missing after he disappeared. I have to find those keys.”

“I accept it’s a mystery, but I don’t think finding them is of earthshattering importance.”

“That depends on where those keys are now, and who has them. From a security point of view, it could mean having to replace all locks and security codes throughout the place. It’s not the expense that worries me. It’s why those keys weren’t where they should be, and where they are now.”

“I don’t care what else you thought you were going to do today. Get up now, go down to security, and make their life a misery if you must to sort it out. Come on, get up. Go.”

As she spoke Jo came round, grabbed me by the arm and hauled me out of my chair before propelling me out of my office and along the corridor to the lift. When the lift arrived, she shoved me in, pressed the button for the ground floor, and ducked back out as the doors began to close.

Thank goodness Jim is on duty today and not one of the new young blokes. "Good morning, Jim. I've come to annoy you if I may."

"Certainly, Miss McCarthy, what can I help you with?"

"Jim, in the past, whenever keys were handed back in, all the details were entered in a register. Does that process remain in place?"

"Yes, Ma'am, it does, or we wouldn't know where we were with our keys. Were you looking for something, or just checking on the current procedure?"

"Well, Jim, I'd like to have a look through the register if I may. There are a few things I want to sort out in my mind. I won't interrupt your duties while I do it."

Jim unlocked the cupboard under the desk and removed a thick ledger. It was the same one in use for as far back as I could remember. "This is a surprise. Everything else we do around here is now 'on the system'. It's wonderful to see some of the old tried-and-true methods still persist. Thanks for this, Jim. I shouldn't need it for too long."

"I'm sorry, Miss McCarthy, but I can't let you take it away from here. It's the rule, you see. It's my duty to see nobody fiddles with the information recorded in the register. I'm afraid the rule must apply to you too."

"Quite right too; I'll just pull this chair over and work on the end of the desk if I may. I don't want to get in the way. Pretend I'm not here."

How long ago did James disappear… exactly? I flicked back through the pages until I came to the exact date, and then started to work forward page by page towards the present. A few sets of keys were handed in, and some handed out to new recipients. I didn't have expectations about how many transactions there might have been in the two-year period, but the entries in the register came as a surprise.

After checking through from the date James disappeared to the most recent entry, there was no mention of James Rothwell. My mind went into denial mode. Less than an hour ago it was happy to accept I hadn't surrendered James' keys. Now my psyche didn't want to believe nobody handed them in. "I probably skimmed over it," I murmured to myself. "Start again."

"Are you all right, Miss McCarthy? Is something wrong in the register? Is it something I can help you with?"

"Thank you, Jim, but no, I didn't find anything. In fact, what I wanted to find in the register isn't there, and therein lies the problem. Oh, hang about. I need to check something else while I'm here."

I checked the same pages again – twice – before accepting the truth of what I was reading. "Jim, how often is this register updated? If someone handed in their keys, how long before they would be entered in the register?"

"Straight away, Miss. That's the way it has to be done. It's the rule. Are you suggesting there's a problem; that we're not following the rules correctly?"

"Of course not … well, not exactly. Christ, Jim, I don't know what's going on, but something is not right. It's almost two years since James disappeared, but his work keys aren't recorded as having been handed in during that time. I suppose I half expected that, so let's just put it to one side for the moment. It's what's happened in the last couple of weeks that concerns me."

Jim came and stood behind me and flicked backwards and forwards through the last few pages of entries in the register. "The only keys returned during last couple of weeks were those of Claude Dietrich. See … His is the second last entry in the register. The last entry is for the issue of keys to Miss Ballard. Did you expect to see other entries made during that period?"

"Yes, Jim. Within the last week, entries should appear for the return of two more sets of keys: one set from the former finance manager, and one from Miss Krista Thomas."

He stood staring at me for a moment before checking the last few pages of the register again. "I can't understand it. Probably because I wasn't on duty when either of them left, I never gave it a thought to check the register. I don't suppose you know who was on duty on those occasions?"

"It so happens I do. On both those occasions, I asked the guard on duty to escort the relevant person off the premises."

"Perhaps you better give me their names – the security guards' names, I mean."

"No, I don't think so. It's not your problem and you shouldn't worry about it. I'll take it to someone whose responsibility it is."

My inclination was to go straight around to have a few words with the security manager, but common sense intervened. It suggested I should go back to my office and think about how to handle the situation before doing so. I heeded my own advice, but returned to my office via the stairs, rather than the lift, to give myself time to think.

Five minutes after arriving in my office, I phoned the security manager and suggested he might like to come for a chat with me. He said he was busy, and would tomorrow be all right. Silly man! It ruined his chances of our chat being cordial or polite. A few minutes later, a sullen chap who looked like he was barely out of high school knocked a tad too harshly on my door.

As expected, the conversation did not go well. Again, the silly man insisted on telling me how James did things. The fatal blow as far as he was concerned came when he suggested I should study how James managed the place before I came trying to change things: *after all, as the owner of the company, he knew what worked and what didn't, and he knew how to run it.* Poor bloke! He brought out my dark side and felt the full force of it.

"I have better things to do than improving your education, but I will spend a few moments helping you to understand the world around you. You might remember what I tell you because at some time in the near future, you may want to think back on it to understand what went wrong. Firstly, James Rothwell never owned this company. Secondly, it turns out he wasn't a manager's boot lace. On top of that, he had no idea how to run this company. In fact, I'm not sure he made any effort to run it at all, preferring instead to let people do whatever they liked. Just so you do understand the situation that exists here, I own this company. My family established it and has continued to own it for three generations, and yes, I was running this company before James ever appeared on the scene."

The few moments I allowed him to digest the spray I gave him probably wasn't nearly enough for him to fully comprehend the situation before I launched into the next bit of information I wanted to share with him.

"I'm not sure what I'm about to share with you is relevant from your point of view, but I'll tell you anyway. Over the next few weeks, there will be quite a degree of restructuring within this company. Some of it already has happened. A further change will occur within the next few days. The reason I'm sharing this with you now is because the new staffing plan does not include a security manager. There will still be need for someone to manage the security operations, but it will become part of another multifaceted position. As with any such restructuring initiative within a company, there is always some degree of attrition, and redundancies are a natural part of that process."

"Are you firing me? Is this what this conversation always was going to be about?"

"I don't recall making any mention of terminating your services. So, no, I didn't invite you here for that purpose. I wanted to discuss some lax behaviour on the part of two of your security officers, behaviour which now may have placed the security of this whole operation in jeopardy. In talking to you, it has become obvious discussing the matter with you would be a total waste of time.

My suggestion is for you, over the weekend, to consider your position and ongoing employment with this company. I would expect to hear by the close of business on Monday whether you wish to continue working here, or if you prefer to explore other options. Whatever your decision, as of now, you are relieved of your duties as security manager and are to have no further involvement with the security staff. Perhaps you might like to leave work early today to give yourself some extra time to think about your situation. Feel free to leave now, but hand in your keys before you leave the premises."

"If I'm no longer the security manager, how do you intend to continue to employ me?"

"The restructuring includes the formation of a new administration section. There will be a limited number of clerical positions available in the new section."

Our conversation ended with the young man storming out of my office while telling me – and the whole world probably – about my shortcomings as a person and as a manager. At the end of it, I suspected he held no ambition to become an administration clerk. I'll be surprised if I have to wait till Monday to hear about it. In the meantime, I had a more immediate problem to deal with. I now had to appoint someone to manage the security section in the interim. Jim is the longest serving security guard, and by far the best operator. He may not be thrilled with what I'm about to tell him, but I best do it now in case things blow up.

As I expected, Jim was not thrilled with his new responsibilities, but accepted the change graciously. With Jim now in charge, I was free to discuss with him the fact that the last two people to terminate their employment with the company did not appear to have handed in their keys. More importantly, it appears the security officers involved on both occasions were remiss in not securing the keys before allowing their charges to depart the property. While he was angry, Jim was not surprised.

"They are both young and new to the job. No previous experience or training as far as I can see, and they object to being told how to do the job. I take it, as part of my new responsibilities, I should initiate appropriate training." I nodded and gave him a sympathetic look. He chuckled. "Not a problem, Miss McCarthy … I shall enjoy every moment of it."

On my way back to my office, I collected a coffee and a sandwich from the canteen. Then, I closed my office door behind me, placed my lunch onto my newly acquired side table, and collapsed into my newly acquired lounge chair. I was only half-way through my sandwich when Jo stuck her head in.

"I can see you're desperately busy, but I wanted to ask you something. Are we working back again tonight or not?"

"Oh, definitely; I have a full head of steam I have to expend somehow. Moving furniture seems like an ideal way to do that."

Having committed myself to moving both the cocktail cabinet and the wine cabinet from the social club tonight, I went in search of a couple of large cartons. By the time people started trailing out of the place at the end of the day, the contents of the cocktail cabinet were removed and it was ready for relocation to the conference room. I was removing the bottles of wine from the wine cabinet and stacking them nearby on the floor when Jo arrived with our trusty trolley.

It wasn't a late night. Both pieces of furniture relocated easily. After replacing the contents of the cocktail cabinet, I used the same empty cartons to move the wine to its new home in the conference room.

"I see Gordon organised the two ladders we wanted. Let's see how much of our weekend we spend dealing with that mirrored ceiling and the bed. Before we leave tonight, we should fold up those bed clothes. I don't know what you intend for them ultimately, but take them home for now and work out what you want to do with them later."

Jo's suggestion made sense. We packed them into one of the now empty cartons for the trip home. While I went straight home, Jo detoured to a takeaway place and arrived home with a selection of Chinese dishes.

We both went to bed early, but much of the time after we arrived home was taken up with planning how to deal with *that bed*. I couldn't help feeling the weekend might turn into an interesting exercise.

Chapter 17

"Ooowah… I didn't expect that to happen. Thank goodness the bed was still there. If that's any indication, these mirrors are going to be easy to remove from the ceiling." I peered down at the square of mirror now lying on the bed below. "I'll shift it off the bed before we remove any more in case they fall onto the bed as well. We could end up with an awful mess if they come down on top of each other."

Jo stopped wriggling the end of her paint scraper's blade under the edge of another tile. "Good thinking. Maybe it would be better if we dealt with each mirror together. It will take a bit longer to remove the nine mirrors, but it might be safer. Before you climb back up, move your ladder over against mine."

Working together, with one supporting the mirror while the other levered it off the ceiling with their paint scraper, we had all nine mirror tiles off much quicker than I anticipated. That left us with the not so small matter of the bed to tackle. While Jo attacked the thick foam mattress with a saw, I stacked the mirrors on the trolley, took them down and loaded them into the back of Jo's car.

By the time I returned, the foam mattress had been cut into a number of strips which were now being sliced into neat squares. Jo took a break from sawing to avoid having to shout above the noise.

"My thinking was that, by cutting the mattress into appropriately sized pieces, we could pack the pieces into those empty cartons ready for removal. We'll have to do that with the polystyrene base well. It's a pity we don't have more big cartons."

"I'm not sure there will be any left, but I'll duck down to the furnace area to see if there is."

Quite a few discarded cartons remained piled in a ragged heap close to the furnace. I selected four of the largest and took them up to the room. Jo had finished surgically rearranging the foam mattress, and had removed and propped the sheet of ply which covered the base against the wall. Her target now was the large blocks of polystyrene that comprised the base.

"They look good," she said, indicating the pile of empty cartons on the trolley. "I'm still not sure they'll be enough to deal with all this lot. By the way, what are we going to do with all this stuff when we get it home? We might have to hire an industrial bin or something."

"Ah, I don't think we need to take it home. There are industrial bins at the back of the building. They're usually full of packing materials and offcuts from the production floor. I have an idea. I'll be back in a minute."

I rushed to the kitchenette. "Ah hah, I was right. I thought I'd seen a packet of these in here," I told the universe as I scrabbled around in the back of one of the kitchen cupboards and found an unopened packet of large rubbish bags.

"Jo, look what I found in the kitchen. They're those large plastic bags used to line wheelie bins. We could fill them with the polystyrene and anything else we want to get rid of, and dump them in the industrial bins out the back. Between the bags and the empty cartons, we should have enough capacity to cope."

We worked as a team with Jo cutting up material and me stuffing it in bags. By eleven o'clock, everything we demolished so far was in the industrial bins, including the carved up pieces of the foam mattress. All that remained to deal with was the thick polystyrene frame of the bed.

"I don't know about you, Mel, but I could kill for a coffee. How about we take a break before we attack the rest of the bed?"

I made two large cappuccinos. "Where do you want to have this?"

"In your office is as good as anywhere."

"Pity I've only got one decent lounge chair. It would be nice to sit in comfort for a few minutes."

"Oh well, I think we can remedy that. What were you planning to do with the remaining lounge chair at the other end of this room? If we moved it into your office we could set up a nice little niche with the two lounge chairs arranged on either side of that bedside table."

With the two of us sliding it across the floor, the second lounge chair was soon positioned beside the former bedside table, and we were enjoying our coffees in comfort. All good things come to an end. Jo soon had us back dealing with the remains of the bed.

"Being round as it is, it's a pain in the backside. I'm going to carve it into small strips, but they'll be difficult to pack into anything because of their shape."

Jo stood poised with chainsaw in hand over the bed's now empty polystyrene frame. She indicated how big the slices would be.

"If you make them a little bit shorter, we should be able to pack the pieces into those cartons we emptied. I'm sure they will hold the all that material. Then it can go down to the industrial bin too."

By one o'clock the demolition work was complete and the results were in the industrial bins. On our way back from the bin, I told Jo to go ahead. "I want to go out to my car. I'll drop the front passenger seat to make the cargo area a bit longer. I want that Japanese screen, and I think it can fit it in my car."

"It's as well we both drive large SUVs. I'm sure the screen will fit easily once you drop that seat. I'll wait until you come back upstairs before loading it on the trolley."

Loading the screen into my car didn't require much more than a fair amount of grunting, sweating and straining, but the length of it wasn't a problem. Back in the social club, the two of us scanned the room for anything overlooked. Apart from the sheet of ply leaning against the wall and a few crumbs of polystyrene scattered on the floor, the room was empty.

"Thanks, Jo. I couldn't achieve this without your help. Now I will feel quite relaxed when Gordon's carpenters arrive here on Monday morning. That reminds me. It's going to be awfully noisy in your office – not to mention dusty – when they make you a new interconnecting door. You could share my office, or maybe set up a temporary desk out in my front office. Majella will need to work from Krista's desk while the workmen are here. We can deal with that first thing Monday morning. There's nothing more to do here. Let's go home for a late lunch."

"You go. I've a couple of things I want to do before I leave."

"I could give you a hand with whatever it is. Before we left home this morning, I packed enough fruit, crackers and cheese to sustain us both if the work dragged on."

"No, no; you go home, Mel. I just want to work on in my office for a bit. I'll see you at home later … and I'll help you unload that screen."

After another coffee and sharing a plate of crackers and cheese, I left Jo to get on with whatever she wanted to do. On the drive home, it occurred to me we hadn't discussed Jo's progress with her investigation for a while. I didn't know whether she was making progress or not, but she had spent a lot of time on it. Somehow, I must persuade her to tell me what she found, and how much further she needs to go before we have a definite idea of who is behind the misappropriation. I don't want her to keep spending so much additional time on the investigation.

When Jo arrived home just after five o'clock, she was bright and chirpy; almost excited. She insisted we unload the screen and set it up inside before we poured ourselves drinks. It was a pleasant evening, so we took our drinks out into the garden, and sat in silence for a while watching the shadows lengthen. Twilight moved in rapidly. Soon we would be forced back inside.

Already the night air had a nip to it. Before long, it would be too dark and too cold to remain in the garden. Going back inside would make it harder to persuade Jo to tell me about her investigation. If I couldn't initiate that now, I would have to wait until after dinner when, with any amount of luck, we would both be mellowing out in the lounge room. Argh, to hell with it, I told myself. Take the direct route. Initiate the conversation now.

"Did you stay back to poke around in the accounts again this afternoon?" Jo nodded. It didn't look as though she was going to enlighten me, so I rushed on. "How's it going anyway? I haven't had a chance to ask you about it lately. You're spending quite a few hours on it. Anything interesting come to light so far?"

"Yep, very interesting I would say. I told you earlier about those dummy payments occurring on the second and fourth Fridays of each month. If the practice continued, another payment was due yesterday. I spent all day with one eye glued to the computer waiting for it to happen. When it didn't come up on the system, I was worried my poking about might have scared them off. One way or another, I was busy all day, and it was possible it slipped through unnoticed. I wanted to take another look today, to see if I'd missed it yesterday. There *was* a payment. I didn't miss it. It was in one of the batches scheduled to run last night."

"I don't know what to say. Is that good or bad news? Is that all you found? You seemed excited when you came home, so I wondered if you'd had a breakthrough of some kind."

"In the first instance, I was relieved. The payment confirmed I hadn't left a trail or set any flags to warn off the perpetrator. Not based on any real evidence, my mind had settled on a handful of possible suspects. I was a bit concerned when two of those possible suspects left the company this week. Before you ask, I never considered Claude Dietrich a suspect."

"Only a handful of suspects…? I half expected there would be heaps; all of your clerks for instance. With two of your suspects no longer with the company, does it help focus your attention on the remaining possibilities?"

"You would expect so wouldn't you, but that's not the case. Today, I confirmed something I only suspected up until now. I might add, it took me some time to unravel it. How well do you trust your IT people?"

"That's a strange question. Let's just say, I don't have any reason not to trust them. There are three people in the IT team, and two of those have been here since before James took over running the place. Are you about to tell me I shouldn't trust them?"

"If only it were so simple. No, I don't think there is anything to worry you there, but I am curious about who else within the company's employees might have significant IT capabilities. Here is the reason I'm asking: it took me all afternoon to unpick it, but I now know the scheduling of those payments is written into a part of the operating system."

I frowned and shook my head. I had no idea what she was talking about. Jo noticed and jumped in to provide me with a simplified explanation.

"It means that at some point – way back when perhaps – someone inserted a series of commands into the operating system dealing with the payment of accounts. I've discovered that, at the beginning of the second and fourth weeks, the system automatically generates invoices and emails them to the stores department. A day or so before then, the system also generates goods received notices which end up in the stores in-tray. So, we then have all the necessary documentation in the system to cover the payments being made at the end of those particular weeks."

"So, the clerk processing the invoices would see nothing out of place, and would include them in the end of week payment runs. Is that how it works?"

"Not exactly. It appears the documentation supporting the payment isn't handled by the clerk. It just appears in the file on the system as though it has been processed in the normal way. The payment itself would occur regardless of whether the other documentation was there or not. It's a significant patch added to the operating system, not something your average clerk is capable of developing."

"Now we know how it's happening, how do we stop it?"

"We don't … not yet anyway. Until we get to the bottom of it, we don't want anything alerting the perpetrators to our interest in their little scheme. That could be disastrous. I was planning to go back into work tomorrow to do more digging around. I feel we are close now. It requires just a little bit more before we know it all."

"Jo, I don't know about you, but I'm freezing."

"Yeah, me too; why are we still sitting out here? Let's go and do something about dinner."

"The reason we're still sitting out here is because I don't want to go inside and have this conversation come to a dead end. I'm prepared to sit here and freeze if that's what it takes for me to learn all you have discovered so far."

"What the…? We can talk just as well inside as we can out here in the garden. If we go inside, we're less likely to catch pneumonia. Come on, grab your glass and let's go inside."

We sat at the breakfast bar in the kitchen. While she refilled our glasses, I urged Jo to tell me what else she knew.

"There isn't much else to tell. I might know more after I spend some time on it tomorrow. Perhaps, what you don't understand about such an investigation is the way it happens. You don't work your way through some prescribed tick-and-flick list. It isn't the case of do this, then that, followed by the next thing. A lot of the time, it's what you find tells you what to do next. Sometimes, it's instinct or intuition that directs you.

That's why I can't be too definite about what I'm going to do tomorrow. I have a couple of vague ideas I want to explore. They might provide nothing. On the other hand, they might set me on a track that produces better results than we could hope for. I will keep you informed. There are times when my thinking becomes overloaded with the case I'm working on." Jo paused and took a deep breath before continuing. "When it happens, I sometimes lose track of everything else I'm supposed to be doing … like keeping you informed. That's the reason I don't trust myself to pursue this investigation during work hours. I could easily get side-tracked and forget all about being the finance manager."

"Okay, I admit I don't understand the process. I wasn't being critical, or suggesting the investigation wasn't progressing as I expected. If I'm honest, I feel helpless about not being able to do anything to assist. You must tell me if there's anything I can do. Perhaps, I could help you investigate some of the employees."

"You are doing your bit to help with the employees. If you keep sacking staff the way you have been, you will have eliminated most of the suspects."

"None of the ones I've seen off so far have the brains to be behind any of this. Nevertheless, there is a possibility one or two of them might have been involved. But, they would have been drones and not the main player."

There wasn't much else Jo could tell me, and I'd run out of intelligent questions to ask. So, after a light meal of frittata and salad, we took our coffees through to the lounge room. I picked up the book I'd left on the side table and pretended to become engrossed in reading it. After a few moments, I heard Jo chuckling. When I looked over at her, her chuckling developed into full-scale raucous laughter.

"If you want me to believe you're reading that book, it would help if you turned it right way round. I don't doubt your abilities, but I suspect reading a book upside down is not one of them."

"Eh..? Oh bugger … All right clever clogs, I wasn't reading. My mind was processing everything we talked about earlier this evening. In particular, it was dredging up everything I knew about employees who had any likelihood of being involved in ripping funds off the company. The most upsetting thing about doing that is finding such a high number of relatively new employees. So many of them were employed during James' time at the helm. I know, these days, the tendency is for people not to remain in the one job all their working life, or even for extended periods of time. But that doesn't stop me being surprised at how many 'new' ones there are."

"You're right. These days, the rate of employee turnover is much changed from a decade ago. Tomorrow, I intend to spend some time examining some of those 'new recruits'."

Chapter 18

Jo: the money trail

"Good morning, Jim. My apologies for not letting you know I would be coming in again today. I'll be spending time in my office, so it should be a lot quieter upstairs than it was yesterday."

"Right you are, Miss Ballard. Thank you for checking in with me. Are you on your own today or is Miss McCarthy likely to be coming as well?"

"Not that I'm aware of; I think you're stuck with just me to keep an eye on today. By the way, Jim, congratulations on your promotion."

"Thank you, Miss, but I'm not sure it's one I wanted."

As I climbed the stairs to my office, Jim set off on one of his scheduled rounds of the premises. It lifted my spirits to know some employees of Jim's calibre still remained. *They* would not be the focus of my work today. My gut told me it had to be a more recent employee who was involved … but how recent? I still didn't know how long this wonderful rip-off scheme had been in place, or when and by whom it was initiated.

My thinking last night was to make today's priority searching for when the rogue payments began. Nothing happened to change my thinking. I logged onto the system and began my search working backwards through the records. The search progressed well until about ten o'clock. Until then, tracing the twice monthly payments was easy. Then, I reached the end of the files on the system. It didn't take long to establish the reason. The company has a rolling schedule of archiving files off the system. In my case, it's not helpful. The files I can access only stretch back five years. The fortnightly payments were established before then.

Damn! It was beginning to look as though it wasn't worth coming in today. I made myself a cappuccino and settled into my new lounge chair to think while I drank it. I guessed the archived files needed reloading onto the system to be accessed. That wasn't going to happen today, and I didn't want to ask the IT section to do it. Someone wanting to access files from so far back was bound to raise questions. If I couldn't continue tracing the payments, what else could I look at?

The other area I had earmarked to examine at some stage was payroll. I doubted I'd find anything in those files, but it was worth a look. My thinking was, if routine rogue payments were established in the accounting system, there would be no need to siphon off funds via the payroll system. With nothing else to work on, it was worth checking the payroll anyway. Then, I could cross it off as something to be investigated at a later date.

Auditing the payroll system would be more complicated than I'd thought. Almost as soon as I started, I realised my knowledge of the company's employees was sketchy at best. How would I identify a rogue name if I didn't know the legitimate workers? Any employee lists I found on the system would include the name of a rogue employee if one existed. Time to stop pounding the keyboard and do some thinking instead.

"What about the personnel records?" I asked the universe. With no reply forthcoming, I searched the system for employees' personnel records. If the records were on the system, they would have restricted access. My assumption proved correct. I found the files, but my login wouldn't allow me access. After a few moments of hesitation, I called Mel.

"Apologies if I interrupted something lovely you were in the midst of doing, but I have a problem. I need access to some restricted files. My login doesn't get me in. I was wondering whether you were able to access them." Mel didn't ask why or which files I wanted to access, but I thought it best to explain my reason for wanting access. "… No, I don't think I need you to come in … Would you mind if I used your login to access them? … Yeah, I think I remember it … Okay, if you've nothing better to do, come on in … I was just hoping for your permission to use your login so I could make a start on the files. … Thank you. That's great … Yes, you can come in if you still want to, but it's not necessary."

I held my breath as I entered Mel's login. Normal breathing resumed when the system opened the files I required and didn't lock me out. Again, these files weren't as straight forward as I'd hoped. There were multiple files for each employee. Their information included details of past employment and qualifications taken from their original employment application, and a file for training courses undertaken since employment with the company. Others included a file relating to taxation instructions, and one containing information and instructions pertinent to the company's superannuation scheme.

Employee's files containing information submitted on their employment applications seemed the most likely to be useful. If there were a ghost employee, it would have required meticulous thought and preparation to create such a file on the system. The doubts in the back of my mind reminded me that, if the file contained realistic details, I wouldn't be able to determine if the person was a rogue or not.

Progress was slow, and required a thorough scrutiny of each file before it was declared legitimate. I was examining the fifth employee file when Mel arrived.

"Didn't trust me ferreting around on the system using your login while you weren't here, eh?"

"No, it's nothing like that. I'm here for two reasons: I might be able to help verify identification – at least of the people I know. My other reason for coming was to bring lunch. So, tell me what you are doing, and how far you've gone with it."

Explaining my method was easy. Admitting my lack of progress was embarrassing. "It's a slow and tedious process. So far, I've examined only five files, and was just about to start on the sixth employee."

"Okay; whose name is next on the list?" I read out the name. "Yep, he's a genuine one; works in the store and has done for more than a decade I'd say."

As Mel rattled off what she knew about each employee as I read out their name, I also cast a quick eye over their file. This new approach sped up the process. The only time it slowed down was when Mel didn't personally know the owner of a name. For each of those cases, we had to rely on the information in the file being genuine and not something created to legitimise a ghost.

About an hour later, we stopped for lunch. While making considerable progress since Mel's arrival, we had barely made a dent in the list of employees. To do as much as we could for the day, lunchtime was shortened to about twenty minutes before returning to the computer files. After some discussion over lunch, we had agreed not to work beyond four o'clock. That had me frustrated all afternoon. If it were up to me, I would prefer to work on into the night, or at least until I felt I'd made significant inroads into checking the employees.

By about two o'clock, I felt as though my eyes were hanging out from staring at the screen. "I need a break. I'm going to wander around for a while to stretch my legs and rest my eyes."

Mel bounced up off her chair. "Thank God. I didn't think we were ever going to take a break. Do you feel like another coffee?"

Stretching our legs took us to the kitchen and back to Mel's office to drink our coffees. After another brief stroll to the kitchen to rinse our mugs, it was back to work. The second name I read out after our restart had Mel shaking her head.

"No, never heard of him; probably was employed during James' time."

"Would Gordon Grimshaw know the names of all the men who work for him?"

"Of course he does. Why are you asking?"

I didn't answer Mel, but keyed in Gordon Grimshaw's home number instead. "I'm sorry to disturb you at home on a Sunday, Gordon. Would you mind if I ask you one quick question? … Do you know the name Preston Wardell? … Not one of your tradesmen?... No? … Perhaps a carpenter? … Okay, thanks for that, Gordon … No, there's no problem and nothing for you to worry about. And, Gordon, this conversation never happened, if you get my drift … Good man, thanks again."

"What, what? … What have you found? Come on, Jo, tell me what he said," was the mantra Mel started chanting as I finished speaking with Gordon. She had moved forward to perch on the front of her chair. "Jo Ballard, I swear I'll slap you if you don't tell me what you've found. Who is Preston Wardell?"

"So far, none of us knows. He has a dodgy looking file, which gives an impossible address, a doubtful qualification, and little else."

"Why is it an impossible address?"

"It's a bookshop on the High Street."

"Yes, but he might live above it."

"I know who lives above it. She also owns the building and runs the bookshop and, unless she has undergone a major change, she is gay."

"So we found our ghost. You were right. For however long, we've been paying someone who doesn't exist."

"No. Don't jump to conclusions. We have a suspicious looking file. That's all we have. There could be any number of explanations for it. What we don't know yet is if the company is paying him."

After logging out of the system as Mel, I logged back on as myself. "Mel, I've logged out as you. If you want to keep working, you could go back to your own office and continue going through the employees list. Make a note of the particulars of any of the names you don't recognise. I'm going to start checking the weekly payroll files to see if this bloke is being paid."

"You think there might be more than one ghost on the payroll?"

"At this point, I'm not sure we have any ghosts on the payroll, and I won't be until I've checked. It would be unusual for there to be more than one, but we can't discount the possibility."

It didn't take long to locate Preston Wardell's name on the latest payroll run. Within about half an hour, by a random selection of earlier payroll runs, it became obvious Mr Wardell was a long time invisible employee. I looked at the details I'd copied from his personnel file. Mr Wardell appeared to have been created almost seven years ago. *...By whom,* was the question the file failed to answer. I went to share my latest news with Mel.

"So, we do have a ghost and we've had him for a while. What do we do now?" she asked.

"We call it a day. You go home and think of something nice for dinner. I'm going to call my friend with the bookshop, just to check she doesn't know any Preston Wardell, and doesn't have anyone by that name living with her."

My phone call didn't bring any surprises. She had never heard of Preston Wardell. Using Mel's login, I went back onto the system and checked Wardell's personnel file again. The only signature associated with it was the personnel manager's sign-off on the authority to employ Mr Wardell. It probably meant nothing. It was usual for personnel managers to sign off on such applications.

After pondering the matter for a few minutes, I grabbed my phone. I needed to make two calls, and neither of them should be on the company's phones. As today was Sunday, one of those calls would have to wait until tomorrow. The other call I could make now. I found Syd Hartley on my contacts list and listened as my phone dialled the number. Syd answered just as I was about to end the call. I hadn't given a thought to the possibility he was out on a case and might choose to ignore my call.

"No, I went to fetch a coffee and left my phone on my desk in the squad room. It's a quiet day and I'm the only one in. So, talk to me. It will help relieve the boredom."

Syd sounded cheerful enough. It eased my trepidation about asking him to do something else. "At the risk of straining the friendship, I wondered if you might look up another person for me. He is the current personnel manager here at Mel's company, and seems to have arrived on the scene around the same time as the former finance manager I asked you to look into." I gave Syd the personnel manager's name. It didn't ring any bells for him. As he was just about to start trawling through records for information on the former finance manager, it was easy enough to add the personnel manager to his search.

An odd thought occurred to me as he spoke. "Well, if you're about to go digging through records, perhaps you might add another name to your search list?" Syd seemed relaxed about it. "Okay, please search for any background information there might be on James Rothwell."

"James Rothwell… wasn't that Mel's husband, the one who disappeared overboard?"

"That's the one. Something smells rotten, and my gut is nagging me to delve deeper into the situation here. I have an interesting story to share with you the next time we meet."

With nothing more I could do, I packed up and headed for home. I knew I was close to solving the case. I felt it in every thread of my being. All I needed was one or two vital clues to tie it all together. Perhaps Syd will get lucky with his search, but I'm banking heavily on the call I need to make tomorrow to come up trumps for me.

Home early for a change, we took long cold drinks out into the garden while we waited for Mel's baked dinner to finish cooking. Having been cooped up inside all day, I hadn't realised what a glorious day it had been until I was on my way home. It remained so as day drifted into evening. Its lingering tender warmth relaxed both body and mind. A breeze so light as to be almost non-existent drifted the perfume of the neighbour's jasmine over the fence to envelop us.

"You seem more relaxed tonight, Jo. Are you close to getting to the bottom of it all?"

"I wouldn't go so far as to say that, but today was encouraging. We now know the misappropriation of funds is not a recent initiative, but one that has been in place for an extended time. And, we have identified it as a quite sophisticated scheme. There's no way of knowing how long it will take to solve the mystery, or if we will ever know who is responsible, but we are drawing the net in closer around it."

"Are we able to put a stop to it? I am so angry and frustrated that somebody continues to rip off me and my company."

"Oh yes, we will put an end to it, but we have to let it continue until we trace this 'rabbit back to its burrow'."

*****

Chaos ruled supreme this morning. Everything was moved out of mine and Majella's offices and into Mel's front office area. Gordon brought up a couple of tradesmen who, armed with tape measures, made various hieroglyphs on the walls of the former social club room. Then, by mid-morning, the racket of power tools hard at work was deafening. Mel and I encountered one another at the coffee machine.

Mel gave me a wry smile. "I should have insisted on overtime and had the modifications done after hours. Before long, we might have to send someone along to the first aid station for a packet of analgesics."

"Before they started all the racket, Gordon told me it would be noisy for a couple of hours, or maybe three, while they cut out the new doorways. After that, there should be a bit of hammering, but nothing like what we are copping now. So, if we hang in there for a bit longer, the worst should be over."

As I returned to my desk, my mobile phone vibrated in my pocket: Syd Hartley. I walked out of the office and along to the stationery room as I answered the call.

"Do you suppose you might be able to slip away for an extended lunch hour today?"

"Does it have to be at lunchtime? I would have a better chance of slipping away late this afternoon."

"Try to make it by four o'clock at our favourite pub. Bring your notebook. I've lots to share."

How could I refuse such an offer? But, Syd's call reminded me of that other call I had intended to make first thing this morning. While I was still in the stationery room, I searched my contacts list for the name I wanted, and heaved a sigh of relief when the familiar voice of Jackson Quale answered.

"Jo… It's been a while … I heard you were back home. What can I do for you? Are you working a case?"

"Yeah; once again it's the usual story of chasing the money trail. I was hoping you might have some spare time today to see me."

Jackson had meetings for the rest of the morning, but suggested an appointment for two o'clock. I agreed before I even thought about squaring it with Mel. I rushed back and knocked on her door. When she looked up from her desk, her face lit up.

"You've found something haven't you? What is it?"

"No-o … I don't have anything yet … but I have talked to a couple of people who might provide me with what we are looking for. Problem is, I need to disappear for most of the afternoon to talk to those people. I'd hate to encounter the Three Strikes Rule so early in my new position."

"It's only natural you would need to talk to various people in relation to your position here. Disappear at lunchtime if you like."

"Thanks; I'll probably leave here about one o'clock and won't be back today. See you at home later this evening."

Chapter 19

Jo: revelations

It was a bit after one o'clock when I left the office and found a parking place just off the High Street. A quick sandwich at a coffee shop followed by a brisk stride along the Street, and I was in the bank right on two o'clock. Jackson came out into the front area and waved me over as soon as I arrived. I settled down across the desk from him.

"Thanks for seeing me at such short notice, Jacks. I have a couple of relevant documents for you, but I'll talk you through it anyway."

He gave the two sheets of paper I handed him nothing more than a cursory glance. "What are we looking at with this one; money laundering?"

"No not this time. This time, it's plain old misappropriation. But, I have to admit, it involves a very clever way of carrying out the theft. The top one of those two sheets contains details of a rogue company which receives twice monthly payments into an account at this bank from Mel McCarthy's company. The second sheet relates to a ghost employee whose wages also are deposited in an account at this bank."

"Okay, but before we go any further, let's make sure those accounts are with this branch."

A few moments later, he confirmed both accounts were at his branch and were active. His confirmation was not news. I had established that yesterday. If I wasn't sure they were at his branch, I wouldn't have called him. "Thanks, Jacks. I'm interested in who is operating on those accounts. I wouldn't expect them to be the same person, but there might be similarities."

"Are you in a hurry? I'm finding the system is a bit slow today, so it might take me a few minutes to find the information."

With nothing scheduled until four o'clock, I had plenty of time – and I preferred not to leave without the information I wanted. He asked someone to bring us coffee. I sipped mine while he tapped on his keyboard and muttered at the screen. After apologising to me several times for the delay, I saw him sit up straight and start hammering his keyboard. For the next couple of minutes, I wasn't sure whether he was talking to me or still addressing his computer. There seemed to be a mumbled conversation occurring.

"At last…!… Yep, we're in … Now, let's see… What's the first account? … Okay, there it is … Oh, right… That's interesting … Can I print that? Ah, yes; two copies please." I heard the printer on a small table adjacent to his desk come to life while his mumbled conversation continued. "Now, what was the other account number? … Eh? … Oh, typed it in wrong … try again … that's better … Oh, hello…! That makes two interesting situations … print this one out too."

Then, his conversation with the computer came to an abrupt end. He reached across and grabbed the printouts, spread them out on the desk and studied them for a few moments. He scratched a fingernail through his designer five-o'clock-shadow-type beard as he sat focused on the sheets of paper in front of him. Finally, he looked up at me and cleared his throat.

"Ahem, sorry about the delay, but after all that, I'm not sure I can help you." He sorted out one copy of each page he printed and handed them across to me. You can study those in detail later, but I can tell you now there is nothing more than a few pence in each of those accounts. I've asked the computer to find further documentary evidence relating to them. That seems to be taking a while to track down. While the system is slow today, I think the delay in this case might be due to something else. I think the authorities relating to the operation of those accounts might have been lodged with one of the other branches. Hence, it is taking the system longer to find them."

"Could you have a guess at what those authorities might tell us? From the look of this," I waved my copy of the printout at him, "all monies are sent off to somewhere else. And, if I read these codes correctly, in both cases, the funds are being transferred overseas – to France. Am I correct?"

"Yeah, I knew you'd work it out straight away. You've been in this game far too long not to recognise those codes."

At that point, his computer pinged announcing the arrival of something. I hoped it was the digitised versions of the original authorities he'd asked for. Even from my side of the desk, it was obvious whatever appeared on his screen excited him. It held his attention for a few minutes. During that time, he sporadically attacked his keyboard. I assumed he was interrogating the information received. My patience finally received reward.

"For obvious reasons, I can't give you copies of these authorities. I'm sure you understand. But, if you've got your notebook ready, I can tell you what the gist of them is."

I had my notebook open on the desk ready to record anything of interest but, in this case, I opted to note the information directly on the printouts Jacks gave me earlier. Then, it was my turn to sit and stare at the information as I tried to glean more from it than it had to offer.

"Jacks, I can see what this says, and I understand what it means. Is there anything else you can tell me, anywhere else you can search for more information?"

"Jo, I know you would like more definitive details, but there is nothing more here. You will need to follow the trail a bit further along, and I fear it might not be a simple one-step exercise."

"Thanks for being so encouraging and optimistic! You're not telling me something I don't know. In both these cases, the set up was much too complicated for it to be as simple as requiring one more piece of information."

"Your visit has been disappointing. I'm sorry we can't help you progress your investigation any further. But, we will be interested to hear about anything you uncover as you move forward with this. It's important we know what we might be inadvertently facilitating."

In the same coffee shop where I had lunch earlier, I took time over another cup of coffee to review the documents Jacks gave me. As it was soon after three o'clock, I had plenty of time and not far to go before meeting Syd at four o'clock. I dragged my laptop out of my bag and entered the information from Jacks' printouts onto my case file. With nothing much else to do, and the coffee shop staff glaring at me for staying so long without buying anything more, I packed up and returned to my car.

Our favourite pub was quite close to the coffee shop – well within walking distance – but I decided to drive and have my car close by when I was ready to leave. In spite of the short distance to travel, driving took me much longer than it would have if I walked. Syd already was reading today's newspaper at our table in the corner when I arrived.

"I know I am early, so how long ago did you arrive?"

"About half an hour ago; before you ask if it's been a slack day at the office, I've been on duty since four a.m., and it feels like it's been a l-o-n-g day. What are you drinking? I'll get us a couple of drinks before we start."

While I was tempted to demand he forget the drinks and just tell me what he found, good manners insisted I play the game his way. A few minutes later, we got down to business.

"That first bloke you asked me to check up on, the finance manager, was interesting from the outset. I just started scoping him out when you asked me about the other two. And, would you believe it, I already had found connections with those two."

"Are you telling me you found evidence connecting all three of those people I asked you about?"

"You've summed it up nicely. Their connection goes back a long way. They were all at university together, but there is evidence they would have known each other before that. What's not clear so far is how well they knew each other before their university days. At this stage, I don't know whether that is likely to prove important or not, but I suspect it won't have much impact, if any."

"Are you telling me it appears James indulged in a spot of nepotism? Keep in mind I don't believe in coincidence any more than you do."

"I don't know we can jump to that conclusion."

"What… in spite of how it looks? What would you say about it then?"

"Do you want to argue semantics, or do you want to hear the rest of my report?"

"…Your report, please."

"Right, well, as I said, they knew each other at university. There was also a fourth member of the gang, and another sort of associate member. None of them amounted to much, not academically anyway. After failing various subjects, and exhausting the allowable number of resits, your finance manager's university days were over. It seems his parents gave up on him too and, with his financial support withdrawn, he took to bumming around."

"How long was he at university? Did he complete much of his course before being tossed out?"

"He was there for two years, but I don't know how much he successfully completed. It was much the same story with your personnel manager. The difference was he changed course a couple of times, but still failed often enough to be shown the door at the end of second year."

While it had nothing to do with my case, I was a bit interested in the identity of the 'fourth member of the gang' as Syd called him. After Syd told me his name, I definitely wanted to know more.

"I don't know a whole lot more. If I'd known you are interested in him, I'd have put a bit more effort in to finding out about him. All I remember about him is he was the son of that loudmouth politician from up north, had been spoiled rotten by his parents from what I could tell, and didn't do any better than his mates when it came to his studies. I think he dropped out of university around the same time as the other two, but it might've been for different reasons."

"That sounds intriguing, tell me more. Yes, I know he's not one of the ones I asked you about, but now you've roused my interest."

"I was checking newspaper archives to confirm who he was when I came across an article in the social column about his forthcoming marriage. Just like you, it had me intrigued and side-tracked me for a bit. It seems he might have put the blushing bride in the family way and was obligated to do the 'right thing'."

I managed to hold back my smile at Syd's use of the antiquated phrase 'family way'. While that bloke and his bride had nothing to do with my investigation, I was surprised Syd had wasted time looking into him and mentioned it.

"I didn't set out to investigate him but, after the article about his forthcoming marriage which confirmed his identity, the next week's paper carried a photo of the wedding party. And there they all were: the three blokes you're interested in, the bride and groom, and a gaggle of bridesmaids. To my way of thinking, it confirmed a close bond between the four blokes. I'm not suggesting that's of any use to your investigation, but I found it interesting."

"Agreed. It is interesting. I've never heard Mel talk about James' bachelor days, and I'm sure there's never been any mention of his attending university. Do you know if James obtained his degree?"

"Oh, sorry, I meant to mention it earlier. If what I've found is correct, he did very well in some subject areas, but was hopeless in others. In fact, it might be fair to say that, in those areas where he did well, he could be described as outstanding – even brilliant. The fact that he was so hopeless at every other subject finally brought about his downfall. He too was kicked out of university part way through his third year. Apart from not being bright enough to continue, the university was concerned not all his results were his own work. The charges levelled against him by the academic board included using his fellow gang members to undertake certain exams for him. It seems that, between them, they had sufficient academic ability to maintain James' progress through his degree course. After the others dropped out, James was left to battle on alone. That's when the rot set in."

"Correct me if I'm wrong, but it sounds like you are telling me his cheating ways, as well as his lack of academic ability, finally got him tossed out. I wonder what he did after that, and how I'm going to ask Mel about it."

"Can't help you with that. I didn't find any more about him. But, I suppose I stopped looking at that point and focused on passing on what I already knew to you. I wasn't going to say anything to you but, because this whole thing has grabbed my interest, I intend to dig a little deeper. I'm not saying I'm going to find anything of use to you with your investigation, but I am curious."

"I'm pleased to hear that. We might both be surprised at what you manage to dig up."

"Jesus; I almost forgot to tell you a really interesting fact. Remember that politician's son who had to get married in a hurry…?" I nodded but didn't comment. "I don't know why, but I followed it up a bit more. It seems a baby was born about four months after the wedding, but he only lived a matter of hours, not even a day."

"All things considered, it wasn't the happiest start to married life was it? I wonder how things ended up for them."

"Ah well now, that's the really interesting part. They had only been married a few months – less than a year anyway – when notice of their impending divorce appeared in the paper. I checked the records. The divorce was on account of the wife's adultery. It seems she had resumed her relationship with her former lover … none other than one James Rothwell."

"Christ, I wonder if Mel knows about that … And if I dare ask about it. Who was this adulterous wife, do we know?"

"Yep, she was the long-standing associate member of the gang. Her name was Krista, and she was your finance manager's younger sister."

"Hang about; backup for a minute. That northern politician you mentioned, what was his surname?"

"Thomas … Roland Thomas; and his son was Wilston Thomas. You seem a bit excited about that. How is it important?"

"Some people might put it down to coincidence, and I suppose I should confirm it before passing judgement, but I am certain there is no coincidence involved in this. Let me tell you a story. When Mel brought James into the company and set him up to take over as managing director, he needed a secretary. That secretary continued on after James disappeared and ultimately became Mel's secretary when she took up the reins again. It wasn't a happy association and was doomed from the outset. In a somewhat spectacular display, it was terminated last week. Then, soon after, in response to an offer Mel made at the time, the secretary asked if she might come back to take up the lesser position Mel had offered her instead of terminating her employment."

"I'm sure all that makes for an interesting story, but I don't see why it might interest me."

"Ah well, Syd, I haven't told you the secretary's name. She is Krista Thomas."

I watched Syd's jaw drop and his eyebrows crawl up towards his hairline. He looked hard at me for a few moments before speaking. I could almost hear his brain working in overdrive.

"Well now, my friend, that is interesting. And, I suspect it might also be a worry. If these two women are one and the same Krista, it might explain the secretary's antagonism towards Mel. I've no evidence to support it, but I'd almost bet a significant part of my anatomy on a previous relationship between her and James not exactly being dead and buried. I think this opens up a much wider field for investigation."

"You're not on your own there. There is something you didn't mention. What was each of the gang members studying before the university days were cut short?"

Syd consulted his notes before answering. "Here they are, now let's see. Wilston Thomas took political science. Your personnel manager was doing some sort of sociology course.

One of those strange airy fairy things. Oh, you will love this. Your finance manager was studying to become an accountant. Funny how they seem to have ended up with managerial positions requiring the skills and knowledge they flunked out on."

"I don't know that I'd call it funny, but it is very interesting. But you haven't told me the most important thing. What was James studying?"

"I didn't write down the exact name of the degree, but my notes say it was all about computers, programming and all that other IT stuff. It seems that was the stuff he was good at, but he was hopeless at the other subjects in the course."

How I managed to restrain myself from reaching across the table to kiss Syd is a mystery. He had just given me the key; what I was sure would turn out to be the most vital piece of information in solving this case. As I scribbled furiously in my notebook, I became vaguely aware of Syd speaking to me. "I'm sorry, Syd, what was that?"

"I asked if you are planning to have a meal here this evening."

"I suppose I half thought so when I first arrived, but now I don't think so. I need to get my head around everything you've told me this afternoon, and then see how the pieces fit my puzzle. And, I think there might be a hard conversation to have with Mel, and the sooner the better."

As I spoke, Syd's phone vibrated loudly on the table. He said only a few words, but I watched his jaw tighten and a touch of urgency develop in him.

"Just as well we weren't planning on dining here tonight. That was a call to action. They found another body. Looks like my day is turning into a 24-hour stint." He slipped his phone and his notebook into his pocket and picked up his coat. "I'll keep digging for you. Your case has taken hold of me. I can't promise I'll find any more, or that it might be soon, but I will let you know if anything else turns up."

With that, he was on his way out the door. I shoved my notebook in my bag and followed him out. As I reached my car,

I saw his vehicle disappearing along the street. A few minutes later, I was on my way home and trying mentally to prepare for the conversation I had to have with Mel.

She was busy in the kitchen preparing a pasta dish for dinner when I arrived. Slamming the lid on the pot she had been stirring, she bounded over to the breakfast bar.

"How did your afternoon turn out? Don't keep me in suspense, what did you find out? I'm pleased you came home when you did. I think I might've died of curiosity if I had to wait much longer."

"Is dinner at a stage where you can leave it for a few minutes while we talk?" She nodded enthusiastically. "Good; my afternoon went well. At least I think it did. I don't have any answers yet but we are getting closer."

In spite of her best efforts to hide it, Mel was disappointed. I could understand why. I also could understand why she wasn't as excited as I was. I knew it was going to turn into a late night, but I thought I'd try to lighten the mood a bit first.

"I suppose there's a few nuts and bolts type things I could share with you at this point in time, but there is something important I need to ask you." She leant forward in her chair and nodded again. I put on the most serious and worried face I could manage before dropping my bombshell.

"How do you feel about a trip to France? And how soon do you think we might be able to get away?"

Chapter 20

"You spend all afternoon swanning around town and, as soon as you get home again you want to know if we can go to France. I'm sure we can go, but I do have a few things to do beforehand. And, the first thing I need to know is why you think we should go to France at all. Come on, I know it's got something to do with what you discovered this afternoon. Share it with me."

"Yeah, I did find out quite a few things this afternoon, but not quite enough to be ready to go to tripping off just yet. My thinking is to leave it until the next payment to the rogue company is paid and to be in France at that time. Look, I don't know how to share with you some of the stuff I learnt this afternoon. It is sensitive and, while it doesn't bother me, you might find it upsetting. As I said, I don't know how best to share it with you, so I'm just going to dive in and give you the key facts… and trust you can handle them."

Jo launched into what I suspect was a potted version of everything her afternoon turned up in relation to the case. It was upsetting in a funny sort of way, but not as upsetting as either of us thought I would be. I let Jo run through to the end of all she learnt today before I interrupted. There were questions to ask. Some things I couldn't comprehend, but my overall reaction was one of relief. She put to rest for me a few niggardly doubts and questions residing in my mind for years, even from long before James disappeared.

"I now have a problem, Jo. I told Krista I would get back to her at the end of the week about starting in the general office pool. I left a message to the effect we were restructuring. As a result, the position in the office pool might not exist in future and I would contact her when the situation became clear. It wasn't deliberate, more a case of it having slipped my mind in the midst of everything else happening over the last few days. The question now is should I even consider having Krista anywhere near the place again, or leave her situation as a permanent termination? Is there any benefit to your investigation in bringing her back?"

"It's an interesting question, and one I don't have an answer for. To be honest, I'm not sure whether having her around to keep an eye on her makes any difference to the investigation. I think what's been put in place in the past will continue to operate whether she and her cronies are here or not. Were there any of the staff with whom she was particularly friendly?"

"Not that I noticed. She treated Gordon Grimshaw as though he didn't exist; completely ignored him. I don't think she had much time for the IT manager either. There was a reasonable relationship with the personnel manager. From what you've just told me, that probably stems from their former lives long ago. And, I now know why she was so friendly with the former finance manager, and why she took such umbrage at his departure. I can't see there was anyone else among staff or employees she was even remotely friendly with."

"I think I'd like to keep her away from the place. Perhaps stalling it as you have is best until we see if the various payments continue for another couple of weeks. Might the upheaval caused by the work to start in the office area on Monday be a reasonable excuse for delaying your decision even further if needed?"

"Oh, yes, that would work if I needed another excuse… but I didn't indicate how long this restructuring might go on for."

"So there's going to be a restructure…?"

"Ah, yes. I was going to talk to you about that this evening. After spending all afternoon thinking about it and scribbling a few possible charts, I've decided to create an administration section. It will take over most of what's currently in the personnel manager's area, plus a couple of other things. There will be no changes to Gordon Grimshaw's or the IT section's arrangements. And your only change to the finance section will be the addition of the payroll people. The only problem with all that is, I need to find a damn good administration manager twenty-four hours ago.”

“What’s to be done with the personnel manager?”

“He rang and wanted an appointment on Monday. I put him off until two o’clock as I thought the morning might be taken up with sorting out the work on the social club room. He jumped the gun a bit. I had planned to set up a meeting with him on Monday, but he rang me before I got around to it. He will be offered a redundancy package. No doubt it will not be substantial enough for his liking, but it will be a case of take it or leave it. It would have been nice to have an administration manager lined up before I caused complete chaos in the place.”

“Hmm … I might just be able to help you there. I happen to know one of the best administration managers around who took early retirement but is now interested in returning to work.”

“I don’t want another woman.”

“I didn’t say it was another woman … And why not anyway? What’s wrong with it being another woman?”

“It’s about avoiding the perception of setting up a ‘petticoat government’. A bloke would be a handy addition, if he were the best person for the job.”

“So happens Jock is a bloke. He took early retirement a couple of years ago when his wife became terminally ill. She died about three months later and it really knocked him flat. He seems to have moved on now and would love to get back into work. Jock was the admin manager for the mob I work for, and I doubt there’s a better manager around. In case you’re wondering, he comes with impeccable credentials and academic qualifications.”

“He might find the size of this place something of a comedown after working for your mob. Do you think he might be interested?”

“Quite likely, I should think. I know he was looking for something a little less demanding than the huge conglomerates he’s worked for in the past. Say the word and I’ll give him a call.”

"Yes, please. I don't suppose he'll want to talk to us on the weekend so, even if it has to be amidst the chaos on Monday morning, as soon as you can organise it would be wonderful. By the way, what's his name – apart from Jock I mean?"

"Uhmm … K-e-i-th…? Yes, I'm sure it's Keith; Keith McGillivray. Everyone calls him Jock, and I think he prefers it. I doubt many since his mother have called him Keith."

"If we can come back to your suggested trip to France, if we are going to do that, how soon does it have to be? And, I suppose, how important is it to the overall investigation?"

"Not for at least another two weeks, preferably; I still need to obtain a little information. I also want to see if those payments continue. If the payments don't continue, then I will have to consider whether a trip is worthwhile or not."

Information overload seemed to have set in. Jo already had given me more information than my mind could cope with in one night. Even if there was more she could tell me, I don't think I could handle it just now. The weekend looked like being spent on finalising my ideas for my new administration section. It seems I'm going in at the deep end on Monday.

Everything we talked about this evening continued to churn in my mind long after I turned off the lights. By two o'clock I was begging for sleep to keep me company for what remained of the night.

*****

Saturday morning was glorious, even if I wasn't in a mood to fully appreciate it. After breakfasting in the garden, I remained outside reading the weekend papers. I was trying to get my head around a heavy article which I couldn't understand, but which seemed as though it should be important, when Jo bounced out and sat beside me. The smug look on her face should have captured my attention. Thanks to my foggy state this morning, I didn't pick up on it, so wasn't forewarned.

"You can't sit out here all day. You have things to do." I suspect I offered nothing more than a confused look in response.

Not put off, she continued. "Jock McGillivray is *v-e-r-y* interested in the administration manager's position, and would be happy to meet with you this afternoon. He suggested three o'clock. I'll let him know whether you prefer he comes here or to your office."

"Here would be better. But, I have nothing prepared; no paperwork to give him. I'll be sitting there waving my arms about as I try to paint word pictures of what the job, the company and everything else is all about."

"I don't think it's a problem. He knows all about Melissa McCarthy's company, its history and what its business is. So, come on, let's put together some information on all the internal operations he might not know about, and might need to be aware of in order to make a decision about the position."

The interview with Jock was a breeze. He sounded perfect for what I wanted, and he could start as soon as required. After I explained about the office refurbishment, which included creating his new office, we agreed I would call him to arrange a definite start date when the work was completed. In my mind, the work would be finished by late Tuesday, so I would be calling Jock on Wednesday.

Jo and I spent much of the remainder of the weekend finalising details of the new offices to be created in the former social club space, and tightening up on the structure of the new administration section. There was a trip into the office late on Sunday to move most of the stuff out of Jo's office into my front office area in readiness for the onslaught of the tradesmen the next day. Only her desk remained to be shifted. We agreed we might leave that for the men to do first thing in the morning.

By Monday afternoon, new doorways had been cut and doors fitted. Puttying and scraping went on during the day in amongst everything else so the offices would be ready for painting on Tuesday morning. All day Tuesday, nothing remedied the smell of paint that pervaded our work areas. All three of us went home with headaches. From home, I called Jock on Tuesday night to tell him his new office was ready for occupancy but remained unfurnished. He said he would come in tomorrow to organise whatever was necessary.

Mid-afternoon Wednesday, when I walked out into my front office, I realised life seemed to be humming along as normal again. Jo and Jock were established in their new offices, the former personnel manager had accepted the redundancy offer and departed, and the secretary who previously looked after both the personnel and security managers was installed in my front office outside Jock's door.

Over a drink on Wednesday night, Jo and I discussed our next move in her investigation. I had no time to even think about it over the previous few days, and I suspected Jo's days were just as chaotic. "So, Jo, what's our next move and when does it happen?"

"My original thinking was not to do anything for a couple of weeks. Now, I'm inclined to believe we should make a move much sooner. What is your schedule like for next week?"

"I need to be in my office all of next week. I will be looking at work requests for the coming year, and we will be going over all the sections' budget proposals for the next financial year. Apart from that, I think it necessary we both are around to ensure this new admin section kicks off properly and to assist Jock to set it up the way he wants it."

"That sounds perfect. If the long-established routine continues, our ghost employee should be included in the pay runs on both this Friday and Friday next week. Likewise, an invoice from the rogue company would be paid next Friday. If that does occur, it will be all the confirmation we need before we act. My suggestion would be for us to be in France by the start of business the following Monday.

While I'm unsure about certain timings relating to those payments, I think Monday morning will be the earliest the next stage of the process happens. We would need to be in France on Sunday evening at the latest to be at the bank when it opens its doors on Monday. I should have the extra information I need by the end of this week, or early next week at the latest. So, I'll be able to put the ground work in place before we go to France."

There was nothing in Jo's plan to argue with, so we tentatively scheduled ourselves a trip to France on the Sunday of next week. I was a bit confused about what we were to do in France, but I suspected I was largely a spectator along for the ride on this operation. Nevertheless, sometime over the next week, I would try to get a handle on our game plan.

*****

Somehow, during the typically intense budget planning week, Jo managed to devote some time to her investigation. I wasn't aware of it until during the weekend when we were preparing to decamp to France. On Saturday evening, as we sat with our drinks in the last of the sun's rays and basked in the latent warmth of the surrounding cobbles and bricks, Jo gave me the details.

"Now payroll is located in my domain, I asked them to find me the time slips for our ghost employee. When I mentioned his name, they both looked vacant and claimed never to have heard of him. It follows that they couldn't find any time slips ever having been submitted for him. It seems our ghost, Preston Wardell, is an automatic insertion into the payroll at the time the payment and disbursement run occurs on a Friday evening. The pay clerks complete their work on Friday afternoons and set the pay run to occur at about eight o'clock on Friday night. As part of the process, each employee's pay for the week is deposited into his nominated bank account. That same procedure applies to our ghost employee. His pay is deposited in the local bank on Friday night. Then, as part of the bank's normal processing, sometime over the weekend – I'm still not sure when exactly – the money is transferred from his account at the local bank to another account in France."

"We are not going to be at the bank in France until Monday morning. Will that be critical to finding further information? Will it be too long after the event?"

"No, I think not. A similar process occurs with our invoice payment run on Friday nights. So, last night, payment for an invoice would have been deposited in our rogue company's account at the local bank. Sometime over this weekend, that money will disappear across the channel to an account in a French bank. To the same bank as the ghost employee's pay is transferred. I hope nothing more happens to either of those French bank accounts before Monday morning. In case some automated process might intervene during the weekend, I contacted the bank and asked them to put a hold on everything until we arrive."

"I can't believe the bank would do that in response to a call out of the blue."

"No, they wouldn't, except they know me from my real job and previous investigations. They simply accepted I was working on one of my employer's forensic audits and were only too happy to oblige. You see, it's better to oblige and have it all sorted out, than to find yourself in court at some later date accused of being complicit in something illegal."

For a few brief moments, I pondered the legality of Jo's actions, before deciding she had been in this game long enough to know what she was doing. While I now understood why we were going to France, I still didn't know what our role would be – more precisely, what I would be doing – when we were there. The little voice in my head told me it might be handy to know my exact part in this operation, and how comfortable I might be with that arrangement.

My original thinking regarding my role was pretty much spot on. It seems most of my time would be spent as a spectator, with my only real involvement to occur if there was need for some input by the company owner who was being ripped off. While still not sure how that was going to play out, I felt reasonably confident I could manage whatever it might entail.

According to plan, on Sunday afternoon, we took the train to France and settled into our hotel not far from the bank we would visit tomorrow. We dined at a little eatery around the corner from the hotel and returned to our rooms early. Later, over a drink in my room, Jo seemed quite relaxed about the next day. I suppose all this is routine for her. It was anything but for me.

I was aware of a tightness in my stomach. It had nothing to do with the meal we ate earlier. It was an emotional thing, but I wasn't sure whether it was brought on by excitement or apprehension. I tried convincing myself there was nothing to be apprehensive about. Somehow, I didn't quite manage to pull it off.

Chapter 21

"Where am I? Oh God, this is my hotel room in France." After a few restless hours, I fell into a deep sleep, to wake late and in unfamiliar surroundings. We were to meet for breakfast in the hotel's coffee shop. I was late and didn't seem able to get myself together enough to do anything about it. Maybe, if I let in the day, I would wake up properly. The drapes probably opened on a glorious view across the skyline of Paris … but not today. Today, the world outside looked bleak and miserable.

Not many pedestrians strode the short strip of the pavement I could see below me. Those who did were hunched down into their coats, had their collars turned up and their coat tails wafting behind them as they leaned forward into the wind. "This is not helping my feelings about today," I told the universe. "I would have preferred a warm, sunny day."

Jo sat at a corner table with her case file open in front of her. It was obvious she had breakfasted without me. "I didn't know how late you might be, so I went ahead without you. There's still plenty of time before I'm due at the bank. You should stay and have a leisurely breakfast even if I have to dash off before you're finished. We'll still meet up later at the restaurant for lunch as arranged. I don't know how long my work at the bank will take. It might be best if I called you when I'm nearly finished there, so you know to head up to the restaurant on the top floor and grab us a table. Any problems…? You remember where the bank is located?"

My attempt at a sweet smile didn't work, as I reassured Jo I knew exactly where I had to go and what I had to do. "But, before I go anywhere, by the look of the world out there, I need to go back to my room to add a few more layers. It's warm and cosy in here, but it looks like it's freezing outside."

Before I started my first cup of coffee, Jo gathered up her bag, shoved her file into it, and stood up. "Time to go; any questions before I disappear?"

With nothing urgent to drag me out into the miserable looking world outside, I dawdled for as long as I dared at my snug table in the coffee shop. I was making a good job of it too until a steely look from one of the staff left me know I'd overstayed my welcome. Back in my room, as I added multiple layers of insulation, I tried formulating a schedule for my morning ... without much success or enthusiasm.

Our plan for how I would fill in my time while Jo was busy in the bank seemed about as enticing as last week's soup. I was to spend the morning taking in the myriad of shops in the immediate vicinity of the bank. While I was free to do as I pleased, I had to remain close by the bank in case Jo called me to come to sort something out. Never a shopaholic, having to wander in and out of shops for a few hours held no appeal. I told myself it might be enlightening to see what they were selling on this side of the channel. The only problem with that was I had nothing to compare it with. As I wasn't a shopper, I didn't know what was being sold on the other side of the channel.

The area I was confined to seemed to contain only small shops, but selling a wide variety of women's apparel. It all looked amazing ... and expensive. I wandered around in three such shops, inspecting their merchandise and being amazed at the prices, before I came to a shoe shop. The treacherous nature of such establishments is quite familiar to me. Their purpose in life appears to be to induce a certain state of euphoria which facilitates separating the customer and their cash in near record breaking time. I refused to enter. Instead, I stood drooling on the pavement while gazing longingly at the array of shoes and boots on display in the window, until I finally broke the spell and dragged myself away.

A bridal boutique provided a little light relief. The boutique owner hovered over the mother and one of the bride's attendants as the bride-to-be modelled a succession of bridal gowns. With each new outfit, the three onlookers clapped their hands and moaned in rapture at the spectacle before them. The fourth outfit seemed to be the winner. A seamstress, complete with tape measure hanging around her neck, worked furiously to nip and tuck various parts of the gown in a bid to make it more closely resemble the body it encased. The mother's eyes glistened with tears as her soon-to-be-married daughter sneaked long admiring looks at herself in the many strategically placed full length mirrors.

While so engrossed in the 'wedding dress' performance, a disconcerting question slid in and planted itself in my sub-conscious: had I missed out on what should have been an important episode in my life? Was my abhorrence of all the frippery and fuss and bother associated with weddings an omen? My wedding had none of that. Did it indicate some fundamental component of the whole marriage game was missing? If anything, my wedding was notable for its almost complete lack of complication.

My mother had passed away some years before, and my father's health started to fail soon after. I was working in the business, and gradually took on increasing responsibilities until I was running the company single-handed by the time I was married. When James and I decided to marry, I didn't see it as some monumental undertaking. Of course, there were things to organise, but life's like that. There's always something to organise, whether it's the next stage of the company's expansion, what to wear to the end of season ball, or simply what to have for breakfast. My wedding was no different.

There were the usual basic elements to organise, but they were straightforward. The marriage would take place in my old school's chapel. It would be at eleven o'clock, followed by a luncheon in the function room of the pub just along the road from the school. My plain white sheath gown came from the local department store. It had no train, and I wore no veil or any other head adornment. My long-time best friend, Jo Ballard, was to be my attendant. When we were at high school, we made a pact to be each other's bridesmaid when we married.

As luck would have it, Jo's work had her based in the US at the time of my wedding, and she had just broken her leg in a skiing accident. Another friend from my university days stepped in to fill the gap. I left it up to her to choose whatever she wanted to wear, even if it was something she already had would be okay. James was an only child and had almost no family other than his parents. Apart from my aunt, dad's sister, I had no other relatives to invite. So, the guest list comprised our parents, eight or nine of our friends and their partners, a handful of my father's friends and associates and their spouses, and a few friends of James' parents.

On the big day, the wife of the school chaplain filled the chapel with fresh flowers. The luncheon menu had taken little time to decide, but proved perfect. Soon after lunch, we both changed into day wear and flew to Paris for the rest of the weekend. Monday morning saw me back at work, and James at home trying to adjust to being a married man. It was all so simple. So little time, thought or effort went into organising and executing the whole event.

For an idle moment, I wondered how the groom-to-be associated with this wedding group was coping with the lead up to the event. Was he, willing or otherwise, a participant in the decision-making processes associated with his forthcoming nuptials? It occurred to me there was little a bloke had to do. Traditionally, he and/or his family organised the grog for the wedding breakfast and, of course, there was the mandatory stag party. From memory, the only thing James had to do, and the only thing he was interested in, were the arrangements for his last night of freedom with his mates.

Yet, here in the bridal boutique, simply choosing the right gown seemed like such an important and emotional interlude for the trio involved. That question again begged an answer: had I deprived myself of one of life's special times? I didn't waste time dwelling on it. The answer was simple: no, I hadn't missed out on anything. This was not something I would have wanted to experience. I did understand what today brought to the lives of those other people in the boutique, but I knew now, as I did way back then, it was not something I wanted or needed in my life.

With the question finally settled, I pushed it to a dark corner of my mind, and returned my focus to the ongoing saga of the wedding dress. But, during the time it took for my trip down memory lane, things had moved on in the boutique. It seems a decision was made. THE gown had been chosen, and everyone seemed emotionally charged as a result of the experience.

Somehow, watching the bridal pantomime managed to fill in almost half an hour before it lost its lustre. My only thought as I emerged onto the street was how thankful I was I would never have to face a similar mother-of-the-bride charade. I continued reviewing the bridal boutique experience as I strolled further along the street, and was almost bowled over by a woman rushing out of a hairdressing salon. The woman of pensionable age, with a mound of neon red hair held stiffly in an elaborate style, never as much as glanced at me as she mumbled a couple of lame apologetic words. Her attention focused on untangling her scarf and arranging it tenderly over her new hairdo to protect it as she rushed to a vehicle waiting further along the street.

Unsure what to do next, but convinced I had overdosed on shopping research, I turned on my heel and retraced my steps towards the bank. Earlier, I thought I noticed a small coffee shop tucked into a front corner of the building. The prospect of a hot coffee drew me in. Yes, it was a coffee shop, but it looked crowded. A raucous group of people, including a woman pushing pram and a man in a wheelchair exited the coffee shop.

They came towards me, scattering bystanders in all directions as they advanced towards the door. I too had to move to allow them to pass and avoid being run over by the moving wall of bodies. My less than elegant escape move left me tangled in the multitude of long slender canes of a basket palm tree. The fronds of the palm contained in a huge concrete pot were about three metres tall, and the clump was about two metres in diameter. As I smoothed myself down and endeavoured to regain a vestige of dignified composure, a woman came in and strode towards the coffee shop.

I froze midway through dusting myself off. Something about the woman seemed familiar. The little voice in my head told me I was being ridiculous. Of course I'd been to France any number of times in the past, but I didn't know anyone here. There was nothing about her to remind me of someone else. Tall and slim, she wore a long charcoal grey coat belted tightly at the waist, and a vibrant purple felt cloche hat covered her hair. All I had was the rear view of her, and there was nothing in that to suggest I knew who she was.

Why did some strange woman seem familiar? I shook my head to clear such a strange thought from my mind. Then, after one brisk final brush down, I prepared to step out from behind the huge potted palm. A screech of brakes on the street made the woman snap her head around to see what was happening. Her face was turned directly towards me.

"No … No, it can't be … It's not possible … How can this happen? Does Jo know about it?" I whispered to the palm.

Mention of Jo had me reach into my pocket for my phone. I hesitated. For a moment I stood staring at the phone lying in my trembling hand. Dare I call Jo and risk interrupting whatever she was doing? But, this is important. Maybe it impacts on what we do next. Jo needs to know. As I flicked through my contacts to find Jo, my phone rang, almost frightening the life out of me. It was Jo.

"Yes, it's early, but I'm almost done here. Perhaps you could dash up to the restaurant and snag us a table. If you think it's too early for lunch, we could call it morning tea, or brunch, or something. I'll be here for about another twenty minutes, before I join you up in the restaurant."

I don't know whether she was breathless from rushing about, or from excitement, but her hurried call gave me no opportunity to say anything. Should I call her back? My gut was telling me she needed to know that at this moment Krista Thomas was seated in the coffee shop in this building. I don't always take my gut's advice. This was one of those occasions when, after dithering for a couple of minutes, I decided to ignore it. After all, Jo would be meeting me in the restaurant soon. I could tell her about Krista then.

Instead of heading straight up to the restaurant as Jo suggested, I hung about in the foyer to see if Krista came out again, or if someone went in to meet her. That proved a fruitless exercise and wasted about ten minutes of the time before Jo came looking for me in the restaurant. I strode resolutely out from behind the potted palm and headed for the lifts. Only one lift operated today while the second one underwent routine maintenance.

A crowded of mostly blokes in suits and ties waited for the lift to return to the ground floor. The moment the doors opened, the mob rushed in almost knocking over the two people trying to alight. There wasn't room enough for the last three blokes, so they joined me in waiting for the lift to return. I watched the lights slowly track the lift's upward journey. The floors between the ground floor and the restaurant were occupied by the offices of various corporate entities. It would be a while before the lift reached the top floor and then returned for those of us left behind.

To fill in time, I watched the passing parade of patrons going to and from the coffee shop. Then I had a moment of panic. Krista was on her feet and about to pay for her coffee. She would leave the coffee shop … and there I was, standing out in the open in front of the lifts. A moment later, a group of five people joined those of us waiting for the lift's return. Ignoring polite decorum, I elbowed my way through to stand at the front of the throng so I could be first in when the lift doors opened again.

By positioning myself at just the right angle, I could monitor activity in the foyer reflected in wide shiny chrome surround of the lifts' entrances. While it was difficult to make out details, Krista's bright purple cloche made her easy to identify. She appeared to be waiting for someone, alternating between standing still, and wandering back and forth in a small area in the centre of the foyer. I silently begged today's only lift to hurry back to the ground floor, but it was a bit like the watched pot that never boils. This lift was just as perverse. It stopped at every floor on its way to the top, and then revisited each floor on its way down.

Its arrival brought with it a further delay. Crammed with passengers, including a young man on crutches, it took what felt like ages to empty before we, its next load, could board. Impatient to board and be gone from the foyer area, I shuffled from one foot to the other, while all the while keeping a close eye on that purple hat. Finally, the last of the passengers disembarked and it was our turn to enter. It had taken so long to unload the previous passengers, the lift doors tried to close just as the first of our mob entered. One of the waiting men rushed up and placed his arm across the door to keep it open while we embarked.

His initiative was appreciated by those waiting. He received thanks from everyone as they passed by to enter the lift … everyone except me that is. By stepping forward to deal with the door as he did, he effectively blocked my entrance. The rest of the group rushed to enter, and blocked me from ducking around the bloke holding the doors open. In one brief moment, I went from being at the front of the mob, to being relegated to last in line to enter. I told myself no one would recognise me from behind. So, as long as I didn't turn around, I would be safe.

At the same time as I shuffled forward towards the gaping chasm of the lift entrance, I kept an eye on what was happening in the foyer and, in particular, what that purple hat was doing. Just as I was about to step into the lift, a tall, slim man in a flat cap hurried towards Krista. He must have called her name. She spun around to face him. It was obvious this was whom she was waiting for.

The man continued towards her until he was standing close beside her. Before I lost sight of them, the last thing I saw was the man slipping his arm around her waist. Now, having strode into the safety of the lift – or so I thought. I turned to face the front. I expected to see the lift doors closing in front of me. They weren't. The same man continued to hold the doors open. I looked about to see why, and realised we were in for a further short delay. A heavily pregnant woman dragging a toddler with her was hurrying as best she could to the lift.

With his short legs, the toddler was slow. His lack of speed was being compounded by his obvious distaste for and bolshy attitude to the whole exercise. Embarrassed and frustrated by the youngster's performance, the mother hefted him up into her arms and carried him the rest of the way. The toddler's performance distracted me for no more than a few moments. Then, mother and child were in the lift. Surely the doors will close now. I took what I hoped would be a last look at Krista and her companion.

I returned my eyes to Krista and her companion, in time to see the man bend down and kiss her on the lips; just a quick peck. She gave him a coy smile before they both turned their eyes to the large clock set high in the wall above and a little off to one side of the lifts.

As the lift doors slid closed, I saw my husband's face … my *dead* husband's face!

Chapter 22

James…! It's James… How can it be James? James is dead. The coroner said so. I know he is gone …But I know that was James … How do I know? … Am I losing my mind?

I stood rigid staring at the lift doors as it rose silently upwards. My legs felt like jelly, and my stomach heaved. For a moment, I thought I might pass out. A quiet voice from beside me asked if I was all right. I turned to look at the concerned face of the man who had held the lift doors open. He was standing squashed up beside me and had bent down to murmur in my ear.

"You don't look well and you've gone quite pale."

"Thank you for your concern. I'm fine. I just remembered something that upset me. It is quite close, and the air seems stale when there are so many people in here doesn't it? I admit some fresh air would be welcome but, as with everyone else on board, I'm sure I'll survive the ride." I finished with the best smile I could manage, but I knew it amounted to nothing more than a wan effort even a blind beggar could see through. I don't think it reassured my gallant fellow passenger.

The lift stopped at almost every floor on its way to the restaurant at the top. A few got off at each of the first and second floors, leaving only myself and two others to continue the journey. The other two disembarked at the third floor. Unless someone from the floors above got on, I was a solo passenger for the rest of the trip to the fifteenth floor. I rested against the rail running around inside the lift and tried to persuade my scrambled brain to make sense of what happened in the foyer. That undertaking was still a work in progress when the lift doors slid open at the fifteenth floor.

To my left at the far end of the floor was the restaurant, and tucked in behind that in the back corner was what looked like a bistro type eatery. I was standing in a wide corridor-like area dotted here and there with potted plants and with several contemporary artworks suspended from a picture rail running the length of the area. Off to my right, at the opposite side of the floor to the restaurant, were the toilets. Still not convinced I wasn't going to be sick, I headed for the toilets. Maybe splashing water on my face might help. As I dried my hands in one of those new fancy hand dryers that threaten to remove all your rings while it's about it, I leaned over and put my face down close to it in the hope the air it generated would also dry my face.

While in this most interesting position, I sent Jo a thought message begging her to hurry to join me at the restaurant. I needed to tell her what happened. I needed someone to tell me I wasn't losing my mind. Perhaps my thought message wasn't delivered. For whatever the reason, as I kept watch, Jo did not suddenly materialise on the fifteenth floor. I kept the toilet door open a crack so I could keep watch for her arrival. The lift arrived again. Jo didn't step out of it … but others did. The two people I least wanted to see up here strolled towards the restaurant. His arm was still around Krista's waist.

I didn't know whether Jo was finished in the bank or not, and I didn't care. I needed her here, and I needed her now. She didn't answer her mobile. Christ, what has happened? Why isn't she answering her phone? I listened to my phone dialling her number until it clicked onto her voice messages.

Krista and her companion – I still couldn't bring myself to call him James – had disappeared from sight. One of the wait staff had shown them to their table somewhere further back in the restaurant where I couldn't see them. My problem was, I didn't know where their table was located and which way they were facing. While I couldn't see them from my hiding place here in the toilets, I wasn't sure they couldn't see the lifts from their table. It had been so long since he had seen her, James might not remember Jo. But, in spite of Jo's short time at the company, Krista would recognise her. I couldn't risk Jo blundering into the restaurant.

I keyed Jo's mobile number again. While waiting for it to start dialling, I glanced at the indicator lights above the lift doors. They indicated the imminent arrival of the lift. Jo's phone started dialling. The lift pinged to announce its arrival. Jo stepped out into the wide corridor and answered her phone.

"Jo, it's me, Mel. Don't go into the restaurant. Turn around. Look along here at the toilets." I eased the toilet door open a fraction wider and waved at her through the gap. "Come here. I need to talk to you. It's urgent." Jo strode along the corridor towards me, swivelling her head from side to side and looking over her shoulder in search of whatever might be lurking in wait for her.

Bursting in through the door I held open for her, she hissed, "What's this all about? You almost frightened the life out of me carrying on like that. And, I'm not accustomed to holding meetings in toilet blocks. Now I notice, you don't look so great … more like you've seen a ghost in fact. What the hell is going on? …And, do we have to stay in here?"

"For the moment, yes we do have to stay here, at least until we sort out a few things. And, your assessment is spot on. I have seen a ghost; James' ghost."

"Eh…? James' what? Perhaps you should explain."

Giving Jo an overview of what happened in the foyer before I managed to take the lift to the restaurant didn't take long. She was silent for the few moments it took her to process the information.

"You seem quite sure it was James you saw, so I'm not going to argue that with you at the moment. What happened after you came up here to cause you to hide in the toilets?"

"It was the shock of it all. I felt faint and came in here to splash water on my face. As I was about to leave here, James and Krista exited the lift and went into the restaurant. I can't see where they are seated, but I am concerned they might be able to see the lift from their table. For the moment, I don't want either of them to know we are here."

"We can't spend the rest of the day holed up in the toilets like a pair of sewer rats. What if Krista decides she needs to go to the toilet? No, we have to either use that lift, or walk down an awful lot of steps to the ground floor. I, for one, would prefer to take the lift. …Hmm … I have an idea. The first thing we need to establish is where those two are located in the restaurant. Stay here while I check it out."

Wasn't Jo listening to me? I thought I made it clear I didn't want the other pair to know about us. I was about to argue with her when I saw her shake out her long knitted scarf and drape it over her head. Instead of wrapping the ends of the scarp around in some way, she let them hang loose on either side of her face.

She reached for the door and announced, "It's a terrible day outside. It's essential to protect your hairdo." With a knowing nod, she was out the door and heading along the corridor.

I watched her go around to the bistro area and pause as if to check for vacant tables. Then, she turned slowly, pulled out her phone, and started back. It was a realistic impression of a woman checking out the bistro and then calling someone to arrange to meet them there. At the entrance to the restaurant, she slowed and let her eyes drift over its interior. Within moments, Jo was back at the toilets.

"Purple hat and her companion are seated at a table against the windows in the back corner. They are taking advantage of their view across the city, and are facing away from out here. I think we will be safe enough to leave here and take the next lift down to the ground floor. We should call for the lift, and then wait amongst the potted plants against the opposite wall for its arrival."

For want of other ideas, I nodded my agreement … and promptly felt my stomach tighten further and my breathing become fast and shallow. I didn't have time to dwell on it. Jo was already out in the corridor. After trying for one deep breath, I followed her towards the lifts. She was about to press the button to summon the lift, when a ping announced its imminent arrival. We both dived back against the opposite wall and tried looking inconspicuous when the lift arrived. Jo sprung away from the wall to greet the sole passenger who exited the lift.

"Jacque…! They must pay French bank staff too well these days if they can afford to come to the restaurant for lunch."

The face of a tall, slim, smartly dressed executive-looking young man wearing heavy-framed glasses lit up at the sight of Jo.

"Jo…! Ah, sadly, no, this is for work. Our bank's directors are visiting today. My boss has been with them all morning, and now I must join them for lunch. I would rather be having lunch with you and your companion."

"I might be able to arrange that some time. A photo of all the directors having lunch here at this branch would be good, wouldn't it?"

"Why would I need a photo…? Oh … *Oui, oui,* such a shot would be good for our staff newsletter, *nes pas?* But, why do you want a picture of my bank's directors?"

"I don't, but there is a couple at another table I would like photographed. I think there is a way you might be able to manage that for me. If you do, it's definitely worth lunch the next time I'm over here."

"…In this restaurant up here?"

"You drive a hard bargain, but okay, in this restaurant. Now this is how you might be able to do it without alerting them they are being photographed…"

While I watched from against the wall, Jo pulled out her phone and waved it about as she mimed some complicated activity. Excited, Jacque followed her every word and move before announcing he could do it."

"Don't do anything to upset your directors but, it would be great for my investigation if you can pull it off. I will owe you big time. If you do manage to get a clear shot of their faces, flick it to my phone please. We will be downstairs in the coffee shop."

During Jo's conversation with Jacque, the empty lift descended again. As she wound up their discussion, she reached over and pushed the button to recall the lift. We watched Jacque *d*isappear into the restaurant. A few moments later, the lift arrived. Jo seemed to have everything under control, but I had no idea what was happening.

"What happens now? I want to know what my dead husband and his secretary are up to, and where they go."

"We are going down to the ground floor coffee shop where we will keep watch until we see them come down in the lift. Come on, get in. I'm not holding this lift all day for you."

The coffee shop was filling up, but an ideal table became empty as we approached the entrance. Jo went ahead to grab the table before somebody claimed it, while I went to the counter to order our coffee and croissants. As I was settling myself at the table, Jo's phone whistled at her. She swooped on it and flicked through to the message. I watched a wide grin spread across the face as she studied the phone. Then, she turned the screen to face me.

"What do you think, not bad, eh? Good one, Jacque; I definitely owe you lunch for that. I'll forward you a copy."

Moments later, my phone also held a copy of Jacque's shot of James and Krista enjoying lunch in the top floor restaurant. "Now that you've seen the photo, do you agree it is James I saw … and Krista?"

"I stopped doubting you before this. That's why I organised Jacque to take the covert shot of them together. I'm dying to ask him how he went about it, and if he created any problems in the process. I need to make a quick phone call. So I don't annoy other diners, I'm just going to step outside to make it. You stay and hold the table for us. I'll only be gone a minute or two."

My concern that she might be going out onto the street to make the call wasn't necessary. She made her call from behind the same potted palm I hid behind earlier in the day. I sat with my eyes glued to the area in front of the lifts. The second lift was brought back into service sometime during our sojourn in the toilets upstairs. While I sat there, my mind was miles away and busy trying to make sense of what happened this morning.

Then, as one of the lifts disgorged its passengers, my mind came back sharply into focus. Grabbing both our bags, I was on my feet and heading for Jo out in the foyer. She was finishing her call as I raced up to her.

"They've just come down in the lift. What do we do now?"

In response, Jo grabbed me by the arm and held me firmly. "We stay here behind this potted thing, and we wait and watch. I suspect they'll grab a cab as soon as they leave the building. I want to see that cab as it drives off."

Hand in hand, the couple crossed the foyer and exited to the street, where James hailed a cab. Jo was already positioned in the building's main entrance as James and Krista climbed into the vehicle. I watched her scribble something on her hand as she held the cap of her pen in her teeth. Then she had her phone out again and stabbed the keypad to make another call.

I went and stood beside her. Since I first saw Krista in the foyer this morning I seem to have been incapable of functioning normally. My mind and reflexes were as slow and laboured as though they were swimming through treacle. Thank God Jo seems to be functioning normally. The call she made intrigued me.

"... Perhaps you can help me with the problem. A couple have just boarded one of your vehicles from in front of the bank. They just left a meeting here, but inadvertently left a very important document behind. They will need that document later today. I was hoping you could tell me where they were going when they left here. If I knew where they were going, I could follow after them another cab to give them the document they left behind. ... Yes, I know it's most unusual ... Well yes, I could ask them to return to collect it, but their schedule is tight. They will be late for their next meeting, or maybe miss it all together. That could have serious consequences. ... Oh, that's wonderful. Thank you so much for that information. ... No, no, please don't alert the driver. I don't want him to mention the situation and maybe upset them. I'm waving down a cab now, so I'll catch up with them at the station. Thank you so much for your help."

"Where is this cab you've just hailed … And where are we going when it finally materialises?"

"We are not going anywhere – not yet anyway."

"Thanks to my eavesdropping skills, I gathered from your strange conversation, our mysterious couple are heading to a railway station. If we don't follow them, we will lose them, and will never know what they're up to."

"I don't think that's the case. I can almost guarantee I know where they're going. And so are we, but not until later. There is no need for us to go dashing off right now. First, we need to return to the hotel to pack, pay our accounts and check out. Another thing we need to do is to organise a cab to collect us from the hotel at about six o'clock this evening."

"It's bloody freezing out here on the street. Do you suppose we might head back to our hotel now?" I hoped Jo would suggest we take a taxi but, as the hotel was just around the corner, we walked. Conversation was non-existent until we were in the lobby.

"Right, let's go up to our rooms and do what we must to prepare for this evening. I've a couple more calls to make, and then I'm going to try for a nap. I suggest you try for a rest as well. We are in for a late night. I'll meet you down here in the lobby at five o'clock."

It wasn't until I was back in my room that I realised I still didn't know what we were doing or why. All I'd managed to figure out was that we were taking a train trip tonight. If nothing else, the trip should give me opportunity to squeeze Jo for information about what is happening.

At the last minute, there seemed a slight change of plan. Jo called and said to be downstairs to book out at five-thirty instead of six o'clock as originally planned. I was packed and ready to go, so it wasn't a problem, and I was keen to be on the move and feel we were doing something about sorting out the mystery.

Settling accounts and booking out was a swift and painless exercise. Jo asked the receptionist whether the hotel had a sister establishment in Avignon. Within a couple of minutes, the receptionist had booked us rooms in that city. Now, I knew where we were going. Our cab arrived as Jo finalised things with the receptionist. While she did so, I went out to hold a cab and load my gear on board. Such gear as there was. We only expected to be away a couple of days, and it doesn't take a large bag to hold all you need for that.

After arriving at the station at a couple of minutes after six o'clock, we bought tickets for the six thirty train to Avignon. Then Jo dragged me off in search of a cafeteria. "From memory, it's about a three-hour trip. I suggest we pick up something to eat on the train as we might arrive at our hotel too late for room service."

At 6.20 p.m. we boarded our train, found ourselves what looked like a quiet compartment, and settled in for the next three hours … and what I hoped would be a long and detailed information sharing session.

Chapter 23

As we raced through town and country, darkness fell. My stomach began letting me know it hadn't been fed since breakfast. "Today has been a different kind of day and now, to add to everything else, I'm starving. I'm pleased you thought to pick up the salad bowls from the station's cafeteria. I do want to eat but, while we do so, do you think you might bring me up to speed on what's happening and why?"

"Sorry, Mel, it's all been a bit hectic; almost surreal at times. Okay, let's start with my visit to the bank this morning. I've worked with Jacque on other cases, so it was easy to get straight down to business. My expectation was that, once we were in Paris and started digging into those two accounts at the bank, the whole thing would unravel quickly. I suppose it has to some extent, but, not the way I expected. As you know, the wages and invoices we pay into the local bank at home, within a couple of days, are transferred to accounts at the Paris bank where we were this morning."

"Yes, that's why we came to France: to follow the money. So how has it not worked out as you expected?"

"The money doesn't stay in that bank in Paris. Every second Monday (that is, after an invoice payment is made), most of the money in both the accounts in Paris is transferred to accounts at a bank in Avignon. It is set up as an automatic transaction, so no one is required to come into the bank to make it happen. An interesting aspect to it is that the money transferred to Avignon is a set amount in whole Euros. This means that, over a period of a month or so, the 'loose change' left in each account builds up a bit. That's when, on some random basis, someone comes into the bank and transfers most of the residual to the Avignon accounts. Again, they only transfer whole Euros and always leave a little t in each account to keep it active."

"My visit today was perfect timing, someone came into the bank and made the transfer to Avignon while Jacque and I were looking into the accounts. We tried to identify who did it, but were out of luck. Whoever it was came in, filled out the necessary forms, placed them in the envelopes provided and dropped them through the slot in the hole-in-the-wall type machine. At eleven o'clock, the machine was cleared and processing its contents began. The person who initiated the transfer had vanished by the time we were aware it happened."

"I don't believe in coincidence any more than you do, but I'm beginning to wonder. James and Krista's presence in the bank building on the day this happened is just one of those 'lucky' things to occur from time to time."

Jo asked if I had any idea what time it was when I saw James meet up with Krista near the lifts. I wasn't sure. Using some rough mental arithmetic, I gave Jo a reasonable estimation. After a few moments of staring at some indeterminate point in the distant landscape rushing past our window, Jo's eyes lit up.

"I think that fits," she yelped. "Yes, I'm sure it does. At about the same time as you first saw Krista wandering around in the foyer, it is likely James was in the bank setting up the transfer. He then went to meet Krista in the foyer to take her to lunch in the top floor restaurant. The timing fits. And you're right, I'm not a fan of coincidence."

"At the time, you had no way of knowing who might be involved, did you? Regardless of what happened after that, I think we were always going to end up in Avignon weren't we?"

"As soon as I discovered the money trail led to Avignon, there was no question about following it there. Every move we make seems to lead us closer to James – and maybe Krista as well. The fact they are here in France together does suggest they remain more than casual acquaintances. How are you coping with that?"

"I don't know. I'm not sure anything we've discovered to-day has sunk in yet. I think part of my psyche is still numb so, after a fashion, I suppose I am coping. There is one thing I am certain of: I want to know the whole story, and I think I am reconciled to what it's going to be."

"We've never talked about James' background. While I've had a bit to do with him on and off over the years, I don't feel I know much about him. Under normal circumstances, it wouldn't matter, and his being lost at sea would be all the more reason not to be interested in it now. Since our evidence now proves he is still alive, perhaps I do need to know more about him."

"What would you like to know? That's odd. Now that you've started me thinking about it, I'm not sure how much I do know about him and his early life. But, ask your questions, and we will find out."

"Tell me about his family."

"Okay, let's see … James was an only child of what you might describe as upper-middle-class parents. His father had his own business in the tourism industry; organised bus tours, group seaside holidays, excursions to the continent, trips away to football games, and the like. When we first became involved, James had some sort of executive position in his father's business. Both parents died soon after we were married but, sometime before then, the business started going downhill and was defunct by the time of the wedding. I don't know if that was helpful, but what else do you want to know?"

"What about before that, his academic background for example? Did he go to university and what did he study?"

"At the risk of sounding a right goose, I'm not sure. There were things in conversations – not necessarily with me – that suggested he did go to university, but we never discussed it. And, it follows that I don't know what his qualifications are. Come to think of it, you would expect him to have friends from that time in his life. I don't recall ever meeting or hearing about any such friends. None was a part of his life after we were married. He didn't even have a best man picked out for the wedding, and ended up asking my bridesmaid's brother after she suggested her brother would be happy to step up."

"I'm finding it hard to believe that you were never curious about his earlier life. Did he refuse to discuss it, or did you not ask?"

"Truth…? I never asked. James was a 'closed' sort of person. His personal business was just that: *his* business. If I think back on it now, his guarded attitude to sharing anything about himself was always there. Maybe it was due to an inferiority complex, or perhaps he was intent on hiding something embarrassing in his past. You've made me want to know more; want to uncover everything there is to know."

"Are you sure about that? There may be things better left buried."

"Yes, I'm sure. I want to know all there is to know; good bad and ugly. Perhaps knowing will help me understand other things."

"Right; well, I think I can fill in some of the gaps for you, if you're sure you want to hear what I've learnt about James."

I assured her I could handle whatever it was she had to tell me, and encouraged her to get on with it. Jo hesitated. For a horrible moment I thought she was going to renege. Then, she sat up straight and took a deep breath before delivering her facts.

"Well, I don't know much, but I can tell you James had a chequered history at university. Like his mates, he didn't complete his study, and didn't graduate. In fact, didn't progress much beyond second year. Towards the end of his time there, it appears he was the centre of an unsavoury matter also involving his friends. As I understand it, some of the results he achieved for subjects in which he had no ability were the work of his friends, and were not down to James' efforts. When his close group of friends all exited university for various reasons, James was left to battle on alone. That's when his lack of ability became apparent, and soon he too was no longer at university."

"Perhaps I should be disgusted, or horrified, by what you're *t*elling me. But, I'm not. It confirms something I've always been aware of but didn't accept. In other words, I've been a denialist since the beginning regarding James' academic ability. Perhaps, had I accepted the truth back then, I would never have brought him into my company, let alone allowed him to run the business. What else can you tell me?"

Over about the next half hour, I learnt more about James' past than I gleaned in our ten-year long relationship, which included eight years of marriage. I found his association with Krista over the years before our marriage of particular interest, particularly James' affair with Krista being cited by her husband in their divorce.

"It appears whatever the attraction is with Krista, it hasn't gone away. Jesus… Did it ever go away? Was their relationship still going strong when we were married? … Was there ever a time when they weren't in a relationship? Based on what I saw today, I'd say it has been alive and well the whole time. No wonder he was so keen to hire her as his secretary. Did she actually do any secretarial work, or does that bed in the social club room say it all? The bastard…!"

"Maybe sharing all this with you wasn't such a good idea."

"No, it's what I needed to wake me up, to make me face reality. For the first time in almost twelve years, the veil has lifted and I'm seeing things clearly. I am no longer in denialist mode. Just out of curiosity, what was James supposed to be studying at university? I can't help wondering if he would have made any better manager had he completed his degree."

"I doubt it. As I understand it, he was doing an IT degree. It seems he was brilliant at all the IT subjects, but absolutely hopeless at everything else."

"IT…! An IT degree covers a wide territory … including programming. It would require someone who was a whiz at programming to set up a rogue company and ghost employee to rob me blind. James had access to all the computer systems from almost as soon as we were married. It was a while later before I decided to give him a management role in the company and then eventually handed over the reins to him. If you traced those payments back through our archives, you might find they started soon after we were married."

"That's a real possibility, and one you need to brace yourself for. In case you have any doubts, I do intend tracking everything back to its origins."

"When you think about it, it's hard to believe someone had the patience and foresight to put in place such a long-term project. From the outset, he must've known the rogue payments would have to continue well into the future before accumulating worthwhile money. Those two payments could be kept going for years to come. I wonder what led to his 'jumping overboard' when he did. I don't think there's any doubt his 'disappearance at sea' was a well-orchestrated sham. No wonder they never found a body. There wasn't one to find. Have you worked out how much cash he might have skimmed from the company over the years?"

"Not exactly; because we still don't know when the payments began, it's impossible to come up with even conservative estimates. But, it's not too difficult to work out how much per year he has been raking in. The ghost employee would have been paid around thirty-five thousand pounds a year, and the rogue company's invoices were bringing in between fifty-five and sixty thousand pounds per annum. It's easy to work out the total sum per annum was somewhere between ninety thousand and a hundred thousand pounds. That's not bad in anyone's language."

My jaw dropped. I thought I had my quota of shocks for today, but this one took me by surprise. It never occurred to me to do a rough calculation of how much I was losing each year. "Granted, over a period of eight or ten years, that amounts to a sizeable pot of cash, but it's not enough to set you up for life. While the set up was going to continue to feed cash into his coffers, something must have happened to make him jump ship when he did. I was almost frightened to confront the question the voice in my head screamed at me: how many other 'strange payments' are embedded in the system?"

"That question has occupied me since you acquainted me with the presence of James and Krista in the restaurant this morning. If you asked me about it yesterday, I would have had no hesitation in reassuring you we had identified all there were. Now, I'm not so naïve as to do that. My only suggestion for the moment is to try to park it to one side until we find out more about what's happening here in Avignon."

"We must be almost there by now. That salad bowl I had earlier was great, but I still would like something hot and substantial; a proper dinner. Do you think the hotel's restaurant might still be open when we arrive? If not, I suppose I could always try room service."

After rounding up our luggage, we went in search of a cab. Our hotel, on the Rue Félicien David, was in the centre of the city and a few kilometres from the station. The young woman on the reception desk took no time registering us. I couldn't help myself, I had to ask.

"What time does your restaurant close tonight?" I caught Jo's eye roll and ignored it.

"Our restaurant remains open until midnight every night except on the weekend when it stays open a little later. If you wish to dine there, your luggage will be taken up to your rooms. You don't need to worry about it and can go straight to the restaurant."

After she gave us our room keys and some brochures on what to do in Avignon, we crossed the lobby to the restaurant. Diners lingered at only three tables. Staff was happy to fuss over us as it gave them something to do to fill in time until the restaurant closed. The menu looked amazing, but for some reason, now I was seated in the restaurant, all I felt like eating was something light and hot. I settled for a mushroom omelette. It was glorious.

As the last diners in the restaurant, we felt obliged to eat and run. Perhaps, if the place were empty, the restaurant would close early and the staff could go home. We went to make the acquaintance of our rooms on the first floor. All rooms on this floor have a balcony overlooking the street below. From the street the building resembles a three-storey nineteenth century box with lots of windows. My room removed any misgivings I might have developed about the place.

My queen-sized bed had a wrought iron bedhead. There was stained timber panelling, a plush leather armchair, a small table and two chairs, and a built in desk. The ensuite was well appointed. WiFi was free, and a buffet breakfast was available. It was an altogether charming place to stay … but it took me until the next morning to really appreciate it. After luxuriating in a hot tub, I fell into bed and was asleep almost immediately. I wasn't aware of being tired. After all, I had done nothing all day. If anything, I expected to be kept awake for most of the night as my mind churned over all I learned about James.

*****

Spoiled for choice, I wandered around the breakfast buffet to give my tastebuds a chance to work out what they wanted for breakfast. I was mid-way through my prowl when Jo joined me. She went straight to the bench and collected a plate and cutlery. I still hadn't worked out what I would have. "Jo, don't you want to have a look around first before deciding what to eat?"

"No, I don't need to. If you've eaten breakfast in hotels as often as I have, you know to stick to your usual breakfast. Otherwise, the temptation is to lash out and load you tray with everything that looks good. You then spend the rest of the day feeling like a blimp and regretting the whole breakfast temptation debacle."

She made sense. I settled for fruit followed by a croissant and wonderful coffee. Neither of us is talkative at breakfast, so we were drinking our coffees before I introduced conversation to the morning ritual of a silent breakfast.

"What's our schedule for today?"

"I've an appointment at ten o'clock to meet with Jacque's equivalent at the local bank. It's likely our meeting will go through until lunchtime. Then we can meet up somewhere for lunch and to review what we do for the remainder of the day."

"It sounds as though I will spend the morning exploring the city again. Is there nothing useful I could do?"

"I was going to ask you to see if there is an address for James in the local phone book. You could still have a look, but I think it would be a waste of time. Even if he continues to use his real name over here, I'm sure he would want to keep a low profile. Anyway, if you wander around the streets, you never know who you might spot in the crowd."

…Or who might see me I thought, but didn't share it with Jo. I have to admit, for much of this trip so far, I have felt like a spare wheel; merely a spectator along for the ride. It's not a role I'm used to, or comfortable with. As we approached the hotel last night, I noticed an interesting looking eatery a few doors from our hotel. We agreed to meet there for lunch after Jo finished at the bank.

Until it was time for Jo to leave for her meeting, I sat in her room as she updated her file with yesterday's notes. At least she made me feel useful by checking details and sequences of events with me.

Then it was time for Jo to leave, and I was back in my room rugging up for whatever the day outside this solid building might have to offer.

Chapter 24

A cobbled square occupied a huge area out the front of our hotel. Several large trees grew along the centre of it. Just about every imaginable type of eatery lined both sides of the square. Those inclined to alfresco dining were accommodated under large umbrellas out front of the various eateries, as well as at tables clustered closely together under the huge trees in the centre of the square.

To find anything other than eateries to look at, I had to move outside the square and search other streets. Those who were into the shopping-thing would probably find the range of shops and their merchandise on offer nothing less than mesmerising. For me, the best I can say is they were interesting. Nevertheless, I chewed up quite a bit of shoe leather on my prowl through the centre of Avignon. Today, the weather wasn't as ferocious as yesterday, and it was quite pleasant being out and about.

Time slips by unnoticed until I became aware of a strong craving for a cup of coffee. A check on the time told me it was almost twelve o'clock. While I had no idea how long Jo's session at the bank would last, it was almost lunchtime. It made sense to head back to the square in front of the hotel where we were supposed to meet. While I waited for Jo to call me, I sat at one of the small wrought iron tables under the trees. It was close to one o'clock when she joined me there.

"Sorry, I'm a bit later than I expected. I would have been here a bit earlier, but I took a wrong turning and ended up several streets away from where I needed to be. Let's order lunch. Then I'll tell you about my morning."

As most people seem to prefer the tables under the umbrellas, we took our lunch out to the tables under the trees where we could discuss things without being overheard. Jo whipped out her notebook to refer to it as she updated me on her morning's session at the bank.

"Phillippe, the man at the bank, is Jacque's counterpart here. I really do have to buy Jacque lunch next time I'm in town. He called ahead to Phillippe and told him about me and my investigation. It saved a lot of time not having to establish my credentials before getting down to business. As it turned out, we lost a bit of time getting started anyway. Phillippe had a staff meeting before our session. Apparently a heavy debate developed and it ran way over time. Once we started, things fell into place quickly."

"Were you able to gather the sort of information you required about those bank accounts?"

"Yeah, we went straight to them. In both cases, I could see where all the regular transfers came in from Paris. There's been heavy activity on one of the accounts in particular, and it shows heavy drawdowns during certain periods. The other account was different. It shows small withdrawals on a regular basis, the type that might be regular housekeeping money. After looking at both accounts, I went back to the first account, the large one receiving the transfers from the rogue company payments. Something I came across in it nearly knocked me off my chair."

"I'm almost not game to ask. After all, so far today there haven't been any shocks. I suppose it's time another sinister aspect of this investigation became apparent. Go on, tell me about it."

"It hit me like a bolt out of the blue as I was running my finger down the list of transactions. Another regular transfer arrives in that account every quarter. The astonishing thing about it is the amount involved: about fifty thousand euros."

"Are you kidding me? … Fifty thousand euros every quarter…? I suppose it could be coming from anywhere. Just because most of the money is from my company doesn't mean this money is from there too. About how many pounds does that equate to anyway?"

"Of course, the conversion rate varies, but it's about the equivalent of forty thousand pounds."

"…Every quarter? I dare not think how long that's been in place – if it does involve my company. It sounds like we have more work to do at home before we finally understand the scope of this rip-off. Did you find out anything else interesting?"

"There was one other thing. I'm pleased you didn't waste your time trying to find James in the local telephone directory. The bloke associated with those two accounts at the Avignon bank called himself Jonathan Ruddick. Curious that he stuck with the same initials don't you think? Anyway, Phillippe took me out to speak to the head cashier, or whatever she is. He asked her to describe Jonathan Ruddick. That's never an easy thing to do. Not only was she taken aback by the request but she struggled to come up with any sort of description. I remembered the photo taken in the restaurant, and showed it to her. She identified James as their client, Mr Ruddick. She also identified James's companion in the purple hat as Katrina Ruddick, Mr Jonathan Ruddick's wife."

"Christ… I didn't think anything more about him could shock me. I was wrong. How can you be married to someone for so long and not know him? It's obvious I didn't know James Rothwell. That aside, do we know how long this other rogue payment has been in place?"

"Not exactly but, because the account has been so active and there have been some substantial transactions, it wasn't archived according to the same schedule as most other accounts. I was able to look back at five years' worth of transactions. Beyond that, they would have to request the records from archives. Both the quarterly payment I've just discovered and the other rogue payments we already knew about stretch back to the start of that five year period. The bank requested the relevant files from archives. They will be available for me to peruse tomorrow morning. I've arranged to meet Phillippe again at ten o'clock."

"Then what happens? It appears this is where James has established his bolthole. Are we going to do something about all this while we are here?"

"Oh God, no... It depends on a couple of things, but it's likely we can return to Paris sometime tomorrow, and then head home. We need to gather up every skerrick of information and have everything lined up properly before we do anything about James. I'm hoping that can happen quickly once we are home again. But, in case it takes a little longer, all those rogue payments must remain in place. It's vital we do nothing to tip off James and Krista to the imminent demise of their wonderful money-earner scheme."

"The thought of continuing to line their pockets galls me something terrible, but I know you are right. You know, I'm looking forward to being home and moving this whole affair along to a successful conclusion."

"Well, right now, I don't mean to rush you, but there is somewhere we need to be in about twenty minutes. If you're done with lunch, shall we move off?" This was news. I didn't know we were going anywhere and said so. "Ah, didn't I say? We are going back to the bank. Phillippe set up a meeting for me with the head bloke in their commercial property section. It's possible he might tell us something about James' set up here in Avignon. A bit over three years ago, a major transaction in one of those accounts suggests James purchased property somewhere around here. Now we know the name he is using here, it might be possible to find out quite a bit about his new life."

On the wrong side of fifty, Jean Paul was short, pudgy, going bald, and had the most piercing blue eyes I'd ever seen. His hair and skin were so pale as to be almost colourless, but he wasn't an albino. The John Lennon spectacles perched on the end of his nose did nothing to enhance his appearance. As he welcomed us into his office, I found myself hoping the buttons struggling to keep his waistcoat together didn't suddenly give up the struggle and fly off.

In preparation for our visit, he already had a thick file in the centre of his otherwise bare desk. "Phillippe said your interest was in Mr Jonathan Ruddick's property ventures in the Avignon area. In particular, you are interested in the possible purchase of a property some three or four years ago."

Jo confirmed it as our primary interest, but it was not our only one should there be other purchases on file. "We have no idea of land values in this area, but the amount of money paid out at the time seems substantial enough to be for the purchase of a property."

"It is likely your assumption is correct. A little more than three years ago Mr Ruddick purchased a large estate in the countryside outside Avignon. It is a large, long-established property which underwent a reversal of fortunes. For many decades the property has produced fine rose wines from its own vineyard, and is now experimenting with the merlot variety. Truffles have been harvested there for many generations and, for several decades now, asparagus has been grown in vast commercial quantities."

My vocal chords refused to cooperate when I first went to speak. I cleared my throat and tried again. "You mentioned the property experienced something of a reversal of fortunes in more recent times. Is it possible for you to elaborate on that, please?"

"It's a sad tale of family disharmony. The patriarch of the family was in his late nineties – almost made a century – when he died. He had two sons, both then in their seventies. They were indulged their whole lives and allowed to live the life of the idle rich. Neither of them ever had been involved in the operation of the estate. Nevertheless, when the old man passed away, the sons jointly inherited everything. For a few years prior to the father's death, the property went into decline. The old man couldn't manage it well anymore and production dropped. The situation became worse after his death. At first, it appears the sons didn't realise that, having inherited the place, they were now responsible for running it. After about eighteen months or so, the place was barely producing anything, and its former employees were owed a considerable amount of unpaid wages."

"I find it hard to hear of such a historic place being allowed to run down like that. Surely someone alerted the sons to their responsibilities." I couldn't help but think the old man must be turning over in his grave over his sons' behaviour.

"As you say, Miss McCarthy, the sons became aware of the reality of the situation when their cash resources dried up. That is when the real trouble started. They blamed their dire situation on each other. Somehow, amidst everything else happening, each of the sons decided he should have been the sole beneficiary. If that were the case, he could sell the property, pocket the cash, and set himself up comfortably for the rest of his life. Sharing everything with his brother seemed a less lucrative proposition. Both sons individually challenged the will in court, each of them claiming the father had promised him the property."

Jo sighed. "It's not an uncommon situation, but one rarely with a happy outcome. What did the court decide?"

"Well, there was a further development before the court could rule on the appeals. By some strange means, the former employees heard about the appeals, and guessed the intention was to sell the property. They believed the sale would eliminate any chance they had of recovering their unpaid wages. They took their claim to the court and sought an injunction to prevent any action contrary to their best interest occurring before they were paid.

As is not always the case, on this occasion the court applied common sense and dealt with all three cases together in a long and convoluted process stretching out over almost two years. By the time the court handed down its decision, one of the sons was suffering a severe respiratory condition caused by a long association with tobacco, and the other son was displaying the first symptoms of dementia. In the end, the court ruled the property must be sold, and the former employees be paid their entitlements from the money raised by the sale. After court costs were also deducted, the residual sale funds were to be divided equally between the two sons."

"So, that's when the property went on the market?" Jo murmured as she scribbled in her notebook. Turning her attention back to Jean Paul, she asked, "Did the property take long to sell?"

"There was an immediate response from a few potential buyers, but they took one look at the place and walked away. It wasn't producing. All agricultural aspects would be a long time becoming a viable proposition again, and the château was a crumbling wreck. For a couple of weeks, a sale seemed unlikely. Then, a new buyer appeared on the scene. Within days, an agreeable price was determined and the place was sold … to Mr Jonathan Ruddick."

"That sounds like a serious gamble. Do we know what the buyer's intentions were at the time?" All I could think of was the timing of the purchase. It was less than two years since James 'disappeared', yet he purchased the property three years ago.

From the outset, his had been a well-orchestrated and successful long-term plan I had inadvertently helped nurture and fund. I was sitting rigid in my chair and felt my jaw starting to ache. I realised I had my teeth firmly clenched, and I became aware my clenched fists had my nails biting into the palms my hands. It's not easy maintaining a relaxed and disinterested façade when your anger levels are off the chart. I realised Jean Paul was speaking while I was trying to bring myself under control again, and I had missed his reply to my question. I apologised and asked him to repeat it.

"We did not know what the buyer's intention was at the time. There was some thought he might be a developer and the place would start sprouting unit blocks. Whatever his initial thoughts were, his first move was to re-employ many of the former employees to begin the long recovery process for the property. A small cottage near the entrance to the estate was in better condition than the château. Mr Ruddick used that whenever he visited the property during the first twelve months or so while repairs and restoration were underway at the château. He now resides there permanently … and with his wife, of course, when she is in town."

He pulled a number of photos from the file and handed them to Jo. They featured sweeping views over orchards and vineyards, a lush paddock with a few cows. The photo to grab my attention was of a magnificent villa-type building. Jean Paul noticed my interest in it.

"Magnificent isn't it?" he said quietly as he nodded towards the photo. "It is so pleasing to see it restored to its former splendour. Mr Ruddick's insurance agent is a friend. He says the interior is even more spectacular. He describes it as 'breath-taking'. Mr Ruddick had discerning taste, but it appears his wife is particularly talented in that department. My friend believes Mrs Ruddick was responsible for the interior decorating."

After receiving detailed instructions on how to find the property, we thanked Jean Paul for his time and returned to the hotel in silence. As we stepped inside the hotel, Jo said, "I think we both could do with a drink before we do anything else. The bar is this way."

Forsaking my usual glass of crisp white wine, I opted for a large single malt scotch without ice. After sitting silently in enormous enveloping lounge chairs for a few minutes sipping our drinks, Jo said quietly, "I can only imagine what you must be feeling after this afternoon. It left me stunned, and I'm only the investigator. It's interesting that James was able to return production almost to former levels in such a short time. If the harvest lives up to expectations, this year's grape pressing will see a return to the glory years. It will be nothing short of a miracle."

"It's unlikely James can take any credit for it. He wasn't capable of caring for a potted plant, never mind take on an agricultural challenge of such magnitude. No, I think he has bought in the best expertise available, and that's where the credit should go. But, I have to admit your assessment is spot on. This afternoon has left me gutted … and vicious."

"Vicious…? How? …In what way 'vicious'?"

"I'm not sure how to describe it, but I intend James will pay dearly for everything. I want everything possible thrown at him for what he has done to me. I want nothing less than for him to lose everything; to be totally reduced to nothing when this is finished."

"Atta girl; now you're talking. I'm with you on this one. I promise you, when we pounce, we will be going in for the kill … so to speak."

We both giggled at her choice of phrase. It was enough to lighten the mood a little before we went to our rooms to rest and freshen up before dinner. Nevertheless, dinner was a subdued affair. The food was excellent, the wine was perfect, but our moods still reflected the effects of the day. By around midday tomorrow, we should be on our way to Paris, and then home in our own beds tomorrow night. I felt I needed to be back at 10 Minstrel Close to feel safe and whole again.

*****

Our trip home was uneventful, and involved only about an hour's wait between trains at Paris. With the long shadows of evening falling around us, the cab dropped us at 10 Minstrel Close. While I hadn't done much over the last couple of days, I felt wrung out. After left-overs went into the oven to heat-up for dinner, we both disappeared into our rooms to unpack and, in my case, to take a long, hot shower. Feeling a good deal more human afterwards, I poured us drinks before dinner and carried them through to the lounge room.

"Jo, I feel as though I'm lost in the fog. I don't think I comprehend most of what we learnt from our sortie into France. You probably don't feel much like going over everything right now, but could we do that soon, please?"

"I'm fine – now I've had a shower. And, I think you are right. We need to assess everything that happened and all the information gathered regarding our investigation. Let's eat first and then review what we now know."

In spite of her assurances to the contrary, Jo did not seem 'fine'. She was quiet and subdued all through dinner, and wasn't much chirpier when we retired to the lounge room afterwards. It had been a long day, and I reminded myself Jo too might be suffering information overload after all we discovered in France. No matter how hard I tried to tell myself that was the reason, my gut was working itself into a lead ball. I tried preparing myself for the bad news I felt was to come. Once we settled in the lounge, and before I could ask any questions, Jo opened the conversation.

"I feel guilty about asking this after already being away from work for three days, but I wondered if the place might continue to run okay if I took tomorrow off as well. There are a couple of matters I need to take care of. The sooner those things are in place, the sooner we will be in a position to take down James. Our ideal situation is to be in a position to do that before the next fortnightly payment to the rogue company. It might not be possible, and we might have to let another payment go through, but I would rather avoid it if we can. I'm sure the sooner you extract your proverbial 'pound of flesh', the happier you will be."

"I doubt the world will come to an end if you take an extra day off. Is there anything I need to do; anything I can help you with?"

"No, there is nothing at this stage for you to do. If I'm needed, I could come into work for a while. My problem is, I don't know how long it might take to do the things I need to put in place. Anyway, if you go into work tomorrow without me, it might stop any of the funny looks our joint absence might be generating."

"To summarise what I think we now know, there are two shelf companies receiving payments for fictitious invoices, and one ghost employee being paid on an ongoing regular basis. Are we sure there is only the one ghost employee?"

"Yes, I think we can be confident there is only one. I suppose, if nothing else, James' handiwork embedding those regular periodic payments in the system confirms just how talented he is with IT. I hadn't mentioned it before, but chucking all of James' mates out of their comfortable managerial positions might add some urgency to putting an end to his lucrative scheme. If any of them are aware of James' continued existence, they might moan to him about being laid off. James is no fool, and might interpret it as everything he put in place being under threat. We need to act before he suspects anything. Otherwise, he might clean out the cash already accumulated and disappear again. Even if none of the former managers contact him, Krista's sacking already might have caused a couple of nervous twitches."

"I see where you're coming from. All the more reason why you should take tomorrow off and go and deal with whatever it is you need to put in place. And, you were right about my being a lot happier once he is brought to justice … whatever that justice might be. I will be glad when all this is over and done with."

By the end of the night, in spite of my best efforts to extract information regarding what Jo would be doing tomorrow, I knew nothing more than when she first mentioned it. I didn't doubt her integrity or anything else, but it would be nice to know what was going on before it happened. There have been more than enough surprises over the last couple of weeks. Jo will do whatever she intends to do tomorrow but, tomorrow night – regardless of whatever it takes – I too will know what she has put in place. It is my company, but I am beginning to feel I have no knowledge of others' agendas which impact on me and my business. I don't think it is just an ego trip. I don't need to be in charge of everything that happens, but I do need to be forewarned – and approve of – whatever is put in place.

Chapter 25

Jo: repaying favours

With Mel's approval for my taking another day off, there was no need to hurry this morning. Besides, a little lie-in helped avoid the awkward questions I know Mel is itching to ask about what I intend doing today. I stayed in my room until my clock suggested it was almost time for Mel to leave for work. Adopting what I hoped passed for a nonchalant demeanour, I wandered downstairs and set about making my breakfast.

Mel was not in the best of humours. It was obvious the moment I arrived in the kitchen, giving her a wide berth this morning was the best move. No more than a couple of minutes after I came down, she called out 'goodbye' on her way out the front door. I breathed a sigh of relief. Now I could get on with what I needed to do without worrying about Mel looking over my shoulder. Guilty feelings set in before I even scrambled out of bed this morning, and Mel's grumpy mood only heightened them. I took my breakfast and my phone out into the garden.

There was only one person I needed to talk to who I could ring at this hour of the morning. I flicked through my contacts to Syd Hartley's name. As the call started dialling, I hoped he was free. He would not be happy about me interrupting him if he was at some gory murder scene, or investigating some other serious crime.

"Good morning, Jo. What has you ringing me at this hour of the morning? You're lucky I heard the phone. I was in the shower. Not to worry; I am now wearing a towel and you have my undivided attention. So, why are you calling me?"

"I wondered if you might have some spare time today; some time when we could meet up for a long chat."

"Is this about more to do with the James Rothwell matter? I haven't done much more about him since we last talked. If you still want to catch up, I do have to go into the office for a couple of hours first thing this morning, but I'll be free by eleven o'clock. Perhaps, if you can get away around that time, we could meet up somewhere for lunch."

"Eleven o'clock sounds fine. I'm off work today and have something else I can do this morning before we catch up. Shall we again honour our favourite publican with our presence?"

"Yeah, that's exactly what I was going to suggest. There's a new menu this week, so we need to check out whether it's an improvement or not."

By the time I finished chatting to Syd, I assessed it to be a respectable hour to try making my other important call. It encountered a message that told me their opening hours were from nine o'clock. According to my watch, it was already nine o'clock. It seems the local bank is relaxed about punctuality. To give the staff a little time to achieve operational mode and start their day, I took my breakfast things back to the kitchen and made another cup of coffee. About fifteen minutes later, I tried the number again. This time I spoke to a human who put me through to the person I asked for.

"Good morning, Jackson Torrens. This is your early morning call from Jo Ballard. Would you be able to see me sometime this morning?"

"Hi Jo; your call can only mean you have more work for me, and you're not calling just because you like sound of my voice. How does any time between now and ten o'clock suit you? I'm free until a bit after eleven o'clock, if you think that will give us enough time to do whatever you have in mind."

It would take me about fifteen minutes to drive into town and find somewhere to park. I doubted what I wanted to do at the bank would take anywhere near an hour, but I wanted to play it safe. A few minutes later, I was heading into town with my bag and a very thick case file sitting on the passenger seat beside me. Even at this early hour of the morning parking was at a premium. The best I could find left me with quite a walk to the bank.

Jackson was in the process of showing someone out of his office when I arrived. "Jo, come straight through and let's get started."

"At the risk of becoming a pain, I do have another account I'd like you to check for me. I'm almost certain we'll find it follows the same pattern as those two accounts we looked at the last time I was here."

I gave him the particulars of the account into which we'd paid bogus invoices for the second shelf company.

"You are right about what happens to the money. Soon after payments are received in the account here, they are transferred to an account at the same Paris bank. I don't know what happens after they arrive in France, but I guess you've uncovered all about that end of it since we last spoke."

"Yep, it was a pretty straightforward trail to follow. The money spends little time in Paris before being transferred to an account in Avignon … to an account held by a man who died almost two years ago." Jackson's jaw dropped slightly and his eyes opened wide.

"What are you saying? Did he not die … or … is this now a case of someone masquerading as the deceased person?"

"The person in question did not die, but he did change his name – legally or otherwise, I don't know yet."

"… But, you have positively identified the person as the man who was supposed to have died?"

"Oh yes, identity confirmed. He is alive and well, and has been living on the outskirts of Avignon since his disappearance almost two years ago. … And it would appear he has done very nicely from his schemes over the last however many years. There is something I wanted to ask you, but please don't think I'm prying. In days gone by, people working in your position were rewarded for uncovering something unsavoury in which the bank unwittingly had become involved. Is this still the case with your bank?"

"Yes. The powers-that-be react favourably to such a discovery. Usually the reward is the offer of a promotion to a similar, but slightly more senior, position at a larger branch of the bank."

"Is that what you might aspire to in the future … moving to a bigger branch?"

"Not really; it just means you get first offer if such a vacancy occurs at one of the bigger branches. You can select the alternative. It stands you in good stead at your next staff appraisal, and your salary could increase by at least one level, and maybe two. Why are you interested?"

"These current investigations you've helped me with might be your ticket to an improved salary. As you are aware, we now have three accounts at this bank involved in my investigation. I can give you all the details of the money trail, but there is a proviso. While I could give you the information now, it would be on the basis you did not take it any further until I said you may. There is a lot more than dodgy bank accounts resting on my investigation. Even a whisper leaking too early about what I'm doing could jeopardise everything … And might have the reverse effect on your staff appraisal. In return for the assistance you've given me, I would be happy for you to reap whatever reward the bank chooses to give you, but only if you agree to wait until I give you the go-ahead to talk to people about it."

"Your comments about the bloke who has been dead for two years are enough to make me think this is bigger than skimming or money laundering. I do have an obligation to alert the bank to its possible involvement in illegal activities, but I give you my word it will not happen until you give me clearance to do so. I can't give you any more guarantee than that. So, I guess your decision is whether to trust my word and tell me the whole story, or to withhold the relevant information until some later time when you feel it's safe for me to know about it."

I had no reason to doubt his trustworthiness so, I handed over a sheaf of photocopies and spent the next half-hour going over the story and the money trail I had been investigating. "There is one more thing you might do: check with the Paris bank about what happens to the money after it is transferred from here to the account over there. I know that, in fairly quick time, it arrives in the Avignon account. But it would look convincing if you could show how you followed up with the Paris bank. After you've done that, you might drop me a quiet word about what they told you. In that way, I can ensure my case file contains complete information on the money trail … and would help substantiate the good work you've done, if the bank ever wanted to check with the company."

"Now that I've been made aware of possible 'funny stuff' happening, my position here obligates me to investigate further." Jackson gave me a nod and a knowing wink as he finished speaking.

By the time we covered everything there was to discuss, it was almost eleven o'clock. I knew he had another appointment scheduled, so I wound up our meeting. As I stood to leave his office, he reiterated his guarantee not to discuss anything we had talked about until I gave him approval to do so. I thanked him, we shook hands and, within moments, I was back on the street trekking to where I'd parked my car.

Syd was already at our favourite corner table in the snug of our favourite pub. A quick glance at the pint on the table in front of him told me he'd only just arrived. He hadn't had time for more than a sip of his drink. It was still a bit early for lunch, so we elected to talk first and order lunch later. Syd opened the conversation with yet another apology for not having dug up anything new for me.

"It's not that I've been too busy. It's more a case of having poked about in various records but found nothing new. Still, even if I haven't got anything new to tell you, I'm glad you came to share lunch with me. How is your side of the investigation going anyway? Better than mine I hope."

"It's gone very well. That's why I wanted to talk to you. We are just about at the point where we can blow the whole thing wide open. There is nothing more than a few loose ends to tie up now. I wondered if you might be interested in achieving something like hero status in your CID."

"Hero status might be stretching things a bit, but I would welcome the opportunity to show the new 'bright young ones' in our mob that I am not ready yet to be put out to pasture. From what I can see, most of today's detective constables are all about technology, and have no nous when it comes to investigating a physical crime scene. Still, all that aside, what are you not telling me?"

"I think this case file of mine – relax, it's a copy – might be something you can use to your advantage. While I'm not sure to what ends you might use it, that's none of my business. If you did choose to use it to your advantage, it would mean admitting to digging around in closed files. So, I guess what I'm saying is, I could give you this file to use at your own discretion, and for your own benefit."

"And what do you get out of it?"

"Those loose ends I talked about: catching the bad guy, bringing him down, and wrapping up the whole investigation require someone who can bring legal charges against him. That is where you come in and, any kudos that flows from arrests or whatever that occur, is entirely yours. Do you think you might be interested?"

"Bloody hell, of course I'm interested. This investigation has consumed me ever since you asked me about James' laptop and phone. The moment I started digging into the file, I knew it smelled rotten. As far as kudos goes, I suppose a bit of that might be handy. Our chief inspector is retiring in a couple of months. I reckon they'll start looking around for his replacement in a few weeks' time. Taking the credit for busting something like this wide open wouldn't do my chances any harm. Perhaps we should order lunch, and afterwards, we could go through your file and plan our strategy for closing the case."

Lunch was delicious. The new menu was a significant improvement on the previous version. I considered having a glass of wine to go with it, but rejected the idea in favour of keeping a clear head for what was to follow. Once a pot of coffee was delivered to our table, the work began. I handed Syd a folder containing a duplicate of my case file. Then, each of us with our files open, sat opposite one another at our small table. Our two folders left little room for anything else on the table. The next table was vacant. Syd pulled it over so we had somewhere safe to put our coffee pot and mugs.

We worked on until almost two o'clock. By then, and we were both suffering information overload. It was obvious to me we shouldn't have tried to do this in the pub, and I said so. "Syd, I don't think we're doing ourselves any favours working this way. It would be better if you took your folder home and studied it at your leisure. Then, once you have your head around all we've managed to discover, we could meet again to talk about what happens next."

"Yeah, you're right. There's a lot more in here than I was expecting; no end of surprises in fact. In the light of what I've seen in this folder, I know of another couple of places in which to have a bit of a poke around. Your folder is comprehensive, but I want to check some other stuff too. It's important absolutely everything is nailed down before we act. Nothing can be left to chance … if you see where I'm coming from."

"Ah, you're a man after my own heart, Syd Hartley. The last thing I want is for Rothwell, by some miracle, to wriggle out of all this. As far as I'm concerned, he has used up his share of miracles for this lifetime. And, if it manages to earn you that top job, I would be delighted. No one deserves it more … and I would consider it a favour repaid."

As I was about to follow Syd out of the pub's carpark, I remembered something I saw earlier as I walked from the bank to my car. I found a parking spot almost in front of the butcher's shop. The legs of lamb on display not only looked good, but one of those would solve my dilemma for what to prepare for tonight's dinner.

I felt chuffed all the way home. Today had been a howling success all around. Most importantly, we were now a few days at the most from wrapping up the misappropriation investigation. And, I had repaid two key people for favours rendered in the course of my investigation. That should stand me in good stead should I find myself needing to call on their services again in the future.

The only thing left to do is to tell Mel about my covert activities. After everything is wrapped up might be a good time to do that … and that gives me a few more days to work out how best to do it.

<h1 style="text-align:center">Chapter 26</h1>

My intended early night after our trip home from France saw me in bed earlier than usual, but my mood, and generally unsettled state of mind, kept me awake until the small hours of the morning. It did not improve my outlook on life, and made for a grumpy Thursday morning. Out of bed at my usual time, I was a solitary figure moving about the house until just before I left for work.

Jo, having the day off today, indulged in a bit of a lie-in before venturing downstairs to see me off. When I poked my head into the kitchen to say goodbye, she was happily humming tonelessly as she worked the coffee machine. Good to see one of us seems happy to go out and embrace the day, I thought as I reversed down the driveway.

Despite having capable people managing the various sections of my operations, after three days away, work had piled up on my desk. Thank God for Majella. She dealt with as much as she could during my absence, but my day was hectic, with barely time for coffee let alone lunch. I was thankful for being so busy. It allowed no time to ponder what Jo might be doing. Nevertheless, as soon as the last employee left the carpark this afternoon, I too was on my way home.

"That smells absolutely heavenly. Is it what I think it is?" I called to Jo as I dumped my bag. The mingled aromas of lamb and rosemary and garlic wafted from the kitchen to welcome me home as I stepped through the front door.

"The butcher had legs of lamb too nice to resist, and it seemed ages since we had a baked dinner. Prepare to ruin your calorie intake tonight. I've made dessert as well."

"Whatever you were going to do today obviously didn't take all day. I hope you managed a little rest as well. If your desk is anything like mine was this morning, you are in for a big day tomorrow. Do I have time to unwind a little before dinner is ready?"

We took our drinks out into the garden. For a few moments we sat in silence. I watched the clouds sailing across the darkening sky as shadows lengthened all around us. A lazy cool breeze drifted in. It was counteracted by the residual warmth in the bricks and stone work around us. The effects of the day slipped away from me and I felt myself mellowing in the silence.

"Jo, I haven't asked you how your day went. Did you manage to achieve everything you had in mind?"

"Y-e-s, I did as much as I could today, but it will be a bit of a waiting game before we see how some of it turns out."

It wasn't the information I was trying to winkle out of her, so I tried a different tack. "I'm still trying to get my head around the extra processes required to deal with the second shelf company you found while we were at Avignon, and why there is anything more needs doing here to deal with it. Surely your finding the evidence of its existence is enough."

"We're getting close to the pointy end of things now. It's important we have every possible skerrick of evidence to hand, so there is little room for anyone to doubt the situation that exists here, or to mount a reasonable argument against our case. When we wrap up that situation, and have gathered every possible piece of evidence, then we are in the position to take the final step: to call in the authorities. Regardless of how you feel about bringing them in, they are the only ones who can bring about an end to this. The only ones who can deliver you the outcome you want. It might still be a bit rugged from time to time, but you – and I – will be shielded from most of it by being at arm's length from all the action."

"I know I'm being impatient, but I will sleep a lot better when I know James has had his comeuppance. In the meantime, I think we are both made of stern enough stuff to cope with however rugged it might become. So, what's your next move?"

"My first task as soon as I have a few spare moments is to search through the company's records for payments of invoices to that second shelf company we found. I'll document them the same as I have done for all the other illicit payments. Those lists will form a significant part of the evidence in our case against James. Once that's done, I doubt there is anything else I can do at the company level. Pulling all the evidence together in a proper case file for presentation to the authorities is something I can do at home … And it's probably safer done away from the office. Anyway, by next week, I should be able to focus full-time on the job you're employing me to do … I mean, my job as finance manager."

As it was time to rescue our dinner before it spoiled, we relocated to the kitchen. While Jo fussed about dishing up roast leg of lamb and all its accompaniments, I laid the table and opened one of my good bottles of red wine. After indulging in Jo's crème brûlée dessert, I felt like I should hibernate for about a month. Instead, we stacked the dishwasher, and took our coffees through to the lounge room.

Jo, in a prelude to asking me a question, cocked her head to one side and tentatively cleared her throat. "Ahem, tell me I'm out of line if you like, but I never could understand how you ended up with someone like James. Oh, he was certainly good-looking, and I don't doubt he had other 'virtues', but he never struck me as being your type."

"That's interesting. What exactly is 'my type'?"

"It's hard to put into words. I suppose the simple explanation is that you are two different personalities; very different people in every way. A basic example might be your work ethic. While you own the company now, you always worked hard in the company, even when you were still at university, and you deserve to have what you have today. On the other hand, James doesn't seem to have been too closely associated with hard work of any kind. I think his position in his father's business was merely a token arrangement to fill in some of James' time each day. And another thing to set you apart is your preference for a fairly simple lifestyle, whereas his preference was for flashy and expensive."

"I am aware of our differences now, but it is quite a recent realisation for me. I don't know that I ever noticed it, or even thought about it while we were together. It's only been in the last few weeks that I've come to see how incongruous as a couple we were ... And how much I didn't know about what James did with his life. Looking back, it's as though we shared a house, but lived two separate lives. Something that happened in Paris made me realise the marriage was doomed from the outset. At least, from my point of view, it was. The whole wedding thing should have been a big deal. It wasn't like that for me. I've gone to more fuss and bother having people over for dinner. Thinking back on it, James never managed to display any excitement about our forthcoming marriage either. Perhaps we were both just going through the motions, doing what we – and probably our families – thought was the normal 'next step' to take in our relationship. I don't remember there ever being anything romantic about it."

"Did you ever suspect him of playing around, or that he had a wandering eye? It seems his relationship with Krista has its roots back in their university days. Perhaps there were a few hiccups along the way, but their connection has been resilient enough to survive her marriage and subsequent divorce, as well as your marriage. I can only imagine how distressing it was for you seeing them together in Paris."

"Mixed emotions is probably a better description. They were all there: anger, jealousy, hurt, and shock. It's fortunate none of those is fatal. But now, the all-pervading emotion is anger."

"You didn't mention anything about feeling some relief in finding he was alive and hadn't drowned when he supposedly disappeared overboard."

"No, I didn't. That's probably because I didn't feel any relief or joy in finding he was still alive. Perhaps it accounted for some of the shock involved, but there was nothing more. If nothing else, it confirms I am well and truly over any close attachment to James I might have had in the past. There is only one thing to do now: bringing on his downfall."

A few moments of silence allowed another matter ever-present in the back of my mind to force its way to the front of my thoughts.

"Speaking of James, we still have to think about those letters which keep arriving. Time is slipping away, and the second anniversary of James' disappearance is not too far off."

Jo nodded and studied her almost empty coffee mug for a moment before commenting. "Yeah, I know we haven't progressed that matter yet, but I haven't forgotten about it. In spite of all the work we've done and everything we've learnt in the last little while, I still can't decide whether the letters are linked to James, or if they are to do with something else – like a mistaken identity for example."

"Neither of us believes in coincidence, and the dates on which those letters arrive align too closely with significant dates associated with James. I accept you don't share my view on that but, as soon as we sort out this other mess, I'll be devoting every spare minute I've got to putting an end to them."

"Well, we have what we need to do something straight away to stop them arriving. It might not give us the WHO or the WHY, but it will prevent any further envelopes being pushed through the letter slot in your front door. I haven't seen much mail delivered here to the house. Is there any private mail delivered to this address, or is it only junk mail?"

"No, it's just junk mail. I have a mailbox at the local post office. I organised it when I moved here so my personal mail could go there and not to me at work."

"Good; that means half of my idea already is in place. All we need to do now is to seal the letter slot to prevent any further envelopes dropping onto your carpet. Something as simple as a length of heavy-duty double-sided tape to stick the flap closed would probably do the trick."

"I'm not sure that would deter whoever is delivering those notes. I think it requires something more robust and permanent."

"Okay, that won't be too hard to achieve. On the off chance there might be a better solution available, while I was out and about today, I visited the hardware store and encountered a knowledgeable middle-aged man with whom to discuss our problem about the letter slot. He suggested several approaches, but we agreed the simplest one would be best. As it turned out, his 'simplest approach' aligned with my original thoughts on how to fix it. By the time I left the store, I had the few necessary bits of hardware we need for the job, and he even found me an offcut of ply to screw to the inside of the slot. So, all that's required now is for us to fetch the necessary tools from your shed, and expend some energy on affixing the necessary bits and pieces. We can deal with the letter slot over the weekend. All we will have to do then is wait to see what happens at the appropriate time."

This was not what I had in mind. Somehow, to me, it only dealt with the outcome, not the cause. I tried convincing myself that, if the letters couldn't be delivered, the nonsense would stop, but common sense kept telling me it wouldn't be like that. No, the letter slot was of no consequence in the overall scheme of things. As soon as we finalised the funds misappropriation case, it was imperative we tackled the matter of those letters. My gut kept insisting it would require more than simply preventing their arrival. To put an end to them, we needed to discover their source and shut it down.

*****

Before I scrambled out of bed this morning, I tried telling myself the week was almost over and I had survived it. With only Friday left of the working week, I didn't expect much more excitement to occur before the weekend.

As it turns out, I wasn't disappointed. Friday proved to be a normal, busy workday, and one that Majella, Jo and I spent anchored at our desks. The only highlight of the day occurred when Jo and I encountered one another while making coffee. After checking no one was around, Jo sidled up to me and spoke quietly.

"Have you given any further thought to what you were going to say to Krista?"

"I wasn't planning on speaking to her at all. I thought you didn't want anything to happen until everything was in place to initiate action against James."

"No, I meant about coming back to work here. You told her you would call when the restructuring and refurbishments were complete to tell her whether there was a position available for her in the office pool. It sounds like you haven't called her. I'm not sure that's the best way to handle the situation."

"Geez, I'd forgotten all about promising to call her. What do you want me to do? I don't think we have a vacancy since the reshuffle and, as she would be working for him, it's up to Jock McGillivray whether another person is employed."

"That's okay. There's no need to bother Jock about it. We don't need her back here, so it doesn't matter whether there is a vacancy or not. What is important is for you to call her. We don't want her becoming curious about why you haven't. She might start trying to winkle information out of her onetime associates here. I don't think anyone knows we were in France, but you would be surprised at what people do find out. Your best move is to tell her that, as a result of the restructure and refurbishment, there is no longer a vacancy. Apologise for taking so long to get back to her. Explain you waited until things settled down again to see if something did become available before calling her."

"Okay, that sounds plausible. I'll leave it until this afternoon to call her. I'll claim I was leaving it as long as possible in the hope something might eventuate before I delivered the disappointing news."

By the time Jo and I had a catch up after everyone left for the day, we both felt pleased with ourselves. We had cleared our desks of the backlog. Monday morning would see a fresh start with empty in-trays. And I had made that phone call.

"In case you were wondering, I called Krista late this afternoon. She seemed a bit stiff from the outset, then turned distinctly frosty when I delivered the 'no vacancy' news. I did deliver the apology and explanation as we discussed, but didn't dwell on either. It was a brief phone call."

"The good thing is, if there is anyone here she might contact to confirm your statements, they will be able to back-up your comments about restructuring and refurbishment."

We didn't have much else to discuss. Jo indicated she was going to work back for a while. I guessed she was chasing the new rogue company's payments in our archive files. My suspicions were confirmed when she breezed into the kitchen an hour or so after I arrived home and announced, "All payments now documented and in the case file."

Conversation on Friday night centred on the mail slot in the front door, and our disabling-the-slot-project planned for Saturday morning. I still held some reservations about how effective it would be. We would stop the letters being pushed through the letter slot, but I doubted that would deter whoever was behind them. If those responsible were determined enough – and I believed they were – they will find some other way to deliver them.

Chapter 27

Jo: preventative measures

Breakfast was a leisurely affair accompanied by the weekend newspapers … that is, until Gordon Grimshaw's phone call to Mel. He was contacted by a representative of a huge potential supplier the company had been courting for some time. It appears a number of their representatives were in town for a weekend conference. When this morning's sessions were cancelled, they enquired whether it might be possible for them to look over the company's operations. Gordon wanted Mel to be a part of the exercise. Without any hesitation, Mel agreed to be at the plant to meet them when they arrived at nine o'clock. She told Gordon she would bring something for morning tea and, if the visit went long enough, she suggested taking the visitors somewhere for an early lunch.

After the call, Mel felt torn between going to meet the representatives and leaving me to deal with the letter slot project. Dealing with the letter slot would take no time at all, and was something I could manage on my own without even raising a sweat. I tried putting Mel's mind at ease. "I agree with Gordon. This is an occasion for the 'big boss' to front up and make nice to the visitors. From what I've seen, their prices are good, much better than we get now. So, go and be extra nice to them. You probably would be in the way if you stayed home to help with the letter slot anyway."

Mel left early to catch the bakery for an early pick of what was on offer today. As soon as she was gone, I took myself off to the shed to fetch the necessary tools for the task ahead. About an hour later, the flap was glued shut and the ply offcut screwed across the slot on the inside of the door. With that dealt with, I moved on to the next stage of my 'preventing the letters' project.

The gods smiled on me this morning when they arranged for Mel not to be here.

It wasn't that the next phase was something I thought she might disapprove of – well, she might – but, for some reason, I thought it best if she didn't know about it. In the end, perhaps she might find out but, if that did eventuate, it would eliminate any arguments about its being installed. I made a quick trip to my room to gather up the boxes I had stashed under my bed after my shopping spree on Thursday.

All the boxes had been opened and their contents well scrutinised. I felt confident I could install the bits and pieces without too much trouble. Then, after checking I had everything required, I was off to the shed again to fetch a ladder. It took a bit of sweating and swearing to move stuff out of the way so I could retrieve the ladder from against the back wall. My phone rang as I was lugging it across the courtyard to the back door.

My unexpected caller was Syd Hartley. He barely said hello before asking what I was doing. "What's all the clanking and banging I can hear? What have I interrupted? What are you doing, and is this not a good time to talk?"

"No, it's a good time to talk. Talking to you will give me time to catch my breath and have a rest. I was lugging a ladder from the shed across the courtyard I'm about to attempt installing CCTV cameras on the front of the house. So, thanks for the interruption; what did you want to talk about?"

"If Mel is not helping you with the job, I assume she is in the dark about what you're doing."

"Uhmm … Yeah, she is unaware. And, she also happens to be not home for the rest of the morning. This is my chance to get on with it while she's not here. So, either talk fast, or I'll call you back some time later."

"Ah well now, I am something of an aficionado at installing CCTV cameras. I'll be right around the help you install them."

True to his word, I had lugged the ladder around the front of the house and just positioned it against the wall when Syd arrived. By coffee time, everything was installed and we were ready to give it a trial run. While I waited for the coffee machine to do its thing, I set up the computer in readiness to test the system. With coffee dealt with and time slipping away, I was anxious to test the cameras and confirm the system was operational before Mel might return. After a bit of gentle urging, Syd gulped the last of his coffee, and we were ready to go.

We both went out front for a last minute check on everything and, in particular, to make sure the cameras were angled correctly for the areas I wanted covered. While we were out there, the woman from the house across the street wandered past on the pretext of walking her dog. We had exchanged greetings on the odd occasions we bumped into one another on the street, but we had never as much as had a conversation.

During the installation of the cameras, I noticed her watching proceedings from her front window. It seems curiosity got the better of her. "I hope you don't mind my asking, but I was wondering what you were doing over here?"

I explained about the CCTV system as simply as I could, but without any hint of the real reason for its installation. She thought it a good move, and claimed she had been thinking about something similar for her home for a while now but, as a widow, didn't think she would be able to install it herself. Good old Syd couldn't help himself.

"Well, dear, if you buy the gear, I will come around and install it for you."

That proved an offer too good to ignore. She thought what we had installed would be ideal for her place as well. Armed with details of all the bits she needed to buy, she went on an immediate shopping trip. As I watched her drive out, I told Syd, "I hope she has a ladder of her own and I don't have to lug this heavy one across the street to her place."

With nothing further to delay us, testing the system went ahead. Syd went out onto the street before walking up the path to the front door. He stood on the doorstep shuffling from foot to foot and looking about before walking back out onto the street. While he went through his impersonation of a visitor to the house, I sat in front of the computer and monitored what was happening outside.

Images of Syd were clear and uninterrupted. After repeating the exercise a couple more times, Syd joined me at the computer to see how the images had recorded. It was after eleven o'clock when we brought up the morning's recordings. With no knowledge of when Mel might return, I was becoming anxious for Syd not to be here much longer. If he were still here when Mel arrived home, it would cause a whole raft of questions I would prefer not to have to answer yet.

My concerns were put to rest when Mel called me. "This morning's tour of inspection went well. Then we spent some time discussing the scope of our operations and possible supply arrangements; more positive stuff there. In a few minutes' time, Gordon and I will be taking them to lunch. It seems they are in no hurry to return to their conference, so we might be on for a long session. Just thought I should let you know I am unsure what time I will be home this afternoon. …Didn't want you to starve while waiting for me."

On the strength of Mel's call, I invited Syd to join me in a sandwich for lunch, and cracked open a bottle of white wine beforehand to celebrate the successful completion of the project. From the outset, in spite of my careful thought about their positioning, I was concerned about how visible the cameras were now they were mounted on the front wall of the house. Syd assured me as a result of the way they were tucked up under the eaves, they were unlikely to catch anyone's attention … but I needed to reassure myself. It would defeat their purpose if they stood out like the proverbial to all and sundry who looked at the house. No one would attempt to deliver another of *those* letters if they were aware cameras were watching.

With glasses of wine still in hand, we went out so I could check for myself before I started making lunch. Our inspection of Syd's handiwork coincided with the return home of the woman from across the street. She abandoned her car in her driveway before trotting across to speak to Syd.

"I went and bought all the bits and pieces you said I would need. They are in the car now. So, whenever you might have some time available…"

Top marks to Syd; after congratulating her on being so enterprising, while keeping one eye on me, he said, "We were just about to have lunch. But, seeing as I'm here, if it suits you, I could come over straight afterwards to install the gear for you."

She positively beamed at him while delivering her effusive thanks … and yes, after lunch would be fine.

"Right then; come on Jo, we had better eat so I can hop across the street to do my good deed for the day."

We rushed inside before dissolving into laughter when we reached the safety of the kitchen. In between fits of the giggles, I managed to ask, "Should I accompany you as a chaperone? Judging by the looks the woman was giving you, I'm not sure how safe you'll be over there. I'd hate for you to be ravaged because I allowed you to venture into danger alone."

My comments set the tone for what proved an enjoyable lunch accompanied by lots of funny stories and laughter … probably helped along by the wine. Nevertheless, in amongst it all, Syd did manage to tell me why he had called in the first place. It seems the police were almost ready to act on all the information now gathered on James and his operations. Late on Thursday, Syd had alerted his commanding officer to the case he was building against James and Krista. As a result of that meeting, Syd now believed they were likely to move on the case sometime next week.

I apprised Syd of the additional shelf company we had discovered and gave him a copy of the evidence of payments to it I had extracted from the company's files. He gave me an assurance he would keep me informed – hour by hour if need be – as things unfolded over the next week. Then, with lunch over, and the woman over the street no doubt becoming anxious, Syd drove across the street, leaving me to clean up after the morning's work. We agreed it might be best if his car wasn't still outside when Mel arrived home.

Following their business lunch, Mel and Gordon returned to the plant and worked on for some time before Mel came home around four o'clock. If she noticed the newly installed cameras, she didn't mention them when she came in. She seemed more interested in what I had done to the letter slot. I encouraged her interest in my handiwork as a means of keeping her attention focused on the front door, and away from this morning's labours outside. While we stood on the doorstep examining the now defunct letter slot, I noticed Syd's car drive away from the house across the street. ...Seemed to take him a lot longer to install the cameras over there than it did here, I thought as I ushered Mel back inside.

It was still early and Mel looked worn out. I suggested we take long cold drinks out into the back garden and relax until it was time to think about making dinner. After sitting in silence for about a minute, in a quiet voice, I initiated conversation.

"Mel, you look tired. Did dealing with the visitors make for a difficult day?"

"No, that went well. They seemed impressed with our operation, and said they would send details of possible supply arrangements. There's still a way to go, but I have positive feelings about how the day went."

"Okay, so why are you looking so tired? Are you not sleeping all right?"

"Not really; I suppose I haven't slept well any night for the last week. It's about a week before the second anniversary of James' 'disappearance'. Argh, I'm not being sentimental about the anniversary. The thought of another of those letters arriving keeps playing on my mind."

"At the risk of telling you what you already know, another letter can't be delivered. Now we've dealt with the letter slot, there will be nothing more fluttering down onto your carpet."

"I know. I know, but this has nothing to do with what I know … or about common sense. I've tried putting it out of my mind. I don't seem able to do that. I suppose I'll just have to live with it until after the anniversary."

After that, conversation remained sparse and inconsequential until we went inside to deal with dinner. Nevertheless, for the rest of the evening, I felt conflicted. Should I tell Mel about Syd Hartley's involvement in our investigation, and should I mention something regarding James and Krista's take-down might happen as early as next week? Might it be wiser to wait until Syd indicates things are happening?

In spite of mentally arguing the situation all evening, I had reached no decision on the matter when I went up to my room soon after ten o'clock. It continued to churn in my mind for at least another hour after I crawled into bed. But, sometime before midnight I had decided. This might be one of those times when ignorance is bliss – compared to the alternative, that is.

Mel already was losing enough sleep dealing with her own demons. Giving her more to worry about was not in anyone's best interest. Why rush in when waiting a bit longer might be better for all concerned? I decided to say nothing until after my next update from Syd.

*****

The week got off to a hectic start. It was budget week, so my time was spent helping managers prepare their budget submissions. In addition, entertaining the visitors last Saturday proved a worthwhile exercise. They were keen to finalise supply contracts but there were a few details to sort out before it could happen. With both Mel and I so busy, it seemed like the only time we saw or spoke to each other was at home before and after work. In spite of being so busy, a part of me kept waiting to hear from Syd. I knew he said nothing would happen until towards the end of this week but it didn't stop me being impatient.

For the first time this week, mid-morning on Wednesday, Mel and I happened to be making coffee at the same time. Neither of us had time to sit around and chat while we drank our coffee, so we exchanged only a few words while waiting for the coffee machine to do its thing. Mel said she would be working late this evening and not to wait for her for dinner. She would arrange for something from the canteen to be delivered to her office.

Apart from everything else, as part of budget preparations for the coming year, staff appraisals needed to be completed. While it is a time-consuming and sometimes painful process, any salary increases arising from the appraisals need to be factored into next year's budget. As she went to leave the kitchen, Mel added a 'last line' to her comments about staff appraisals.

"Every year, I dread the time when I have to do the appraisals. The only upside to the process this year is that so many of the senior staff are new appointments who do not need an appraisal this year."

It was around two o'clock when the long-awaited phone call came. Syd wanted to talk to me, but said our discussion should be face-to-face. As Mel wouldn't be home for dinner this evening, I suggested a meeting at our favourite pub. The final arrangement was for us to meet soon after five o'clock to discuss whatever Syd wanted to talk about over a drink. We could then grab a meal before we left.

Somehow, I managed some work before leaving to meet Syd, but it was a struggle to concentrate. My mind kept wondering why Syd felt it necessary for a face-to-face meeting to pass on his latest news. Surely information on where their investigation was at could be delivered over the phone. Nevertheless, I was looking forward to spending time with Syd again. Apart from discussing the police investigation, I liked his company.

As soon as five o'clock rolled around, I bolted from my office. On my way past her door, I noted Mel was on the phone, so I just flicked her a quick wave and kept going. Again, Syd was first at the pub and had secured 'our' table in a back corner. He wasted no time getting down to business. His opening gambit caused my stomach to tighten a little.

"Have you spoken to Mel yet? I mean, have you told her about my involvement and the police's investigation?"

"No-o, I decided to wait until I heard more from you. She's not sleeping well and I didn't want to make matters worse. It's the second anniversary of James' disappearance on Friday, and the prospect of receiving another one of those letters is eating at her. My efforts at reassuring her haven't been successful. Why do you ask if I've spoken to her? …Something untoward happened?"

He chuckled, "No nothing like that; nothing to worry about. We're getting to the pointy end of things now. Before the end of the week, you might need to sit down for a long chat with Mel about everything. We've completed our investigation – well, we confirmed the information in your case file really. My supervisor received permission to move our investigation overseas, and has spoken to the authorities in France, as well as the banks here and over there."

"That is good to hear. This Friday is when the next illegal payment to James' account is to be made. It is galling to know such misappropriation of the company's funds automatically continues in spite of our knowledge of what's happening. The sooner it's brought to an end, the happier we all will be."

"Well, you won't have too much longer to wait. My supervisor and I will fly to France on Sunday to meet up with our French counterparts. We will stake out the bank on Monday morning in the off-chance James comes in again as he did when you were over there. The plan is, if he doesn't come into the bank on Monday, we will move to Avignon to arrest the pair of them there."

"Okay, I see why it's important to tell Mel about it as soon as possible. I'll see what condition she's in when she arrives home tonight. If she's up to it, I will have that conversation then. If she is too strung out after a long day, I'll make sure I talk to her in the morning, even if it means we are late going into work tomorrow."

"Good thinking; it might be beneficial for her to meet me before we head to France. I'll leave it to you to judge whether it should happen, and to set it up if it is."

Until our meals arrived, we filled in time discussing various aspects of his investigation. Neither of us was inclined to linger after we had eaten, so I arrived home before nine o'clock. By then, I had a headache developing. A text from Mel said she would be later than anticipated. Jim, the security guard was on the late shift tonight. In spite of now being head of security, he still worked the odd shift.

Mel had called to ask if he could come in a little before his shift so she could do his appraisal before he started work. It was the last one she had to do and was keen to have them all completed. In view of this late appointment, I assumed she would not be home before eleven o'clock. I decided to take my headache to bed rather than sit up to wait for her.

Telling her about Syd and the police investigation into James and Krista would have to wait until tomorrow.

Chapter 28

An alarm clock is not something I rely on in the morning. Today was different. I arranged to meet Gordon Grimshaw before work to clarify a few issues to allow him to complete his budget submission. As a result, my alarm clock had me out of bed earlier than usual and bustling about in the kitchen preparing breakfast before Jo ventured out of her room. She was still half asleep when she demanded, "What are you doing up at this hour of the day?"

"I have an early meeting with Gordon. That mob we entertained on Saturday sent through their supply contracts before I left work last night. They look fine, but I always get our company's legal bod to vet them before we sign anything. As I'm going in early this morning, would you mind hanging around here until about nine o'clock before dropping the contracts in to the solicitor. See if you can persuade him an urgent response would be good."

"Okay, that won't be a problem. I have a couple of things I can do from here before I drop the contracts off. I'll catch up with you sometime during the day."

I left Jo to finish her breakfast alone while I rushed around doing those last few things before I left. Gordon was waiting for me when I arrived and our discussions began as soon as my feet were under my desk. The meeting went well and finished in time for him to be back on the production floor at his usual time. Some of the pressure had come off this week. While I was still busy, today I had time to breathe and have coffee. I saw Jo come in, but she went straight to her office. For her, the pressure of work would persist until about next Monday.

By mid-morning, it looked like being an ordinary day for me. That was until Jo bounced into my office just before lunchtime.

The sparkle in her eyes and the way she was unable to remain still told me something major was afoot. I raised my eyebrows at her in question as she came in but I didn't have a chance to say anything before she asked, "Have you got a few minutes?"

It looked like it might develop into a significant discussion, so I sent Majella to fetch lunch for both of us. "Okay, Jo, do you want to jump straight in with whatever you want to discuss, or would you rather wait until our lunch arrives?"

She elected to wait for lunch. I was keen to find out why she looked so nervous. So, as soon as Majella returned to her office after delivering our lunch, I initiated the conversation. "Jo, you now have me almost dying of curiosity, and the fact that you are looking so nervous is not helping. What is going on?"

"It's not nervous tension you're seeing. It's more like trepidation."

"Trepidation…? About what…? For God's sake, spit it out. Whatever it is, get on with it."

"Okay, well, since I started working here, we have had two investigations on the go: the misappropriation of company funds, and the periodic arrival of those strange letters. We now have all the evidence to enable us to take action on the misappropriation matter. But, in spite of our efforts to prevent the delivery of another letter, we still don't know the WHO or the WHY about them. As you know, we don't share the same opinions about those letters or how investigating them should occur. I'm afraid I have never agreed with your insistence that the authorities not be involved, and that's why I've instigated a few things without telling you about it … until now."

In spite of my best effort to remain calm until I heard the rest of the story, I felt my tension rising and my stomaching tightening. It didn't take too much to work out what Jo had gone behind my back to do. Nevertheless, I tried to sound normal when I asked her to tell me her story. Her opening sentence told me my suspicions were right: *I have an old friend, a detective named Syd Hartley, whom I asked to look into a couple of matters for me; as a favour of course, not officially.*

Jo rolled out her story of asking her detective friend to look into such matters as the previous owner of this house, the last tenant living here, and various matters relating to the investigation into James's disappearance. As I listened, I experienced a rollercoaster ride of emotions: anger, curiosity, doubt, disbelief, and finally, elation as she ended her story.

"The last I heard was they had confirmed all our evidence and were working with the French authorities. It was likely that Syd and his superior officer would travel to France in the near future to combine with the French to take action on the matter. At least, that was what I knew until about half an hour ago when Syd called me. It's now definite. He and the inspector will go to France on Sunday and, if everything happens as anticipated, James is likely to undergo a major lifestyle change on Monday."

"I assume that means they expect to arrest James on Monday. Is it likely he will be at that bank again on Monday morning?"

"That is the expectation. But, if it eventuates that James doesn't visit that bank as anticipated, the action will move to Avignon, and that's where he would be arrested along with Krista. I'm sorry if I've upset you by initiating all of this. It didn't start out that way. In the beginning, Syd was just to look into a couple of things for me. But what he found, particularly in regard to the investigation into James' disappearance, stirred his interest. After I gave him a copy of our evidence, he did a bit more digging before taking it to his superior officer. After that it became fundamental police procedure."

"If I'm honest, I'd have to admit the way it has happened came as a shock, but I hold no ill feelings towards you or Syd for the work you've done. I'd also have to admit to feeling excitement about what Monday might achieve."

Syd had offered to meet with me to help calm things down if it turned sour between Jo and I when she explained everything to me. It wasn't necessary at this time. I imagined Syd and his superior officer have a busy few days ahead preparing for their trip across the channel. But, once it's all over, I would like to meet Syd to thank him for his efforts.

With nothing more to be said on the subject, Jo went back to her office and I tried to get on with the rest of my day. Concentration was at a premium all afternoon thanks to her news. By the time I left for the day, what had been a nagging hint of an idea all afternoon had developed into a fairly definite plan. Like Jo's recent covert activities, there was no need to share that plan with anyone at this point in time.

In spite of the initial excitement generated by today's news, this evening took on a sombre note. Tomorrow was the second anniversary of James' supposed disappearance overboard. Now I knew he hadn't disappeared – hadn't drowned and was living a wonderful life in France on my money – this so-called anniversary shouldn't mean anything to me. For some inexplicable reason, it did. It wasn't until I mentioned it to Jo over coffee after dinner that the reality of the situation came home to me. The ever-practical Jo explained it in a few brief words: *Be honest with yourself. It's not the 'anniversary' that's the problem. It's the thought of another of those letters that has you on edge.*

Of course she was right. I knew it the moment she put it into words, but there was no getting away from it. Would there be another letter tomorrow? I know we've done all we can to make it a virtual impossibility, but I don't feel confident there won't be another one. We lapsed into silence until after we drained our coffee mugs.

"I think maybe a nightcap will help us both sleep better tonight. I'll take the mugs through to the kitchen and fetch us a port while I'm about it."

She was only gone a couple of minutes but it was long enough for me to devote some thought to the matter of the letters. I shared my thinking with her over our nightcaps.

"I know it's likely James will be arrested on Monday. That sits well with me. What still bothers me are those letters. We still don't know why they're arriving or who is behind them. Despite knowing it was impossible, in the back of my mind, there's always been a vague idea James somehow was responsible. He drowned. How could he be sending me letters? I don't believe in the paranormal, so he can't be sending them from Davy Jones' locker. Now we know he is still alive and well, I can't convince myself he isn't responsible."

Jo didn't have any answers. Her only advice was for me to put it out of my mind until tomorrow. When no letter arrived, maybe then I would be able to put the whole thing behind me. There was little comfort in that, but I accepted it in the spirit it was intended. Nevertheless, I knew I was in for a restless night, and I wished tomorrow morning was here so we could get it over and done with.

*****

This morning found me thick headed and very much the worse for lack of sleep. Of course no letters tumbled through the now sealed letter slot. I should feel relaxed but, all through breakfast and the time it took to be ready for work, I kept waiting for a letter to arrive. Telling myself I was being ridiculous was to no avail. Every few moments, I stole a look at the patch of carpet below the letter slot. As we are about to go out to our cars, Jo caught me steal one last look to see if, by some miraculous means, a letter had arrived.

"No, Mel, not even a moth could crawl through that letter slot, and the draught stopper fitted to the bottom of the door leaves no gap for anything to be slid under it."

As I opened the door to go out to my car, I told myself she was right and I was being ridiculous. That was until I opened the door. I felt my knees start to sag. My world turned upside down. With little control of my vocal chords, I managed to croak, "Jo … Jo, help me!"

She rushed over and caught me as I started to collapse. My head was spinning and my legs refused to support me. After half carrying me inside, slamming the door shut and locking it, Jo dumped me in a chair at the dining table. There was still hot water from breakfast. She used it to make me a cup of weak tea before abandoning me at the table.

"Don't leave me," I pleaded. There was no response. I don't know whether she didn't hear me, or if she chose to ignore my plea. Jo was gone. I saw her leave the room but, in my befuddled state, where she went didn't register with me. I thought she was still inside the house somewhere … I hoped she was still inside with me and hadn't left me alone altogether. That must have been when I passed out as I don't remember anything more until sometime later.

When I did return to the real world, Jo was looming over me with a bottle of smelling salts in her hand. I had a vague feeling someone else was present, but things were foggy and I couldn't focus properly. It would be some time later before I understood what happened.

Chapter 29

Jo: takes control

A blood-curdling shriek shattered the silent street. I dropped my bag I just picked up and sprinted to the partially open door. Flinging it wide open, I saw Mel hunched over, colour drained from her face and trembling. As she began to wobble, I raced to support her and prevent her falling in a heap on the doorstep. There was little chance for more than a fleeting glance at what lay on the mat on the top step.

Mel was in danger of passing out. I had to get her inside and settled somewhere safe so she wouldn't be injured if that happened. The kitchen area was closer than the lounge room, and Mel was a dead weight draped over me. I half dragged/half carried her into the kitchen area and the nearest chair at the dining table. Somehow, in the process of bringing her back inside, I managed to kick the door closed and free up one hand with which to flick the lock. Disengaging myself from Mel and sitting her on a chair was tricky but, after a few anxious moments, she was safely on the chair. She had her arms folded on the table and rested her head on them. She was groggy and incoherent.

She lost consciousness. After making sure she was still breathing and she would be okay for a few minutes on her own, I ran to boot up the computer. "Come on … Come on … Hurry up!" I yelled as it went through its usual pedantic boot up routine. As soon it was right to go, I searched for this morning's CCTV footage. In my haste, at first, I couldn't find anything recorded today. I felt panic setting in. After a couple of deep breaths, I checked again for the relevant file.

There it was… a clear recoding of what happened outside the front of this house some time earlier today. A figure wearing dark coloured jeans and trainers, and with a black hoodie pulled up over their head approached the front door. After trying the letter slot several times, there was acceptance nothing could enter. Admitting defeat, the figure retreated to the bottom of the front steps before turning to look at the front door again. After shaking their head in disbelief a couple of times, the figure again turned and marched off the property and out onto the street.

No more than a couple of minutes later, the figure reappeared and once more strode up to the front door. There was one more futile attempt to shove an envelope through the slot before stooping down to do something it was impossible to see. The visitor's body blocked the camera's view. Whatever was done, it only took a couple of seconds. Then, the figure straightened up and once again strode off the property and out onto the street.

By the time the recording came to an end, I had keyed in a call to Syd Hartley. He answered almost immediately and I began delivering a garbled message. "Stop, Jo. Stop… Take a deep breath and then begin again. This time, take your time and tell me slowly and clearly what has happened."

After a deep breath, I again attempted to tell Syd why I needed him here now. "Another one of those letters has arrived this morning. When they couldn't put it through the letter slot, they left on the doormat along with a small posy of forget-me-nots. Mel found it when she opened the door. I've brought her inside but she passed out. The cameras captured good footage. I need you to look at it. Can you come now … please?

Syd arrived about fifteen minutes later. He brought a calming presence to the place. While I waited for him to arrive, I searched the cupboards for anything useful and found an ancient looking bottle of smelling salts. I was on my way to the kitchen to wave it under Mel's nose when Syd pulled into the driveway. He seemed to be out of the car and at the door almost before I heard the sound of the car's engine die away.

"Are you okay?" I nodded. "Good; how is Mel … and what have you done with her?"

"She's in here. I was about to try bringing her around when you arrived. I hope being out to it for so long hasn't done any real damage. Come with me if you like, but I must do this now."

"Being out to it for a while might help her recover. I'll stand over here out of the way while you do it. We don't want her finding a strange man in close proximity as she regains consciousness."

On my way to Mel, and while Syd was speaking, I concentrated on wrestling with the little lavender crown shaped lid on the smelling salts bottle. It was a long time ago this bottle was last opened. The way Mel rested her head made it difficult to access her face. Syd stepped over and lifted her head a little so I could wave the bottle under her nose. Her response was immediate. I was relieved … not only because Mel was now back with us, but also because I wasn't sure the old smelling salts would still work. She began mumbling.

"Not again… Not another letter … Maybe I imagined it … No, it was there. I saw it. Why, why are they doing this? Who's there? Who else is in the room? Jo, who else is here?"

"Shhh, Mel, you are okay. No need to worry, you are safe. There is someone else here with me. Remember Syd Hartley, that detective I told you about?" For a moment she looked confused. Then I saw her relax and she nodded at me. "Good; well, Syd has come to look into what happened here."

While I was soothing Mel's fears, Syd ducked back to the doorstep. Out the corner of my eye, I saw him slide the envelope and the posy into an evidence bag, before coming back to stand beside me. He smiled down at Mel and, in a quiet voice, introduced himself. What he did next surprised me. Still with his voice quiet and calm, he continued speaking to Mel.

"Mel, do I have your permission to open the envelope to see what the note says?"

She gave me such a beseeching look when she turned her face to me, it almost broke my heart. "It is okay, Mel. He is one of the good guys and he wants to investigate the letters. I think you should let him open it. You don't have to look at it if you don't want to."

After a momentary hesitation, she told Syd to open the envelope, but insisted she didn't want to know what was in it. Syd used a glove to protect the envelope and posy when he picked them up and slid them into the bag. Now, he put a pair of gloves on properly before removing the envelope from the evidence bag. Using a paring knife from the kitchen drawer, he slit the envelope open and shook out a single sheet of paper folded in half.

He grunted in disgust when he read its message. I had rushed around to stand beside him as he open the envelope, and read the note over his shoulder. Without a word, after reading it, he folded it again and slid it back into its envelope. With the evidence bag tucked under his arm, he walked towards the front door. I saw him pull out his phone and make a short call. The call ended, he beckoned me with a flick of his head to join him.

"I think we should try to put Mel to bed, or at least lie her down somewhere. Is there a sofa in the lounge room?" I nodded. "That will do. Come on, give me a hand to move her. You might need to reassure her she is safe and I'm not about to do anything terrible to her."

Amid her half-hearted protests, Syd and I relocated Mel to the lounge room sofa, where she promptly fell asleep. My first reaction was to panic, fearing something worse had happened to her. Syd confirmed she was only asleep. With the drapes still closed, the lounge room was dark and conducive to sleep. I threw a rug over Mel before I took Syd to look at the camera footage.

On the way, he said, "A car should be here shortly. I've asked them to collect the evidence bag. The sooner we get it to the tech boys, the sooner we might have answers to some of the questions surrounding those letters."

We were no sooner at the computer than there was a knock at the door. Syd handed over the evidence bag and had a few brief words to the uniformed officer. Syd didn't stay long and, after recording today's sequence of events and copying the footage captured by the CCTV cameras, he was keen to return to his office. I walked him to the front door and watched him climb into his car. He barely had his backside on the seat when he bounced out of the car again and strode across the street.

The woman for whom he had installed the CCTV system last Saturday stood watching proceedings from her gate. She swung it open when Syd started towards her. After a few brief words at the gate, they both disappeared inside. About fifteen minutes later, they emerged again. The woman saw Syd off before closing the gate behind him and returning inside.

As he again approached his car, I went out to meet him. "What was that all about? Did something happen over there too?"

"No. When I saw her standing by the gate, I remembered installing her CCTV system and wondered whether it might have captured any additional footage this morning. I'm pleased I went over there. She was about to check her emails when she heard Mel's scream, so her computer was already up and running when I arrived. Her system recorded the rear view of everything your system did, but her cameras also had images of the car the 'messenger' was driving. It won't take much to lift vital information from those images. Now I need to get back to the office. I'll call you later today to see how things are here. I assume neither of you will be going into work today."

I stood on the doorstep and watched him drive away. All of a sudden I felt a little weak-kneed too. I sat in the kitchen with a cup of coffee for a few minutes before calling Majella to let her know we would not be coming in. Then, after a quick check on Mel, I sat down to record everything from this morning. After that, I spent a long time thinking on everything I knew about those unwelcome letters.

It was almost lunchtime before Mel woke. Looking pale and drawn, she staggered out to the kitchen. She said she didn't want lunch, but I heated up some left over soup and she ate it. I noticed her colour improve afterwards. Not surprisingly I suppose, Mel wanted me to run through this morning's events. I wasn't sure she was up to it. She assured me she was and pressed me for a detailed report.

This was the first she heard of the CCTV installation. I took her out front to show her the cameras before showing her this morning's footage of the 'messenger's' visit. It seemed appropriate to tell her about the woman across the street installing a similar system, and how Syd also collected a copy of the footage from her cameras. As I ran the video again for Mel, something about the figure caught my attention.

There was nothing familiar about the person. My gut was trying to tell me I knew something about the person, but I couldn't identify what it was. In desperation I decided to ask Mel about it.

"What can you tell me about the person in the video footage? Does anything strike a chord with you?"

"No … I don't recognise him, if that's what you're asking me. With the hoodie pulled up like that, there isn't a clear image of the face. Do you think I should recognise him?"

"Argh… I don't know what it is, but something is trying to grab my attention."

Mel paused the video and began analysing the image now filling the screen. "Hmm … nothing distinguishing about the clothes, they're what everyone seems to be wearing these days. I'm having trouble working something out. Maybe it's a perspective thing. It's to do with the person's size. It doesn't look like a burly front row forward to me. Looks more like a smallish person, but I can't be sure about the size. Perhaps it's due to the angle of the camera."

Her comments gave me pause for thought. "Run the video on a bit further. Let's see if there is a better image with some sort of reference point in it."

She ran the video frame by frame until I yelled for her to pause it again. "There, that's better. That shot captures the shrub beside the end of the path with the figure beside it. How tall do you reckon that shrub is? See how it comes well up to the person's midriff. That *is* quite a small person. I'd even say 'petite'. That's it! The figure is petite. Blokes aren't petite..."

"Are you saying that's a woman?"

"That's exactly what I'm saying. Look at how slight her build is. Even jockeys are more robust-looking than that. Rewind it a bit … Now, play it again. Watch how she moves. What do you reckon?"

"Now you've pointed it out, it does look like a woman. But, it doesn't look like Krista. What other woman might have reason to do this to me?"

It hadn't even occurred to me that it might be Krista, but I didn't respond to Mel's question. I was too busy calling Syd. He answered straight away, and I blurted out, "Syd, it's a woman. The figure in the video is a woman."

"Is that all this call is about? I thought some other disaster might have befallen you. Yes, you are right. We also established the figure was a woman. Is there anything else about her you can tell me?"

"No, unfortunately; Mel assures me it doesn't look like Krista, whom she knows better than I do. And, Mel doesn't know of any other woman she has upset sufficiently to result in such a campaign against her."

"Not to worry; the tech might turn up something more. I'm expecting a report sometime later this afternoon. Talk to you again when I know more."

Soon after I spoke to Syd, Mel admitted to feeling a bit washed-out and thought she might spend a while in her room. I told her my concern was that, if she slept this afternoon, she might not be able to sleep tonight. She still had a few sleeping pills left from when James disappeared. They weren't strong, but she was sure they would work tonight if she needed one.

After escorting her upstairs and making sure she was comfortable, I went to the kitchen for yet another cup of coffee. Having drunk so much of it today I might need one of Mel's tablets to get to sleep tonight. Sipping coffee in the solitude of the kitchen gave all today's events opportunity to catch up with me. Mild shock set in, and it took me quite a while to bring it under control.

If only today's video footage solved the mystery of those letters… It is probably wishful thinking, but I can't help hoping the next time I talk to Syd Hartley, that's the exact news he has to share.

Chapter 30

After a couple of hours of restless sleep, I wandered out of my room and into a silent house. Had Jo gone to work after all? I doubted it. She was unlikely to leave me here alone after this morning's episode. But, wherever she was and whatever she was doing, she was doing it without making a sound. On entering the kitchen, the mystery was solved. She had her laptop set up on the dining room table and was intent on keying figures into a spreadsheet. I recognised one of the company's huge budget documents. She seemed cheery enough, which is a long way from how I felt when I worked on budgets.

"Welcome to the world again. Good to see you up and about. How do you feel?"

"*Numb* is probably the best way to describe it. …Anything happen since I went upstairs?"

"Syd Hartley, the detective you met this morning called a few minutes ago. He will call around after work to update us on their efforts today."

"Did he sound positive? I could do with some good news after this morning. It would be wonderful to hear the mystery was solved."

"Please don't get your hopes up. It was a bit hard to tell whether he sounded positive or not when his call lasted only about two seconds."

Syd arrived not much before six o'clock. The afternoon had grown cool and the evening now had a definite chill to it. I had thought to take Syd out into the back garden where we could talk over a drink in pleasant surroundings. Instead, as Jo suggested, sitting at the dining room table was the better option. She poured us glasses of white wine and a single malt scotch for Syd before we got down to business.

"I'm sure the first thing you ladies want to hear about is analysis of the CCTV footage. The tech boys had no problems extracting more than enough information for us to act."

Jo and I exchanged glances. For some perverse reason, I found myself almost dreading what Syd might say. Jo must have read my emotions. She jumped in to end the suspense.

"Don't keep us hanging, Syd. Get on with it. But, we want to know all of it, regardless of whether it is good, bad … or absolutely bloody shocking. What did you discover?"

"Okay, starting with the CCTV footage… From the material I took from here, they managed to bring up a couple of clear images of the person's face."

"The *woman's* face…," Jo corrected him.

"Sorry; yes, you are right... We had a couple of clear images of the woman's face. From the material from the cameras across the street, we identified the vehicle in the footage and the tech boys were able to bring up its plate to identify the owner. After that, it was a simple matter to match the owner with the image on the video. She was invited to 'assist us with our investigation', as they say in all the best news reports. As part of that invitation, she will be spending the night in less comfortable quarters than she is used to."

"You have her in custody…! Thank god it might now be over." My feelings were elation, and relief, mingled with a touch of triumph. The bastards had been defeated. Then, reality elbowed everything else out of the way to demanded more. "Come on, Syd. I feel you have yet to deliver the punch line; the dénouement or whatever it's called."

"You might feel let down by what I am about to say, but here goes. It seems the woman in question was an unsuspecting pawn in the operation. She did not know what was in the letters, or the real reason she delivered them. She was acquainted with the truth this afternoon, and I believe her shock was genuine."

Jo sat up straight. "Wait a minute; are you saying you know what was behind it all? If the woman didn't know about it, how did you find out?"

"With what she told us about her role and how she came to be involved, we were able to identify and locate the instigator of the operation."

I felt I was losing the plot. I needed hard facts on which to anchor each segment of it. "Can we at least find out who the woman is before you move on to the next chapter of the story? I know I'm being pedantic, but I need to have the first chapter straight in my head before you deliver more information."

"Oh, didn't I say? Ah well, does the name Kinross mean anything to you?"

That was my next major shock for the day… Maybe I was wrong… I was struck dumb. Jo was not so affected.

After glancing at me, she shrugged at Syd. "No, not a thing; should it? It's not an uncommon name, but I don't know of it in this context."

"Perhaps I do," I croaked as the power of speech made its return. "The company had a staff member whose surname was Kinross. He was the security manager … past tense, please note. As a result of a recent staff reshuffle and other streamlining measures, he is no longer with us. Is this the Kinross you allude to?"

"The woman captured by the CCTV cameras was identified as Maree Kinross. I don't doubt her name doesn't ring any bells for either of you. As far as I can tell, she had no connection with the company. But, as you rightly pointed out, Steven Kinross, her brother, was employed by your company until recent times. …And bitter and twisted he is about being let go I might add."

"Syd, the letters started arriving long before he was let go. His recent retrenchment can't be the motivation. The first letter arrived only a few months after James disappeared. When I started renovations on this house in fact. Have you rounded him up too? What does he have to say about the letters?"

"Not much – at first. But I'll take you back to his sister Maree, before we move onto her brother. It seems Maree made a bit of a mess of her life after her mother died. Barely a teenager at the time, Maree fell in with the wrong crowd and, for the next however many years, her father was constantly bailing her out of trouble. Eventually, she did start to settle down, but it required a strong hand and constant vigil to keep her that way.

When the father became terminally ill, he added clauses to his will to ensure a tight rein on Maree would continue into the future. He set up a small annuity for her, but the majority of his significant estate would be held in trust for Steven … but only for as long as he continued to take care of his sister. That condition did not sit well with Steven, but he wanted his father's house and land and what remained of his cash holdings. It seems he made Maree's life a misery, treating as his personal slave. To outsiders, he was adhering to the conditions of the will."

"Poor kid; I'm sorry, Mel. I know she was a part of something that caused you significant pain over the last couple of years, but I do feel a bit sorry for her." Jo gave me a wry smile as she finished speaking. She was right. It was her brother, Steven, we should direct our vitriol at. As I pondered what life must have been like for Maree, Syd started speaking again.

"It seems Steven Kinross and your James go back a long way; all the way to early childhood. James fathered a child with Maree when she was about sixteen. Her father insisted the family have no further contact with James and, in particular, Steven was forbidden to even mention his name again. To add to the mess, Maree miscarried and it sent her off the rails again. His father's draconian rules relating to James did not sit well with Steven, who covertly defied his father at every opportunity. The two lads remained best mates, grew even closer while at university, and resulted in Steven being given a significant position in the company when James took over as manager.

Steven appears to be the one person who knew of James' plan to 'disappear overboard' and, in return for his assistance in pulling it off, James promised him an even better position *when he took over ownership of the company."*

"James thought he was going to own my company? How did he think that was going to happen?"

"Ah, well now, that's what the letters were all about. It seems James believed you were a delicate petal, who would be so bereft after losing him, you would be close to the edge. The letters were designed to tip you over that edge. After that happened, James would stage a Lazarus-type return from the dead and, as your lawful husband, claim everything."

"Just because I lost the plot would not be sufficient for him to be able to take over all my assets."

"No, that's correct. But, they aimed for you to have a major mental breakdown – to lose the plot as you put it. They intended you should become so unhinged and grief stricken, you would commit suicide. Then, he could claim the lot … after a convincing Lazarus impersonation of course."

"They were going to have to wait a bloody long time for me to even consider suicide." I was stunned. Long ago, I accepted I was a means to an end for James, and love had nothing to do with our marriage. But, in spite of my now low opinion of the man, I never imagined him capable of such thinking. "Syd, you said Maree was unaware of what the letters were about…"

"Yeah, it appears she was told they contained cheques, so she needed to be sure to deliver them to the correct address and be careful not to lose them. Above all else, she was not to be seen by anyone when she delivered them."

"Okay, I accept she might have been bullied into sub-missiveness, but surely she must have wondered what those 'cheques' were for."

"She came to the conclusion Steven was paying either an illegal bookmaker or some sort of stockbroker involved in insider trading. Soon after every delivery, she noticed Steven seemed to receive a cash windfall. He had plenty of money, both from his father's estate and the salary from his well-paid job. But, after every delivery, she notice he seemed to have some extra cash with which to buy himself an expensive present … a couple of new suits, another expensive camera, matching monogrammed gold cufflinks and tie pin, that sort of thing."

Jo shook her head in disbelief. "So, James was paying his friend Steven for his services?"

"So it would appear." Syd switched his gaze from Jo to me. "Mel, I hope this has helped put your mind at ease."

"It has to some extent, Syd, but what happens now – about Steven I mean?"

"When we picked up Maree, Steven was spending the day fishing on his mate's boat. When they returned to the marina, two of my men helped Steven off the boat and took him into custody. There was a brief interrogation session late this afternoon."

"Christ, isn't dragging him in now a bit dangerous?" It was obvious Jo couldn't believe Syd questioned Steven. "I mean isn't there a good chance this will jeopardise your operation planned for Monday in France? The first thing Steven will do is call James to tell him their game is up. James won't sit around waiting to be dragged in by the police, even if he is in France."

Syd's chuckle surprised me. I expected him to resent Jo's comments. "You sell me and my team short, Jo. Of course Steven won't contact James, or anyone else for that matter. He has no means of doing so. James is now being held in isolation. He will be interrogated over much of the weekend. We can only hold him for seventy-two hours. But that won't be a problem as we already have enough to lay charges. No, Steven poses no threat to our operation. He is not going anywhere, and he will have no means of communicating with anyone until the successful completion of our operation in France."

Now I was happy. The problem of the mystery letters seemed about to disappear, and I felt some satisfaction in who would pay for it – with the possible exception of Maree.

All afternoon, Jo's stew simmering on the hob filled the kitchen with its aroma. When Syd, having delivered his news, made noises about being on his way, I rushed in with an invitation for him to stay to dinner. He didn't need persuading but, as soon as dinner was over, he was on his way. After he left, Jo and I sat in the lounge discussing today, before we surfed the channels for something worth watching on TV.

By nine o'clock, and having found nothing of interest to watch, I found myself yawning and my eyelids beginning to droop. After all the sleeping I did today, I expected to have trouble tonight. I surprised myself by falling asleep almost the moment my head hit my pillow. As that happened, Syd's parting words echoed in my mind: *Unless something significant occurs, the next time you hear from me will be Monday or Tuesday next week. I expect to be busy over the next few days.*

While I accepted it might be Tuesday before the news I wanted to hear came through, every fibre of my being hoped it would be Monday. Nevertheless, his words fuelled an earlier idea. There wasn't time to explore and develop it before I fell asleep.

*****

The weekend kicked off with a drizzly Saturday morning. Our usual late breakfast with the weekend papers out in the back garden wasn't possible. Breakfast at the dining room table seemed to lack something, and set the tone for the rest of the day. We both spent a quiet day recovering from all yesterday delivered.

Sunday brought with it a beautiful morning to allow a return to our normal weekend late breakfast routine. After claiming she had laundry and other personal chores to take care of, Jo retreated to her room, only to be seen again at lunchtime. I too had things to attend to. Being left alone for part of the morning allowed me to deal with them without interruption. When Jo came down for lunch, she announced she was going into work for the rest of the day.

"After losing all day Friday, budget preparation is way behind schedule. I know the world won't end if the company's annual ritual ,that has been in place for decades, doesn't happen on time this year, but I would like to catch up a bit. Finding a little extra time to check and recheck all the figures before they go out to the managers will make me more comfortable about my first budget for your company. I might work late, so don't wait dinner for me."

On other occasions, I would argue against such a move but, today, having Jo out of the way all afternoon suited me fine. After keeping busy until mid-afternoon, it was time to go. A taxi took me to St Pancras station. Only a short wait on the platform was necessary before, about two hours and thirty-five minutes later, I was at Gare du Nord and hailing a cab to take me to my hotel.

Over dinner in my room, I hoped Jo found my note as soon as she returned home and didn't panic when I wasn't there. From the high levels of anticipation and excitement racing through me, I knew I would have trouble sleeping tonight. They also wouldn't let me concentrate on the book I brought with me. I knew I would feel lousy in the morning, but I also knew, if things went to plan, the day ahead would soon fix that.

Chapter 31

Another grey day in Paris awaited me this morning. Over breakfast, I found myself hoping it was not an indication of how things would play out. Far too early, I was dressed and ready to go, and was forced to kill time by pacing around my room and taking long looks at the pavement below. It was frustrating not knowing at what time to be in position to observe today's events … if anything happened today, that is. Somehow, I managed to remain in my room until shortly after nine o'clock.

This was the same hotel Jo and I stayed in so recently. Today, I decided to explore the other side of the street. I walked about half a block to a pedestrian crossing and crossed to the other side before ambling haphazardly along the pavement there. My wandering took me way past the bank on the other side of the street until I came to the next crossing. While checking out the shops along the way, I kept one eye on the bank. By the time I crossed the street again to approach the bank from the opposite direction this time, foot traffic in and out of the bank building had increased.

The ground floor was a hive of activity with many more people going about their business than I expected. It was just ten o'clock according to the clock mounted high on the wall. Imitating the others around me, I wound my way through the crowd, but I searched for any familiar faces. Having seen no one, I decided a coffee and Danish while away time. That was, until I reached the entrance to the coffee shop. There wasn't a vacant table anywhere.

Try Plan B, I told myself as I made my way to a stand selling newspapers. With an English language paper tucked under my arm, I worked my way back towards the coffee shop. Maybe I could find a table now. I couldn't, so I stood a short distance outside and waited. I hoped I looked like someone waiting for a friend. As I stood watching the passing crowd, my mind registered the absence of the large potted palm. It had been replaced by a large pot of flowering heliconia. I noted it would not be nearly as effective to hide behind as the potted palm had been.

I realised that I stood out in the crowd by standing on the spot for any length of time. Everyone around me strode to wherever they needed to be. I needed to mingle – again. After wandering the length of the ground floor, and with the coffee shop still packed, it occurred to me that someone desperate for coffee might try the bistro on the top floor. At this time of the day, coffee and cake would be on offer.

It was worth taking a look. I joined a small huddle of people waiting for the next lift to arrive. Still no familiar faces had caught my eye. Then the lift arrived and spewed out its passengers. I my fellow passengers filed into the empty carriage in an orderly queue. Being the last person to join the group, I was on the tail end of the line entering the lift. I turned to face the doors and looked straight ahead as they started to close.

Our eyes locked just before the doors snapped shut … and I was on my way up, leaving a surprised James Rothwell behind on the ground floor.

"No. No, this won't do!" a little voice screamed in my head as the lift rose to the first floor. "Get out, get out now," my gut was telling me. As soon as the lift doors opened at the first floor, I bolted out and down the hall to the stairs. In spite of my rush, somehow I managed to descend the stairs without falling on my face.

As I reached the bottom step, I stopped and looked about wildly for any sign of James. Of course, there was none. Why would he hang about when he knew I was in the building? Back on the ground floor, I rushed about, pushing my way through the crowd, in search of James … and earning myself a myriad of angry comments about my rudeness and lack of manners. At some point, I noticed a fracas of sorts occurring near the building' entrance. I pushed my way through the gathered onlookers to see what was happening. All I could see was several burley police officers, who had wrestled a man to the ground, now pinned him there.

Then, the coppers had their prisoner cuffed. Picking him up by his arms and legs, they carried the man across the pavement and heaved him into the back of a waiting police wagon. I didn't see the man's face. I saw very little of him in fact, but I knew it was James. It was almost surreal. For a few moments after he was loaded into the wagon, I was frozen, unable to process what I witnessed.

With the show over, the crowd of onlookers dispersed. I looked around, unsure of what I should do next. There seemed to be something happening in front of the coffee shop. People started moving aside as if to clear a pathway to the building's entrance. As the last of the people moved aside, I had a clear view.

A strapping lump of a police officer and a police woman had a firm grip on each arm of a woman who had her hands cuffed behind her. Gone was the purple cloche. Today, replaced by an oversized scarlet beret worn at a jaunty angle to one side. They marched Krista out of the building and into a waiting police car.

For a few more moments I seemed glued to the spot. At last my feet remembered how to move. I pushed my way through to the now half empty coffee shop and collapsed onto a chair at the nearest vacant table. I was in no state to notice what my coffee and Danish tasted like.

After about twenty minutes, and still in a trance-like state, I left the building and hailed a cab. There was about a half hour wait for the next Eurostar train home. With my overnight bag still clutched in my hand, it was almost two o'clock when I marched past a surprised Majella and into my office.

Jo bounded in after me, slamming the door behind her. "Where the hell have you been? You went to France didn't you? What were you thinking? You could have ruined the whole operation."

I couldn't meet her eyes. "I almost did," I whispered.

"What…? What happened? No … Wait; don't tell me. I'll ask Majella to fetch us coffee and then you can tell me the whole story. By the way, it would have been nice if your note told me where you were going, and not just that you might be away for a couple of days."

Only one thing was on my mind. "Has Syd Hartley contacted you today?"

On her way to the door to organise our coffee, Jo looked over her shoulder at me and shook her head. "Not yet, but I didn't expect he would before tonight at the earliest."

Settled in my lounge chairs with our coffees, Jo began extracting the story of today. "Why did you go to France? You knew the authorities had everything under control."

"I can't really explain it, but I had to see it happen. This time, I had to witness what happened to James before I would believe it."

"I assume you were at the bank building when it happened?" I nodded. "While you were roaming about in the building, did you see Syd or recognise anyone else?"

"No, no familiar faces; the only people I recognised were James and Krista. I was worried I might have spooked James after we saw each other. I was waiting for the lift doors to close when it happened. By the time I left the lift at the first floor and ran down the stairs, they had taken James down."

Relating all that happened took surprisingly few minutes. When I finished the story and Jo had run out of questions, she was on her way back to her office until she thought of something and came back.

"I don't imagine you're too interested at the moment, but the budget preparation is complete. As soon as you vet it and we make any adjustments you think necessary, it can go out to the managers. Depending on how long that takes, you still might be able to present the budget, in keeping with the tradition, at a managers' meeting on Tuesday."

"There are still a few hours left this afternoon. I'll make a start on it now."

It was after seven o'clock when we left our offices but, after making only a couple of minor alterations, the budget was ready to be presented. The last thing I did before leaving was to send out a managers' meeting request for ten o'clock tomorrow. It had done me good to focus on work for those few hours. I was starting to feel normal again. The only nagging thought that remained: what will Syd have to say about my being in Paris and almost blowing the police operation?

While we reheated left-overs for dinner, Syd called. The way in which he reported events in Paris suggested he was unaware I was there. Both Jo and I reacted as though we knew nothing of the details he shared. It was true, until he arrived at the part about what happened after James and Krista were arrested.

"James has been charged with a string of offences, the least of which is bigamy. The charges against Krista are not as serious, but they are enough to keep her out of circulation for quite a few years. On the home front, Steven Kinross has been charged with several serious offences, and probably will serve a lengthy stretch. His sister, Maree, is likely to get off with no more than a slap on the wrist. I think that covers everything. We will be home tomorrow sometime if you need to contact me."

I didn't hesitate. "Syd, if you're feeling up to it, how about coming for dinner tomorrow night?" … And he didn't hesitate in accepting the invitation.

At last I felt able to relax, in spite of the fact I knew I had surprised James and it might have resulted in a different outcome. Syd's account of what happened in that Paris bank building included the comment: *It seems something or someone spooked James just as the officers were about to close in on him. One moment he was standing looking at the clock on the wall, then he spun on his heel and bolted for the door. He was about halfway there when they grabbed him. It seems he wasn't too keen to be taken in. Even with a number of police officers hanging on to him, he kept trying to reach the door. He dragged them with him for some distance before they managed to put him on the floor. Everything was straightforward after that.*

In spite of having only left-overs for dinner, we felt the occasion called for some form of celebration. I chose one of my best bottles of wine. While perhaps not best suited to what was on the menu, it went down well, and was the stuff of many toasts. We emptied the bottle … and paid the price for it next morning.

*****

Neither of us was too bright or talkative this morning, but we did make it to work on time. We both indulged in yet more strong black coffee while Majella made copies of each manager's section of the budget for distribution at the meeting. Then it was ten o'clock and the managers were assembled. The only women to join their ranks put on brave faces and marched in to begin the meeting.

All went well. There were no arguments. A couple of them were surprised to have been allocated more than expected. After a short meeting, it was a happy house as all those present left to resume normal duties. Once back in her office, and in accordance with Syd's advice last night, the first thing Jo did was remove from the system anything and everything to do with those rogue payments. It appears the company's bottom line will look a lot heathier this coming year.

The other news Syd delivered when he came to dinner that related to James' ill-gotten wealth accumulated over the years. Again, I was left a little stunned by his news. In a preliminary hearing held in Paris this morning, James was ordered to forfeit everything. As the evidence we provided showed most of it was gained at my company's expense, the court ordered restitution of all forfeited material be made to me. It seems I am about to receive a considerable cash package, and I now own a huge property and a magnificent house on the outskirts of Avignon.

Now the missing money and the mysterious letters – and James – were done and dusted, I had to find something else to worry about, didn't I? The focus of my new worry: Jo and the future. The following weekend, I found the courage to ask the questions I needed answered.

*****

As we finished our usual late, lazy Saturday morning breakfast, I judged the time right to ask the hard questions.

"Jo, the other day, I realised you don't have much leave left. What are your plans for the future? Will you go back to your old job? I don't mean to pressure you, but I was wondering."

"If I'm honest, nothing is decided – not definitely anyway. But, I don't think returning to being a forensic accountant is in my future. I haven't discussed it with the firm I work for yet, but my plan is to do so soon. Anyway, I suppose a part of the decision-making process involves answers I get from you."

"From me…? I don't think so. The decision about your future is yours. I'm not a consideration in any way. What answers could you possibly want from me?"

"Well, the big one of course is whether you anticipated keeping me on as finance manager."

"I never thought you might stay on … until it occurred to me you were running out of leave and might soon leave to return to your old job. Of course I want you to stay on … IF that is what you want to do. There will be no hard feelings if you don't."

"Okay, that makes deciding easier. Nevertheless, there are other factors I need to consider as well. I'll let you know in plenty of time when I reach a final decision."

"The other thing I thought about was the lease on your unit. If I remember correctly, the current lease is due to expire in a few weeks. Have you had any thoughts about that?"

"The answer to that is: yes … and no. Oh, I don't expect you will want me cluttering up your home for much longer, but I'm not sure I want to move back into my unit. I suppose it also depends on what I decide to do about work. If I return to the firm I work for, I'm almost certain they will send me overseas again to manage a contract they have somewhere in the world.

In that case, I would want a lessee in the unit. So, maybe you can see how these are not individual decisions to make. They all tie in together."

"Right; well, maybe I can help you with some of that process. Here is my preferred scenario: you stay on as finance manager, and continue to live here with me until such time as you choose to live somewhere else. It's as simple as that. We get on well. I enjoy having you here, and you are bloody good at your job. So there, I know that suggests a self-serving interest, but that's how I feel."

"I think I just made a decision. We will discuss it in a few days."

Chapter 32

Life does move in different directions. Sometimes those directions are not of our volition. In the weeks following my covert trip to Paris, a number of significant events occurred: Jo announced she wished to stay on as my company's finance manager and would continue to live at 10 Minstrel Court. I admit to heaving a sigh of relief at the news.

James' trial concluded. His sentence means he is unlikely to see the outside world again until he is an old man – if at all. Krista's sentence would see her well past her prime before she is released. The investigation into Steven Kinross' activities found him guilty of other crimes besides his involvement in the plot associated with my mysterious letters. He too received a hefty sentence. His sister, Maree Kinross, was given a good behaviour bond and walked free.

Jo and I visited the property outside Avignon to familiarise ourselves with its operations and to put in place a management arrangement. It was still too early for me to work out the likely long-term future of the place but, for the foreseeable future, I want to retain it. Besides, that house would be a wonderful place for holidays.

Syd Hartley became a frequent visitor to 10 Minstrel Court, and I knew Jo often met him after work at their favourite pub for a meal. On Syd's birthday, Jo invited me to join them for dinner at the pub. About half a dozen members of the group of friends and colleagues she and Syd had maintained close contact with over the years were there too. That's when I met Richard. He had his own pathology lab and was contracted to the police precinct in our area.

Before he became involved in our investigation, Syd had become disenchanted with his work and was thinking of walking away from his career. Then, the work he did on my case, apart from gaining him my eternal gratitude, also caught the eye of his superiors. About a month after the French operation, Syd was offered his area's top detective position when the current senior bloke retired. He didn't hesitate to say 'thank you' and begin learning the ropes from the retiring officer.

As the weeks slipped by, I watched the relationship between Jo and Syd deepen and develop into something more substantial. While that was happening, it seems I was unaware of spending increasing amounts of time with Richard. We often made up a foursome to attend the theatre and various other events. Life at 10 Minstrel Court appeared to be romping along in a blissful fashion. The only real change was Jo started spending odd nights away from home. There was no mystery to it. I never asked, but I was sure she was staying over with Syd.

She never complained, and it took me a while to work it out, but Jo was overloaded at work. Apart from the Avignon property, James had established two other small businesses. Management arrangements were in place for all of them to continue operations, but Jo had inherited an enormous amount of additional work. She needed an assistant. I needed to find her a good one – and soon.

Richard suggested a solution. His son, Harry, might be what I needed. Harry's mother died when he was about three years old and Richard, with the help of grandma and an aunt, had brought up the lad. Now something of a finance and investment guru with a huge international firm, Harry had been based in Switzerland for some years … but was anxious to return home.

I interviewed him when he made a flying visit home for Richard's birthday. Jo also spent some time with him. The upshot of his visit was that, before he flew back to Switzerland,

I offered him the position of assistant finance manager. The salary was a bit less than he was used to, but his acceptance was immediate. He needed to give two months' notice, but would start as soon as he was free.

For me, life had taken on a new meaning. It almost felt as though I had been transported to another world. Nevertheless, I didn't question any of it. I am more than happy to go along with wherever this new life might take me. After all, why should I question where it might lead when everything is going so well?

The End